Spirits

Written By

Brandon McLeod Humphrey

This is a work of fiction. The characters are either the products of the author's imagination, or used in a fictitious manner. Any resemblance to actual people, living or dead, is purely coincidental.

ISBN: 978-0-9980538-1-3

INTRO

I honestly can't really remember when I first realized this investigation, this season's premier episode, was not going to end well. How far down this rabbit hole had we fallen before I realized there was no way to find our way back out? Not for all of us anyway. No way for this story to have a happy ending. Personally, I am one who hates it when a story is so transparent that I know the outcome before I'm even halfway through with it. So, if I were the one reading this, would I even bother to continue?

Knowing already that the hero dies in the end.

I'm sure many would view me as a pessimist, even though I would have to say I've always thought of myself as a glass half-full kind of guy. Although, to be completely honest, a half-full glass of anything didn't last long in my presence. But who could really blame me? I don't believe most of what's happened in my life, and I was there to witness it. Well, most of it. I won't lie; there are a few blind spots in my memory. Some due to alcohol, some just due to self-preservation I suppose. But that's probably just as well. With a failed marriage, a failed business, and I'm assuming very soon a failing liver, I've obviously made some critical mistakes in this train wreck I call my life.

The marriage I can certainly understand. Those that know me will be the first to tell you that I wasn't exactly the warm and fuzzy type, and I can imagine, not very easy to live with or be around. I was very closed off and guarded most of the time. I can pretty much imagine what the highlights of my eulogies will sound like. 'He loved... well, he was very... uh, no one will ever question Sebastian's knowledge of tequila and cigars.'

The failed business? Certainly, the lion's share of the responsibility must fall on my shoulders. But let's be honest, the producers that green lit 'Spirits with Spirits', a paranormal show based on finding ghostly activity at haunted bars and restaurants, all while the investigators also sampled the cocktails the establishment is best known for, should not

1

only have been fired, but maybe even been drawn and quartered. I've had a lot of alcohol induced brainstorms before, but that was definitely at the top of the list. Yet somehow after two seasons of less than mediocre ratings and more than our share of dreadful episodes, somehow the chance of a lifetime landed on my doorstep.

That should have been my first warning.

Our episodes had been at best, bars and restaurants that hired us not to so much prove or disprove paranormal activity, but to help drum up some business for their failing establishments. Did we ever find evidence? That's subjective, I guess. We sure made it a point to highlight every faint sound and strange occurrence we could, to try and beef up the show for ratings. Even if ninety percent of the time it was just one of our own people tripping over themselves in the next room.

So how did it come to pass that the Wakefield Inn had come calling on us to do an investigation? Passing over several more highly respected shows and settling on the fifth ranked paranormal show in the country. Keep in mind, this was out of a total of five shows currently on the air. My initial thought was they scraped the bottom of the barrel because they wanted a team that would fail to find evidence and thus maybe help resurrect their dwindling business. There are those that might have taken offense to this, but hey, who was I to turn down an easy paycheck for me and my team. By the time I realized why the inn had really chosen us, it would be too late.

The Wakefield Inn had one of the most brutally haunted pasts of any place in the world. Murders, suicides, and guests gone missing never to be heard from again. Even with all the tragedy, they had managed to maintain a fairly decent business. Which is why even though they had every paranormal show begging for a chance to film a show there, they had never accepted. Afraid of the further negative publicity, and the damage it could do to their business.

But with the recent boom of newer and more luxurious lodging choices on that side of town, it would seem they were in a bind. Business had dropped to a point where they could not give their rooms away. And thus, the wheels were set in motion. My team would soon be given the chance of a lifetime. The chance to spend a few nights in the infamous Wakefield Inn.

CHAPTER 1

I awoke in my home office, face down on my desk, to the faint smell of women's perfume. Which seemed odd as I hadn't had a woman over since my wife left me, and to the best of my knowledge, my cat didn't wear perfume. Although at this point nothing would surprise me. As I wiped the sleep out of my eyes, I noticed an unfinished glass of tequila still on the desk. See, I told you I was a glass half-full kind of guy. Never letting good tequila go to waste, I grabbed the glass and slowly made my way to the living room.

"Breakfast of champions?" Theresa, my soon to be ex-wife gloated from the couch. I really hated it when my behavior only confirmed her choice to leave me. But a horrible feeling in my gut gave me an idea of why she was here this early. I knew this day was long overdue, but I still wasn't prepared for it. The damn blood sucking, shit bag, demon from hell, who also went by the professional title of her divorce lawyer, was probably after her to get this wrapped up. Was this the day she finally gives me the paperwork?

"And on that note, I think maybe it's time to give me back your copy of the house key?" I said while shaking my head and trying to think of a way to keep this conversation from heading south.

"Then how would I check on my sweet boy and make sure he's still okay?" She spoke softly, and I smiled for a brief moment, until she motioned to our cat lying next to her on the couch. My heart sank, because for a second I had hoped it might be me she was still worried about.

But no, her concern was for my not so faithful cat, Louie. Short for Louisiana, or on many occasions simply referred to as Lucifer. He laid on his back next to Theresa with his head hanging over the couch.

"I think he may finally be dead. You actually managed to kill him." She motioned towards the cat, and poked at him, but he didn't

5

flinch. "I knew I should have taken him with me."

"He's not dead. He's just in withdrawal. I made him give up alcohol this week." I said triumphantly as I took a sip of the day-old tequila in my glass and watched Theresa cringe.

"I guess it's good that at least someone in the house has the willpower to quit." She continued to pet the cat.

"Let's not anoint baby Jesus just yet. I think that furry little bastard may have a relapse coming on."

I figured I should probably get to the point and ask why she is even here. But the truth is, I kind of missed our banter and didn't really want it to end yet. But alas, all good things must come to an end. For those of our readers that are clueless when it comes to subtext and foreshadowing, that was a not-so-subtle hint that everything will not end well. But what in my life ever has?

"So, you are here because..." I asked hesitantly.

"I heard you have an investigation coming up?" She smiled and raised an eyebrow.

As she rose from the couch, I could suddenly imagine myself wrapping my hands around Brandon's neck and slowly watching the life leave his eyes. Of course, if not for the fact Brandon is my best friend and one of the few people still willing to drink with me.

"Good old Brandon."

"What makes you think Brandon told me?" As she moved closer to me, I got a strong whiff of her perfume. It was intoxicating. I lost my train of thought for a brief moment and forgot what we were discussing. "You weren't really thinking of leaving me behind, were you? You're going to need me on this one."

"I know. I just hadn't given it much thought yet." I finished the last of my tequila, the optimist in me, now wishing the glass were once again half full.

"You realize this has the potential to be the most active place we've ever investigated? We're going to be the first team to ever investigate it. How are you not more excited?"

"Oh, I'm excited." I smiled sarcastically, anticipating the thought of how truly awkward it would be to now spend a week in an old hotel with my soon-to-be ex-wife.

"I sense a little sarcasm. Have I ever given you reason to doubt me?"

"Professionally?" I laughed. "Of course not."

"In any capacity?"

"Your taste in men has always struck me as questionable."

As she laughed, I wasn't quite sure if it was because she truly found my joke funny or if she was trying to cover up the fact she considered it a valid point. I had to hand it to her though. She still looked at these investigations through the eyes of a child. Full of hope and anticipation at the possibilities. That's what made us such a good team. Her optimism balanced my cynical disbelief. While I obviously never ruled out the possibility of paranormal activity, I had pretty much lost faith that we would ever find anything close to hard evidence. She was the other end of the spectrum. Optimistic, outgoing, always open to the endless possibilities that may be waiting. I truly wanted the best for her. I wanted her to find someone that is one hundred and eighty degrees from me. I hated myself for not being strong enough to keep her from coming on this investigation with us.

My train of thought was broken quickly as the front door opened and Brandon walked in. Apparently, I'm the only one that still knocks before entering a house. "Ola!"

"By all means, come in." I said while shaking my head. "What if I hadn't been decent?"

7

"Like you've ever been decent." Brandon grabbed the glass out of my hand. "Really, this early?"

"What if I'd had a woman here?" I asked, not intending to slight Theresa, who was now glaring at me.

"A woman?" He put my glass on the bar and chuckled. "Not likely I'll walk in on that seeing as you're still hung up on Theresa."

I froze for a moment. I couldn't believe he went there. No one will ever accuse Brandon of being subtle. I think in a way he was still thinking he could play matchmaker and get us back together. I casually looked over at her to see her smiling smugly and trying not to laugh. The silence was now becoming awkwardly long. Muttering a few choice words under my breath, I walked over to Brandon and grabbed my glass back.

"I need this if I'm to put up with you this early in the morning."

Not sure I cared for him implying I wasn't over Theresa yet, even if I knew it was true. Besides, relationship advice coming from Brandon? The man never had a relationship that outlasted a carton of milk. I felt like any time he'd seen the same woman for a whole week I should throw him some sort of anniversary party.

And yet, he was one of the best video editors in the business. He could take thirty hours of useless footage and rambling, and turn it into a fairly entertaining forty-five-minute episode. Along with Theresa, who's research skills were unparalleled, I'd managed to wind up with half my team in my living room this morning. Kind of killed my plan to have a drink and watch porn.

We were interrupted by a knock on the door, which came as a bit of a shock as I was getting used to people just walking in my house with no warning.

"Come in." We all said in unison.

The door opened and in walked Christy, struggling with an unusually large folder.

8

"Hi guys. Am I early?"

Christy was the youngest of the group. Very intelligent, and had a great understanding of every aspect of the show. Could set up the equipment, could edit the footage, and even co-hosted an episode when I was ill. Looking at her though, one would not think of her as paranormal investigator. A bubbly blonde, but not in a ditzy way. Although when it gets to be four in the morning and everyone is on their last legs and she's still bouncing around with that peppy voice of hers, I'd be lying if I said I never thought about duct taping her mouth. She was very attractive, but we tried to downplay both hers and Theresa's good looks as we felt they would come off more believable as investigators if they had a studious look to them. Of course, Brandon didn't help matters, as it seemed every time he ordered apparel for the crew, her shirt always came in one size smaller than she had requested. Funny how that worked.

"Early for what?" I looked at Brandon. "Should I be worried? It feels like the start of an intervention."

I nervously looked to the liquor cabinet to make sure Theresa hadn't already poured out my tequila before I woke up. Luckily the bottles were still full.

"Hardly." Brandon said with a grin. "Neither of us is foolish enough to think that would be a worthwhile venture."

Brandon and Christy headed into my office, as Theresa and I followed. He opened my laptop.

"Kind of surprised I didn't open this up and find a porn website." He mused.

"Funny guy." I said, all the while thinking to myself, had I had a few more minutes this morning before company arrived, it probably would have been porn on that screen. Thank God Theresa wears strong perfume. That could have been awkward had I not smelled her perfume and gone out to the living room to investigate first thing this morning.

"Oh, look here, an email titled Meeting tomorrow AM." Brandon

9

clicked on the email. "It looks like we're all meeting at your house to prep for the upcoming gig."

"When was that sent?" I asked defensively. "I don't check my email all that often."

"Hmmm, let's see. Yesterday morning. Twenty-four hours ago." Brandon backed away from the computer.

"See!" I said, feeling justified. "I hadn't had a chance to even get to it yet!"

Theresa moved over and looked at the computer.

"Odd though that several more recent emails were opened." She shook her head. "Here's one for Discount Liquor, there's one for Viagra?"

Christy moved past Brandon and bent down to look at the computer screen as well.

"There's an email titled Catholic school girls in trouble?" Christy questioned. "And of course, it's been opened."

"I thought that might be some sort of outreach program for wayward girls in need." My justified feeling quickly morphed into slight humiliation.

"Wayward girls in need of longer skirts." Brandon laughed as he leaned back into the computer to get a closer look at the email in question.

"Well, it's good you have priorities." Christy closed the computer on Brandon's fingers before he could get the email open.

Christy ventured back to the living room to retrieve her dictionary sized folder off the coffee table. She brought it back to the office and began pulling stacks of paper out.

"Do you mind if I use your bulletin board to post some photos?" She asked as she began pinning items to the board.

"Boudoir shots I hope." Brandon chuckled as Christy paused to glare at him and shake her head. Theresa and I turned to stare at him. Both of us stunned into silence.

"Shit, was that out loud?" He smiled sheepishly.

"Wow." Was all that I could manage to say as I took a sip of my drink, sat down, and motioned towards the bulletin board. "By all means, whatever you need. Mi casa es su casa."

Well, for now anyway, I thought to myself. After the divorce is final mi casa es Theresa's casa. Me y mi gato will be living in a cardboard box on the street. The only thing I don't understand is why she hasn't served me with the papers yet? Is she still thinking of giving me a second chance? Or I guess fourth or fifth chance. I've lost count now. My many mistakes over the last twelve months seem to have blended into one long mistake. Who am I kidding? I wouldn't give me a second chance, why should she? I looked over at her. She was still busy shaking her head at Brandon's inappropriate comment.

"Let me break the awkward silence." Christy said awkwardly. "The history of this inn goes back several hundred years. Do you want the highlights? Or should I go through in detail?"

"Oh, by all means, in detail." I said. "The more information we throw in on top of Brandon's inappropriate comment, the better."

As I glared in Brandon's direction, he quickly averted my stare by looking down at his shoes. And while I must admit, they were nice shoes. They certainly didn't warrant a full sixty seconds of looking towards the floor.

"Alright then." Christy interrupted. "The disturbing history of the Wakefield Hotel"

By the time Christy finished pinning up all of her papers, the bulletin board looked like something out of a cop movie. Brandon and I could only look at each other like school kids that were trapped in a classroom.

"I'm going to go in chronological order, even though some of these were discovered years after the original death." She walked to the left side of the bulletin board. "Eighteen hundred and eighty-seven, the year the Wakefield was built, by James J. Wakefield."

"Originally to be named The Wakefield Stratton Hotel, as Wakefield had partnered with his close friend Arthur Stratton. However, in the initial stages of construction, Stratton leaves his then pregnant fiancé, Abigail Turner, to run off with a younger woman as documented in a rather impersonal letter."

"Guy kinda makes me look like not so bad a catch?" I joked while Theresa shook her head, and Christy and Brandon merely looked at me with odd disapproving glares.

"Really?" I directed my response at Brandon. "Judging me after your boudoir comment?"

Brandon smiled.

"Abigail was devastated. If not for the compassion of James Wakefield, there is speculation she would have ended her life and the life of her unborn child then and there. But James took an interest in her and got her through her dark times. Eventually their friendship grew into more. The two were married just before the completion of the hotel. Abigail's son, Teddy, was now a year old. Two years later, the couple would also have a child of their own, Mary Beth. They ran the hotel together for years, living themselves on the top floor. Those that knew them described them as the perfect family, and James himself as one of the most honorable men in town."

Perfect family? I thought to myself, I had almost had that. Why is it that some people can make it look so easy, and I made it seem impossible? What was it about me that made it so hard for Theresa to stick around I thought to myself as I took another sip of the tequila in my hand.

"But as fate would have it..." Christy continued. "Some twenty-three years later, when the children were grown and had moved on to lives of their own, James took ill. Many think the stress of running the inn had finally caught up with him, as the doctors could not find a reason for his deteriorating health. He would speak of hearing voices in the basement, and ramble incoherently of something trying to get him. Abigail stayed at his side until the end. On his death bed, he continued to profess his love to Abigail and how he had loved her since the moment he first laid eyes on her. How he had always known they were meant to be together."

Christy shuffled through a few of the papers.

"He went on to tell Abigail a story as to how he and Arthur had gotten drunk one night while working late on the hotel plans. He remembered the two of them walking out to the building site, where he proceeded to tell Arthur that he was in love with Abigail. Eventually the verbal argument turned physical. James hit Arthur in the back of the head with a shovel. Then dragged Arthurs' body into the center of the excavated pit. He buried him there that night. As he sobered up, the horror of his predicament began to set in. He forged the farewell note that Abigail would later find. Then proceeded to move up the building plans by a week to make sure the cement foundation was poured the very next day. Removing any chance that anyone could ever find Arthur's body."

We were speechless. Suddenly I started to think there had been worse husbands than me out there. Theresa leaned over to me. "Maybe you weren't so bad." She whispered as she smiled. I simply shook my head.

"Minutes after his confession to Abigail, James passed. In the weeks following the funeral, Abigail's health also deteriorated. She would later be found, having hung herself on the top floor of the hotel with one of the bed sheets. Leaving a note detailing everything James had confessed to her." Christy shuffled a few papers on the desk and pinned another to the bulletin board. "That was case one."

"Jesus, drink anyone?" I stood up headed out to the bar.

"As a matter of fact, yes." Brandon nodded as he quickly followed me out to the bar.

I couldn't help imagining the last thoughts that must have run through Abigail's head. A marriage built on lies. Built with the man that killed the man she loved and the father of her child. It started to make me sick to my stomach. I pulled out four glasses and dropped a few ice cubes in each. As I poured tequila in each, Theresa shook her head, declining the fourth glass that was meant for her.

"Thirsty?" Christy asked. "It's a little too early for me."

"How do you know that was even for you? After that story maybe I needed to pour two for myself and two for Brandon." I smiled.

Theresa smiled while Brandon quickly drank one glass, and proceeded to grab the second. "And you people wonder why I'm not married."

"Oh, we don't wonder." Christy jabbed.

The front door opened once again opened with no knock as Bobby and Jerry entered the house.

"Welcome to happy hour!" Brandon greeted them while raising his glass.

"Nice of you to knock." My greeting was a little less enthusiastic than Brandon's.

"What?" Jerry shrugged. "We saw everyone else's cars and figured it had to be safe to just come in."

"Unless you all have some kinky threesome shit you've been hiding from the group?" Bobby questioned.

"Honey, they don't know what the word kinky means." Jerry said flamboyantly as ever.

I could do nothing but shake my head and smile. The gang was all here. It had been months since we were all together in the same room. If

14

I remember correctly, not since we edited the final show of last year's season.

Bobby, who had always been my cohost on the show, was everything that I was not. We played off each other very well. Where I was sarcastic and sometimes condescending, he was warm and very friendly. Knew absolutely nothing about the gear though. Brandon spent hours editing out footage where he was either calling a device by the wrong name or flat out asking one of us what this tool is for and what he is supposed to do with it. But his charm far exceeded all of his flaws. I'm pretty sure we owe the majority of our female fan base to him.

Jerry, I am pretty sure is to thank for our homosexual fan base, if we have such a thing. Never at a loss for creative wardrobe choices. Many times his clothing scared us more than the places we investigated. But there is no argument. No one knew the equipment like him. But I won't lie, it took some getting used to for me to work with him. I had never thought of myself as a homophobe in any way, but the first few times I was in a dark room alone with him, I probably kept a little more distance than I needed to. Of course, he quickly picked up on this and made it a point to be as close as possible to me. Even throwing out the occasional 'Is this the boom mic, or are you just happy to see me?' But he was a good guy, and quickly found a place in the group.

This was my dysfunctional little family.

"Christy was starting to give us the run down on the history of the place." Brandon explained. "Be happy you missed the first morbid little tale."

"The beginning is key." She started back towards the office. "Follow me. I'll get you caught up while these two refill their drinks."

Christy led Bobby and Jerry into the office. Brandon looked towards the bar, then to me.

"I believe that was her way of giving us permission for another cocktail." Brandon grinned.

"Like I need permission." I scoffed. "Is it too early to be on drink number three?"

Brandon looked at me and shook his head with a dismissive grin. I moved around behind the bar and refilled our glasses with ice. Grabbed the bottle of tequila and began to pour. Theresa looked at us, shook her head and went into the other room.

"You going to be okay with this?" He questioned as he seemed to turn serious for a moment.

"With what?" I asked.

"We haven't really done a full-on investigation since..." He hesitated. "Just thought it might be uncomfortable for you."

"We'll be fine." I took a sip. "We're professionals, right?"

"True, very true." Brandon took a sip of his drink. "But it won't make it any easier."

"Yeah, I know."

"You need to think about moving on at some point." Brandon sighed. "Love can do a lot of things. Love can heal, love can redeem, love can kill."

He looked me in the eye.

"I don't like the route it's chosen for you, my friend." He frowned. "I don't ever see you without a glass in your hand anymore."

"Fine, I won't drink anymore." I took a sip from my glass. "Or any less."

I smiled as Brandon shook his head.

"And besides, you getting preachy with me about trying to get over someone?" I laughed. "You wouldn't know love if it bit you on the ass."

"Can't argue that." Brandon smiled, stood up and began to pace the room. "Although I did date a woman once who liked me to bite her on the ass."

I shuddered at the visual, then assured him. "I'll be fine."

"I've got to tell you; this one makes me a little nervous." Brandon confessed. "This place has always tried to cover up their history. Now they want it out there for all to see?"

"Amazing what people are willing to do once they're down on their luck." I stood up and walked towards him. "Disprove the rumors or go bankrupt. They really didn't have much choice."

"I guess." He took his drink and finished it, then handed me his empty glass. "But if that first story she told us was her idea of easing us into this, I'm going to need another of these. And make it a real glass. Enough of this half shot sized pour."

I smiled and walked back behind the bar and filled our glasses up one last time and handed Brandon his.

"Shall we rejoin the others?" I headed back into the office followed by Brandon.

It's rare to see him this worried, as he's always been the relaxed one. He's usually the one to talk me down when I'm standing on the proverbial ledge. This was probably the first time I started to have doubts about this investigation. Do we have too many distractions? Too much personal crap we're dealing with to be able to focus on what we need to? Probably a moot point anyway. The network's not about to delay the start of our third season yet again just so I can work through my divorce.

CHAPTER 2

As we entered the office, the stunned silence they were in let us know Christy had finished the first story.

"Wasn't that a heartwarming tale for the ages!" As I spoke they all turned to glare at me. "What?"

"I'll try to be brief on some of this as there are multiple occurrences." Christy tried to keep things moving along. "Murders, suicides, tragedies, etc. I'll stick to the ones that even after investigation left more questions than answers."

Christy moved back over to the board as Brandon and I moved closer and joined the group at the table.

"After the initial incident I couldn't find a thing on the inn until nineteen forty-nine." She pulled a photo off the board and passed it among the others.

"Isadora Gallo, well known Italian actress." Christy handed another photo to Brandon.

"Never heard of her." Brandon frowned.

"That's probably because she wasn't a porn actress." Jerry chuckled as the rest of us laughed.

"She was staying in the hotel with her two prized show dogs while on break from a film she was shooting in the states." Christy continued. "She kept to herself, so it wasn't particularly unusual that days would go by without the staff seeing her. She only asked for her room to be made every third day, and she had a private door to the courtyard to walk her dogs."

She grabbed another couple of photos off the board and passed them around. One photo was of a blood-stained floor, the other was of a bloody dress crumpled up in the corner of the room. We all shook our heads as we passed the photos around.

"On one morning the staff was to clean the room, this is what they found." Christy motioned to the photos. "No body. Just a blood-stained shredded dress, and the blood-stained carpet. The outside door to the courtyard was wide open, and the dogs were cowering in the garden, both covered in blood.

"Some guard dogs." Bobby took a closer look at the gruesome photos.

"Pay attention. They weren't guard dogs; they were show dogs." Christy grabbed the photo out of Bobby's hand. "Show dogs aren't bred for protection. They're bred for looks, discipline, and are usually spoiled and pampered."

"Kind of like Bobby." Jerry laughed and nodded to Bobby. "Well, except for the discipline part."

"So anyway, getting back to business. After months of investigation, no suspect was ever apprehended." Christy paused slightly.

"Well, that's certainly mysterious, but nowhere near as creepy as the first story." Bobby grabbed the photos back from Christy.

"You seem to think my pause meant the story was over?" Christy grabbed the photos from Bobby and pinned them back to the board. "Several years later, the property was renovated, and the garden area was redone to make room for a pond. While excavating for the pond, the bones of what is assumed to be Isadora Gallo, were found in several separate holes."

"Separate holes?" I asked, not sure if I really wanted to hear the explanation.

"Separate holes." She continued. "With several canine bite marks on them."

I couldn't help but let a small laugh slip out. The others looked at me disapprovingly.

"I'm sorry. But are we to believe her own dogs ate her over the course of three days, and were well mannered enough to tidy up by burying her in the garden?" I was astonished that the others were even considering this tidbit.

"Well, they were after all, well trained show dogs." Bobby jeered while looking in Jerry's direction.

Jerry grinned and shook his head, while most of us laughed. It was becoming apparent Christy was growing frustrated with us.

"I'm just giving you the facts." Christy responded sharply. "You all can draw whatever conclusions you like. It seems there is a questionable occurrence there every decade."

She walked back to the bulletin board as I looked over at Louie cleaning himself in the corner and wondered how long he would be able to hold out before eating me. I'm pretty sure he might have already done it if he weren't so damn lazy.

"Nineteen fifties there was a murder suicide." Christy handed a photo to the others. "The couple were there on their honeymoon."

For some reason they all turned and looked at me and Brandon. It's not like we always make an offensive comment in these situations. We are capable of keeping our mouths shut on occasion.

"Yet another strong argument for my lifestyle choice!" Jerry cheered.

"I'd take death over staring at another man's hairy ass." Brandon responded.

"I wax my ass, thank you." Jerry gleamed proudly.

"Oh, for the love of god." Cried Bobby. "Way too much information Jerry!"

"Moving on." I motioned to Christy to continue to prevent this conversation from deteriorating any further than it already had.

"The sixties saw a woman have a severe allergic reaction to shellfish and die on the way to the hospital." Christy continued.

"Shellfish allergies are pretty common." Bobby added. "That's not all that unusual of a way to go."

"The staff confirmed her dinner that evening..." She passed around another piece of paper. "Was chicken."

I looked at the report. Sure enough it said chicken. But who's to say the staff isn't trying to cover their ass. Or maybe they cooked the chicken in a pan that was previously used for shellfish?

"In the seventies there was a guest that had starved to death in his room even though the mini fridge was full of food." She pulled a newspaper clipping off the board and handed it to Brandon.

"Maybe he was dieting?" Brandon joked and passed the newspaper clipping around, while Christy ignored him and continued.

"In the eighties a young woman was found drowned in her bathtub. In about twelve inches of water."

"I've heard that's easier to do than you would think." Jerry added. "Especially if alcohol or other chemicals are involved."

Tell me about it. I found that out the hard way a couple of months ago. It was very relaxing though. The warm water, a nice glass of tequila. Unwinding after a long stressful day. I could see how someone could get so comfortable they fall asleep in the tub. If Theresa hadn't stopped by to check on me that night, who knows how it would've turned out for me? I glanced over at Theresa. The glare I was receiving in return made me quickly realize she must have been thinking about the exact same event.

"Then in the nineties a man fell from the roof even though the access door to the roof is never left unlocked." Christy continued.

"Or he was pushed?" Bobby interrupted. "Probably by the wife?"

I could see by the fact the glare on Theresa's face had slowly turned to a rather mischievous grin, she had probably thought of this solution a time or two when it came to me.

"And last, but not least, in two thousand and four, a woman was found to have hanged herself with a bedsheet in one of the upper guest rooms." She handed the last photo to me. "The bed sheet used was somewhat of an antique. From the early nineteen hundreds."

"Same era as Abigail Wakefield?" Jerry added.

"Not just same era." Christy pulled out a news clipping and passed it around. "Same brand of bed sheet Abigail used to hang herself. From a company that hasn't been in business for sixty years."

A hush fell over the room. I would agree these are interesting occurrences, but not necessarily unexplainable. And here in lies the problem with a career choice like mine. As much as it would help our show to just assume everything always points to the paranormal. It's hard for me to overlook the very real possibility that these could be explained in other ways.

"Just to play devil's advocate here." I stood up and walked over to the board. "She could have been a nut job who bought the antique sheet on Ebay or some other antique auction site, and brought it with her to the hotel."

"She would have had to have been a special kind of crazy." Jerry interjected. "To plan that out so far in advance that she would go through the trouble of tracking down a sheet like that."

"Once you're so far gone, you're going to commit suicide, who's to say what level of crazy you need to be." Brandon stood up and headed for the living room. "Time for another drink."

23

I had to admit; I was being drawn in a little. While I thought many of these could have logical explanations. The odds of all of them? The lady with the dogs could have been murdered and fed to her dogs? The starvation? There are anorexics starving themselves to death every day while food is within arm's reach. The fall from the roof could have been a murder committed by an employee that has the key to the roof access. And so on and so on. But this is why shows like ours will always have an audience. People who want to believe in the paranormal are always going to ignore the facts and focus on what they want to. We continued to discuss the cases, or maybe argue is a more accurate description. Before I knew it, we had been at this for several hours and the sun was setting outside the office window..

"Is anyone else getting hungry?" I asked.

"Famished." Christy replied.

"Hell yes." Bobby chimed in and everyone else nodded in agreement.

"I'm not really prepared for entertaining." I apologized. "Chinese take-out work for everyone?"

"Food is food." Brandon replied. "And we at least know you keep a well-stocked bar."

"See, I am useful for a few things." I motioned to the living room. "What can I get everybody?"

They followed me out to the living room and over to the bar.

"We have beer, mixed drinks, or wine." I opened the refrigerator to let people see the selection of beer."

"I'll take any dark beer you have." Bobby responded.

I took a beer out of the refrigerator and opened it,

"Glass?" I offered.

24

"No thanks, the bottle is fine." Bobby grabbed the bottle from my hand.

"Just a soda for me." Christy added while simultaneously receiving disapproving frowns from the rest of us.

"What?" She shrugged.

Brandon slid behind the bar with me and grabbed the bottle of tequila.

"Oh, shit." I mused. "It's going to be one of those nights!"

"In case you hadn't already figured this out, I will be crashing here tonight." He said as he began pouring tequila and margarita mix into a large pitcher.

"Kind of figured that." I watched him mix two thirds tequila to one third margarita mix. "Wow."

I began to pull glasses off the shelf.

"Anyone else that wants to crash, feel free." I said while filling the glasses with ice. "There's more than enough bedrooms."

Christy handed Brandon back the coke.

"In that case I'm having a margarita." She smiled.

"Good for you!" Jerry cheered. "Live a little girl!"

I enjoyed the moment and filled six glasses with ice as Theresa stared at me and shook her head. I knew it was wishful thinking, as Theresa hadn't touched alcohol in quite a while, but who knows, there's always a chance.

I could see Brandon and the others counting the glasses in their heads, and I could feel them judging me. It wasn't like I ever pressured Theresa to partake in a drink, but I still thought it polite to offer. Besides, the extra always managed to find its way to me, which was always a plus.

"I know I'll be drinking two of these." I joked as they shook their heads.

Brandon filled the glasses up, and as expected Theresa did not partake. I smiled and picked mine up, and took a long sip, almost taunting her. She shook her head and walked across the room.

"I'm going to go order the food. Be back in a flash." As I headed to the office with my drink in hand, Theresa turned to follow close behind with that all too familiar motherly scowl.

I sat at the desk and began punching in the order on the computer.

"You sure it's a good idea for everyone to be drinking and spending the night?" Theresa frowned.

"Don't be a buzz kill. It's been forever since all six of us were together."

"I know." She looked out towards the living room. "I also know Brandon is a dirty old man who has the hots for Christy."

I smiled as I continued to enter our food order. I didn't have the heart to tell her that Brandon and Christy had already hooked up a few years back. Oddly enough with Christy being the instigator. She had just got out of a three-year relationship and wanted nothing but a fun night. Poor Brandon actually felt like they hit it off. He was a bit crushed when there was no second date. Was probably good for him in a way, to finally see what the women he dates go through in the aftermath. But I'm pretty sure I was the only one in the group that knew about it.

"They'll be fine. We're all adults." I finished entering the order and stood up. "Maybe you should be more worried about you and I being under the same roof tonight?"

I smiled what I had hoped was a fairly charming smile, to which she merely grinned.

"You've got a better chance of having sex with Jerry than you do with me." She smiled, turned, and walked back out to the living room.

"That's not saying much." I muttered under my breath. "Jerry will sleep with anyone."

Later, we all sat in the living room, a dozen cardboard Chinese food boxes scattered across the coffee table and end table. Everyone on their third or fourth margarita by now.

"I'm stuffed." Brandon patted his belly.

I could tell he had too much to drink already. He was sitting on the couch next to Jerry with their legs touching. That would never happen while sober. Was actually kind of nice to see him let down his homophobic guard for a change. Jerry reached to grab a fortune cookie off the table. After breaking it open and eating a piece, he glanced at the tiny piece of paper.

"Love is closer than you think." Jerry read then turned and smiled at Brandon. Brandon immediately stood up and stumbled over to take a seat at the bar. Well, it was nice while it lasted.

"Come back, I miss you already!" Jerry laughed as did the rest of us.

"Take it easy on Brandon. He's very confused." I joked while Brandon flipped me off.

"I was only kidding." Jerry explained. "And besides, you're not even my type."

"What's that supposed to mean?" Brandon took offense. "I'm everybody's type."

"Ha, yeah right." Christy blurted out. She sheepishly looked around at us. "That just kind of slipped out."

I found it all quite amusing. Brandon would probably try and date Jerry now as he seemed to only want those that didn't want him. I guess

I'm not one to talk, as I looked over at Theresa, then reached to the table and grabbed myself a fortune cookie. I broke off an end and pulled out the fortune, glanced at it quickly and put it on the table.

"Well, what did it say?" Brandon asked.

"It said..." I tried to muster up my best Chinese impersonation. "You best flend will a suck a you cock tonight."

Brandon shook his head and flipped me off yet again.

"Apparently Jerry is your new best friend then." Brandon laughed and motioned towards Jerry.

Jerry didn't laugh, but appeared to be deep in thought.

"You know, if we weren't friends and didn't work together, I would probably do Sebastian." He nodded having apparently given this more thought than I was comfortable with.

"Whoa, wait a second." Brandon stood up. "How is it you would do Sebastian and not me?"

"Don't take it personally, hun." Jerry said sympathetically. "Sebastian just has a certain charm to him."

I smugly smiled at Brandon.

"I can't put my finger on it." Jerry added.

Certainly, one of the oddest conversations our little dysfunctional group had ever delved into. But I could certainly understand. My charm as he called it, was the fact that I was broken. People with good hearts always think they can fix us, and make us whole again. But I am pretty sure I was too broken to ever be pieced back together. I'm pretty sure that's why Theresa stayed as long as she did. She thought I was fixable.

I knew I wasn't.

"Screw all of you." Brandon went over and sat at the bar, refilled his margarita, and sulked.

"I'm pretty sure I just told you that was not an option, lover boy." Jerry quipped.

The rest of us lost it and began laughing. Even Brandon, while trying to shake his head, couldn't keep from laughing as he put his head down on the bar and tried his best to ignore us a Christy slowly stood up.

"As entertaining as all of this is, I need to turn in. I was up all last night researching, and I'm exhausted." She looked towards me. "Which room should I take?"

"My house is first come, first serve." I motioned with my arms. "Take your pick."

As she excused herself and made her way out of the room, Theresa, Bobby, and Jerry also stood up.

"I think I am going to get my beauty sleep as well." Bobby said as he exited the room. "Thank you for the food and drink."

I nodded.

"Me too, thank you." Added Jerry while smiling. "I'm not really tired yet, but I want to make sure I get one of the bedrooms. I remember how lumpy that couch of yours is."

As he exited, Theresa walked over to my side of the table and looked down at my fortune.

"You will have a new love interest." She smiled as she quietly read my fortune.

I smiled and shook my head. For one, I took no stock in fortune cookies. And two, I knew I was not going to have a new love interest anytime soon.

"You know you're going to have to move on." She moved closer to me and whispered. "We both are. You and I..."

I looked up at her while taking a very large sip of my margarita.

"You and I will never get back to what we had." As she spoke she walked over to me, put a hand on my shoulder.

"I realize that." I pouted knowing it was mostly my fault.

"And this? What we're doing now..." She motioned to the both of us. "Is not helping either one of us."

"You're the one that wants to come with on this investigation!" Now I was a bit irritated. "I had planned on leaving you out of this all until Brandon opened his big mouth."

"I need to be there. For the team." She paused. "This one worries me. The history of this place, the darkness that resides there, is nothing like we have ever seen before."

Confused as usual, I shook my head as she too made her way to the hallway. I sighed because deep down I knew she was right. And worse yet, I knew it was my fault. I finished the rest of my drink and put the glass down on the table.

"Love is an illusion!" Brandon blurted out of nowhere as he quickly lifted his head up from the bar.

I think Brandon had now become the drunk prophet at the end of every bar that randomly spews out booze infused wisdom, every now and then revealing a hidden gem.

"You okay there, buddy?" I stood up and made my way across the room to the bar. Brandon looked around the room. Realizing for the first time everyone else had gone to bed.

"Shit!" He slurred. "I get the couch."

"You get the couch." I nodded in agreement. "I'll take what's left of your drink."

I grabbed the glass from his hand and put it behind the bar. Made my way back over to him and help him to the couch. As he laid down, I grabbed the blanket from the back of the couch and covered him up.

"Let me know if you need anything." I said.

"Okay." He said as his eyes began to close. "Can you tell be a bedtime story?"

"Stop me if you've heard this." I joked. "An alcoholic, a hopeless romantic, and a gay guy all go to a haunted inn..."

"You forgot about the ghost part." Brandon tried to enunciate.

"This is me you're talking to. No such thing as ghosts." I chided him. "Now try and go to sleep."

I made my way over to the doorway, took one last look his direction, then turned out the light and found my way to my own room. In my room I found Louie already sprawled out on the bed asleep. It's amazing how a creature so small can manage to lay in such a way as he leaves me a very small sleeping area. I tried to slide Louie over a bit and give myself some more room, but he simply rolled back into the same spot.

I grabbed my glass and went into my bathroom. I took a sip of tequila as I stared at the stranger in the mirror. Sucking in my stomach in, I patted myself on the belly.

"Not that bad for fifty." I told myself.

Then I let my gut return to its regular state.

"Okay, maybe it's time so spend a few hours in the gym." I sighed as I grabbed my toothbrush and applied some toothpaste. As I started brushing my teeth, Louie joined me in the bathroom and hopped up on the sink. This was code for 'turn on the faucet jackass, I prefer running water to that stagnant crap you leave in the bowl for me'. I turned the water on and he immediately submersed his head in the stream. Looked like more of a bath than a drink.

31

"Easy buddy." I tried to enunciate with a mouthful of toothpaste. "I'm not giving you mouth to mouth if you drown."

Louie pulled his head out of the stream long enough to look at me and whine.

"What? You spend half the day licking your ass." I retorted as I spit out toothpaste. "If you need mouth to mouth, there's a good chance you're going to die."

Louie shook the water off his head, spraying me in the process and jumped down off the sink. I finished brushing my teeth and took one last look in the mirror.

"Fuck me." I sighed.

Where had the time gone? When I was young, I never even thought I'd make it to fifty. Now I'm just glad I was wrong. When you're young you never really think about growing this old, let alone ever imagine you'll grow up to be average. When I was five, I wanted to be an astronaut. When I was ten, I wanted to be a professional football player. At fifteen I would have bet my life I was going to be a rock star. Somewhere in my teens, I think I also thought I'd be a gynecologist. Until I realized it was not as cool a job as I once thought.

At what point do dreams die? I don't remember waking up one day and saying, 'time to get a real job and blend in with the other sheep'. It just happened. And if the me of today could go back to that point in time where I gave up, I would slap the shit out of that me and tell me not to give in. But all the responsibilities that come with adulthood eventually wear a person down to the point they can no longer fight back. Dreams get replaced with responsibilities. Passion and desire get replaced with boredom and empathy.

And then you wake up one day and you're fifty.

I should probably stop whining. You all probably think I'm pathetic by now, given my 'responsible' job is getting paid to have drinks and spend nights in creepy old buildings. Probably still a step up from sitting behind a desk. But networks are fickle, and as much as I have a decent gig right now, the odds are that in ten years I'll be handing you your cart as you walk into the grocery store. I'll still be alone. And I'll still be taking orders from a cat.

CHAPTER 3

I remember waking up that night in a cold sweat. Turning to your side and realizing there is no one there anymore is a horribly empty feeling. I looked at the clock to see it was only three in the morning. It was hard to decide if I was more tired or more thirsty. As I decided on the latter, I slowly rose and fumbled my way to the hallway in the dark. Making my way to the kitchen I soon realized I had company. Louie had woken and was now trailing close behind.

I grabbed a beer out of the fridge, popped it open, and took a large swallow. Louie looked at me with those desperate, needy eyes.

"Buddy, you're supposed to be on the wagon." I pleaded.

He continued to stare, and obviously his will was stronger than mine, as I gave in. I grabbed him a bowl and poured some of my beer into it. He immediately began lapping it up. I sat down on the floor next to him and raised my bottle. "Cheers little buddy!"

As Theresa walked into the kitchen and turned the light on, I wasn't sure which I was more disturbed by. That she was there at three in the morning, or the fact I had drank so many margaritas that I had completely forgotten I had company stay over. As it came back to me that the gang had crashed in the spare bedrooms, I was thankful I passed out in my clothes and wasn't sitting on the kitchen floor naked as was so often the case. Brandon was probably still passed out on my couch. I should probably check on him. He was in pretty rough shape last night.

She looked at flickering bulb in the ceiling and shook her head.

"I'll put a new bulb in it tomorrow." I assured her. "I'm handy like that."

"Yeah, right." She laughed. "Like you were going to fix the fence in backyard or like you kept saying you'd to fix the outlet for the water softener?"

"Those are still on my 'to do' list." I motioned toward Louie lapping away at the beer I had poured into his bowl and smiled. "Told you he was going to have a relapse."

Louie finished as much as he could and made his way back out to the living room. I finished the rest of my beer and headed back over to the fridge. Much to my disappointment, this had been the last beer. My pain must have been obvious as I closed the door of the fridge.

"Well, that is certainly not good!" Theresa mused.

"Not good? More like tragic!" I pouted.

"Yes, the sinking of the Titanic, the destruction of Pompeii, and Sebastian running out of alcohol...tragedies all." She mocked me. "I weep for humanity."

Her sarcasm was always painted on with a pretty thick brush. I think that was one of things I always loved about her. Not sure if she had always been like that, or if that was just a natural transition after living with me for several years.

I smiled as I noticed Louie had left quite a bit of beer in his bowl. As she followed my gaze to the bowl on the floor, she could simply shake her head. I sat back on the floor, picked up the bowl, and took a nice big sip.

"Drinking beer from a cat bowl, after your cat has slobbered in it, may be a warning sign that you're an alcoholic." She sighed.

"You've known me how long?" I smiled. "I'm pretty sure we passed the warning signs years ago."

"And on that note..." She exited quickly and went back to the spare bedroom at the end of the hall. I followed her and stopped just outside the door.

"You know this hotel has excellent turn down service." I mused, not realizing the drunk me was not nearly as charming as I thought.

"You and I have very different memories of the services performed here." She smiled and shook her head. "I remember having to carry the inn keeper to bed most nights."

"The inn keeper was usually over served!"

"Yes, by the bartender. Which if memory serves, was also you?" She managed to muster up a smile, yet still make it look disapproving. "Goodnight."

She shut the door as I stood in the hallway. As I raised my hand to knock on the door, I thought better and left well enough alone. Feeling a little dejected I made my way to the bathroom. I ran a little water over my face and stared in the mirror. I barely recognized the face staring back at me. The last several years had certainly not been kind. I could see perfume poking out of the top of Christy's purse on the vanity. It was the same brand Theresa wears on occasion. I grabbed it, removed the cap, and squirted it in the air. Then quickly moved my nose into the path of the falling mist.

I loved that scent, her scent.

I sprayed a small amount on the collar of my shirt and put it back in her purse. Then I noticed her lipstick. Which I immediately confiscated and took with me to put to good use.

The next morning, as I passed the bathroom, Christy was busy getting ready. She frantically looked through her purse, then began looking on the bathroom floor.

"Everything okay?" I asked.

"I dropped my lipstick somewhere." She continued to look for a minute, then gave up.

"I was going to make some coffee. Want some?" I asked as I chuckled to myself..

"That would be great, thank you." She went back to getting ready as I headed off to the kitchen.

I got the coffee started and rummaged through the kitchen for food. This had truly become a bachelor pad. Six cans of cat food and some saltines in the cupboard. The fridge had a carton of old milk and a white Styrofoam container that I can only fear was leftovers from a week ago. Theresa walked into the kitchen.

"Brandon still sleeping?" Theresa asked as she walked into the kitchen.

"If you mean, is he still passed out?" I laughed. "Yes, he's still passed out."

I poured us each a cup of coffee and sat down at the kitchen table. She stood at the kitchen counter and smelled the coffee.

"I do miss your coffee." She sighed.

That's pretty funny. I miss her touch, her smell, the taste of her lip balm, and a million other things about her. She missed my coffee. I hadn't even realized I chuckled out loud.

"What?" She looked at me oddly.

"Nothing." As I sipped my coffee there was an awkward silence. I could feel she was about to venture into a serious conversation. I had done pretty well at not being alone with her for too long, so she had no chance to bring up the dreaded divorce paperwork conversation. Thank God for intervention. Brandon sleepily walked into the kitchen rubbing the sleep out of his eyes.

"I smell coffee." He yawned.

I pointed to the coffee pot on the counter. Theresa looked up from smelling her coffee to look at Brandon, then stopped and shook her head. She proceeded to glare across the table at me. I smiled and shrugged innocently as I took a sip of my coffee. As Christy was also lured to the kitchen by the smell of coffee, she looked at Brandon, then turned sharply to me.

"Can I have my lipstick back?" She was trying so hard to be stern and not give me the satisfaction of a smile, but it had to be hard under the circumstances.

"Yeah, I think it's in the living room." I pointed in the general direction.

"Yes, I saw it on the coffee table." Brandon chimed in still clueless as he joined me at the table. And while I must admit that was definitely not his shade of lipstick, it did bring out his eyes a little bit.

"What are you guys staring at?" He asked as we all continued to admire him.

As Brandon grew curious and exited the kitchen, I soon had the kitchen to myself, and enjoyed the last of my coffee. Soon after, I walked into the bathroom to find Brandon scrubbing violently to remove the ruby red lipstick from his lips.

"I guess I should know by now, not to pass out anywhere near you." Brandon said while scrubbing.

"C'mon, you've had way worse." I tried to reassure him.

"True, this isn't like waking up in a Mexican hotel with no money and no clothes." He stopped scrubbing long enough to glare at me and raise an eyebrow.

"Hey, I came and got you eventually." I said as a grabbed the wash cloth out of his hand. "Hold still."

I continued to scrub at the lipstick wondering how in the hell women go through this crap on a daily basis.

"Besides, I'm pretty sure I still owe you for New Orleans." I declared.

"What?" Brandon backed away. "As I recall, New Orleans ended up as a win for you!"

I had almost forgotten about that, but smiled as I began to reminisce. Brandon and I used to take some pretty wild vacations. New Orleans, Key West, Savannah…anywhere we could find a haunted hotel and plentiful booze. My memory ended up being quite fuzzy on a few of these, but I do remember New Orleans.

We were staying at the Hotel Monteleone, known for its famous Carousel bar which spun slowly as you sipped on your cocktail. At least I assumed it spun. Looking back now, that might have just been me. It was also known for its many ghosts that take up residence in the hotel. I came out of the bathroom, still wrapped in only a towel, to find Brandon sitting on my hotel room bed. As usual, he was ready for the night's festivities long before me.

"Ready to go?" He asked.

"Almost." I responded as I made my way over to the desk and grabbed the bottle of tequila. "Just need a roadie."

As I looked to the empty ice bucket, I let out a loud sigh of frustration.

"While I get dressed can you run and get me some ice?" I handed him the bucket. He simply sat on the bed and stared at me. "Come on, please?"

"I'm not here to facilitate your addiction." He finally responded. "You want ice, go get it yourself."

"Fine." I said indignantly, then turned before exiting. "Like I drink any more than you do."

"Now." He interrupted the beginning of my rant. "I don't feel like sitting in the room all night!"

"You know every year when we take our little trip, you get more and more uptight." I said while tightening the knot on my towel to make sure it would survive the trek to the ice machine.

"That's because every year, this is less of a vacation and more of a baby-sitting job." He replied.

"Ouch." I smiled as I made my way to the door.

"You've got two minutes to get ice and finish getting ready." Brandon pulled out a cigar and lighter. "Then I'm leaving to have a smoke and get a real drink."

I exited the room, leaving the door open just a crack, so I didn't have to bring my key. Luckily the hallway was pretty dead for being midnight. I only ran into one couple who gave me an odd glance but kept walking. This was probably not rare behavior for New Orleans.

As I got my ice and began to make my way back to the room, suddenly the fire alarm went off. I panicked for a moment until I remembered the cigar and lighter in Brandon's hand.

"Asshole!" I muttered to myself.

My pace back to the room quickened as now people were beginning to flood the hallway. I passed an elderly woman who smiled at me as I went by.

"Not in a million years, gramma." I muttered to myself as soon as I was out of earshot.

Who was I kidding, after a few cocktails I probably would have. Once back to the room I saw that the door was now completely closed. I tried the handle anyway, but to no avail.

"Dammit!" I pounded on the door. "Funny! Now open the damn door!"

People continued to file past me in the hallway. I knocked again but still received no response. I turned around and leaned against the door just in time to see a stunning young woman walk down the hallway. She

41

smiled cautiously at me.

"Marital problems?" She asked.

"Not married." I raised my ring finger to show her, but had to quickly return my hand to the towel as it began to slip.

"Hmmm, not married?" She laughed as she walked back towards me. "Hard to figure."

Then I felt the door open behind me as Brandon poked his head out.

"Thay there, dear." He said as effeminately as he could. "Did you forget your key again?"

"Oh, I see." She said as she took a step backwards. "I'm so sorry."

"No, you don't see." I said trying to salvage the situation. "He's just kidding around. He's just a friend."

She was nodding in agreement, but obviously not buying my story.

"Tell her!" I motioned for Brandon to come clean.

"Did last night mean nothing to you?" He continued his pathetic charade as now he also pretended to cry. "You can't keep treating me this way!"

"I am very sorry about him." I said as I turned back to her. "My name is Sebastian."

I carefully extended my hand to introduce myself, while securing the towel with my other hand. She cautiously shook my hand.

"It's nice to meet you." She said as she released my hand. "I think."

"This is Brandon." I said but as I turned, Brandon yanked my towel.

"Two timer!" He said as he disappeared in the room with my towel and what was left of my dignity. I could hear the door slam shut again, then the click of the lock.

She couldn't help but glance down under the circumstances, then quickly looked back up at me.

"Hallway must be freezing." She smiled.

"You have no idea." I said while trying to cover up with my hands, which sadly wasn't hard to do under the circumstances.

Given how we had met, I am still a little stunned she would eventually agree to marry me. I guess Brandon was correct. I did owe him for New Orleans....

As my train of thought returned to the present, I noticed Theresa walk past the bathroom while I continued to work at the lipstick on Brandon.

She stopped, then backed up slowly to look in the bathroom. Looking back, I certainly understand how it may have looked. Brandon in only his boxers and me washing his face.

"This explains so much." She smiled. "I had always assumed it was the excessive drinking that killed our sex life that last year."

She shook her head.

"Little did I know it was my lack of chest hair and a penis!" She smiled dismissively and left the doorway.

As I tried not to laugh, Brandon ignored her and continued to wash his face. Theresa headed down the hallway and I followed close behind.

"I may have had some indiscretions." I shifted to a hushed tone. "But it was never of a homosexual nature."

She stopped, turned and glared at me.

"Oh my god, I was just making a joke. Don't be such a homophobe." She said and turned to resume walking. Then stopped abruptly and turned towards me. "I would have almost understood, no actually preferred an indiscretion with someone you cared about, instead of those nameless, faceless bimbos!"

I had no clever response for one of the few times in my life. This was one conversation we had done our best to actually avoid, even as our marriage crumbled. For those keeping score at home, you've probably already deduced that this marriage ended solely because of me. I'll never argue that. Most people say a bad relationship is the fault of both parties. I can safely tell you that was not the case here.

But I did love this woman until the day I died, and had I been in a better frame of mind, would have fought hell to make sure I never brought a tear to her eyes. Instead, I drank myself into a soul numbing coma, did everything I could to hurt her, and made sure she would leave me. In a way, I guess I believed I was doing the right thing. The man she fell in love with, the man she married, was gone. And she needed the right push to be able to move on to what I could only imagine would be a better life. I had to give her that push or she would have stayed with me and gone down with the ship. I at least hoped I was saving one of us.

"What? No smart aleck remarks for that?" She glared at me.

All of her pent-up anger was finally coming out. All I could manage was a mumbled apology. I'm sure it was barely audible. Apologies have never been my strong suit.

"What was that?" She asked. "Speak up! If you're going to insult my intelligence, at least be man enough to do it clearly!"

"I said..." I tried my best to compose myself. Which, under the circumstances, was impossible. "...I said, I'm sorry."

As I tried to enunciate, I fought unsuccessfully to hold back a tear. It managed to slip out and roll aimlessly down my check. As I looked to the ground, I realized this unexpected emotion had also left Theresa speechless for the first time in, well...as long as I've known her.

It had been fifteen months and twenty-three days since the last time I had shed a tear. It may seem odd to most that I could actually remember that stat down to the day. But there are some sorrows that a person never overcomes. Sometimes life is just a constant reminder of a scar so deep that you know it better than any birth mark.

I tried to make my way back to the kitchen with my head in a fog, still unclear as to how I found myself in that conversation. In the kitchen I found Christy sipping on her coffee, along with Jerry and Bobby. I grabbed my cup and topped it off.

"Please tell me you got a picture of it?" Pleaded Jerry.

Part of me was still in the hallway apologizing to Theresa. I could hear the others talking, but the words were not making it through. After all that had happened, was that really the first time I had apologized to her? The more I thought about it, the more I began to realize what a shit I had truly been.

"Hello?" Jerry finally broke my concentration. "Please tell me you got a photo before Brandon washed his face?"

"Sadly, no." I finally smiled again. "I'm pretty sure he would have destroyed my phone had I pulled it out and even tried."

"That's too bad. I would have liked to see it." Bobby laughed.

"No, trust me." Christy shuddered. "It will take me years to burn that image from my memory."

"Hey, I didn't look that bad." Brandon interjected as he walked into the kitchen and joined the discussion.

"Certainly didn't look that good, either." Christy added.

As they continued to discuss the finer points of Brandon's transgender incident, I ventured back in the hall to see how Theresa was.

After a brief scan of the house, it was clear she had left already. Not sure how I felt about our discussion ending the way it did. While I'm glad I apologized, I wish she wouldn't have taken off so abruptly. Realizing there was nothing I could do at the moment, I headed back into the kitchen to rejoin the others.

"Anything we still need to pick up before we pack up tomorrow?" I asked as I entered the kitchen, seeing the others had finished their coffee and looked to be preparing to leave as well.

"No, we're good to go." Replied Jerry. "I've got some new memory cards at my place in case we need extras."

"Meet back here round nine tomorrow morning to go over the layout and walk through all the gear one more time?"

"Sounds good." Jerry confirmed while the rest of us all nodded in agreement.

As everyone made their way to the front door, I followed them out. As they each made their way to their cars, Brandon hesitated and fell behind. He stopped and turned to me.

"You okay?" He asked with an air of concern in his voice.

"Of course, why?"

"I had caught part your hallway conversation." He added. "Don't want you going into this investigation if you have other issues, bigger issues, to deal with."

"I'm good. I am after all a professional." I assured him with a smile. "Besides, I think this investigation will help me to get my focus back."

"I hope so." He smiled and patted me on the shoulder. "Cause I need you to get right."

I nodded in agreement. He turned and went to his car. Hard to say if I was feeling fortunate that I have a friend who cares the way he does, or if I was pissed off that he was trying to lecture me. I may have a slight alcohol problem, but I wasn't the one that passed out on the couch last night. What's that saying about the pot and the kettle?

CHAPTER 4

After the others had all left, I tried to get some things done around the house. But I kept drifting back to my conversation with Theresa. Was that really the first time I had apologized to her? I really was an asshole, wasn't I?

As I sat at my desk, I looked over at the bottle of tequila, then to the clock. Nine in the morning and I already felt like I needed a drink. I tried to ignore the bottle and get back to work, pulling out my copy of the files Christy left behind. As I started shuffling through the papers, I looked over at the bottle once again. I don't know why I play this game with myself. I know I'm going to give in. I think we've already established my lack of will power. But in my twisted little mind, I guess I considered it a moral victory when I could make it until ten without opening the bottle.

I continued to read through the papers occasionally looking over at the bottle. As always, I eventually lost out to my demons. I reached for the bottle and poured myself a glass. I raised my glass to the bottle.

"Cheers mate! I smiled. "It was a hard-fought battle, but as always, you are the victor!" I looked at the clock and saw it was in fact only nine-thirty-four. Okay, maybe not quite as hard-fought battle as I had thought. I took a much-needed sip from my glass. "This is going to be a long day."

I was never much for the homework side of an investigation. To be honest, I usually left it up to Christy and Theresa. As chauvinistic as that sounds, they were just better at it than anyone else in the group. Brandon and I didn't have the attention span to focus on the details long enough to do it thoroughly. Bobby didn't have the time. And the one time we let Jerry handle all the paperwork, all the notes were covered in smiley faces and frowny faces depending on what they were referring to. So why was I now trying to do some research? Beats the hell out of me. I suppose a small part of me realizes this season may be our last chance to salvage this show. Which despite all of my complaining and skepticism, really did mean a lot to me.

As I was finally about to get started, I was startled by a knock on the door. Seeing as everyone I know had just left an hour ago, it was fairly safe to assume it was either a Girl Scout selling cookies or a Jehovah's Witness selling salvation. Neither of which I considered to be worth the investment. I opened the laptop and powered it up, when another, more forceful knock once again broke the silence.

"For the love of…" I stood up and made my way to the door and yanked it open.

I was now starting to wish for the Jehovah's Witness, as on my front step stood Tony Vega and Elizabeth Hatcher, our show's producers. They were like the Charles Manson and Lizzie Borden of the television industry, but without the charm or cuddliness.

"Well…" I stammered. "This is a surprise."

"You look disappointed to see us?" Questioned Elizabeth.

"No, not at all. I was just hoping for Girl Scouts." I smiled. "Really love those thin mints."

As expected, neither broke into a smile. There was a brief awkward silence that seemed to be confounded by the fact I couldn't stop staring at what I could only imagine was Tony's attempt at growing a mustache. I'd seen high school boys do a better job before hitting puberty.

"You going to invite us in?" Tony said as he was obviously growing impatient.

"Oh, yes, sorry about that." I moved to one side of the doorway and allowed them to pass. "Where are my manners?"

As they entered, they looked around my living room. Their dismissive condescending looks made me want to escort them back out, but I figured that might not be the smartest career move.

"Probably a little different from what a couple of network executives are used to." I tried my best to lighten the situation up a little. "My chalet in Vail is much nicer."

Tony once again stared unamused, but Elizabeth this time at least forced an attempt at a smile. She must be in a little better mood knowing that her mustache looks considerably better that Tony's.

"So, Anthony, to what do I owe this unexpected honor?" I asked cautiously.

"It's Tony." He shook his head. "As I'm pretty sure I've stated on several occasions."

"Yes, of course." I smiled as Elizabeth opened her case and removed what looked to be a new piece of equipment for the show.

"I have a new toy I'd like you to test out for me." She said as she handed it to me. This was an SLS camera. Quite a nice piece of equipment actually. Fairly new to the market and not a lot of information on them out there.

"Are you familiar with the SLR camera?" Tony questioned.

"SLS camera." I happily corrected the smug prick. "And yes, I am familiar with them, but have never actually had a chance to get my hands on one yet. Thank you."

"I saw the top-rated ghost show using it and figured we'd better get one if we want to try and keep pace with them." Elizabeth said.

"Keep pace?" Tony mocked. "That would imply they're even in the same race."

Tony was making it more and more difficult to bite my tongue.

"Comparing the two shows." Tony continued. "Is like comparing the Olympics to the special Olympics. The other network has the Olympics and we have the Special Olympics."

"Couldn't agree more. I think we are far superior." I added. "I've felt for quite some time the athletes in the Special Olympics have far more integrity than the others by far."

"Boys, are you just about done?" Elizabeth jumped in and tried to get us back on track. "We have work to do."

"By the way, Tony, great mustache." I laughed condescendingly. "That'll really be something once you hit puberty."

Tony shook his head as I turned to Elizabeth who was obviously trying not to laugh as she must have obviously thought the same.

"Now we're good." I smiled. "The SLS camera, Structured Light Sensor camera, is kind of a more advanced version of the whole Xbox Kinect thing."

I moved the camera closer to them.

"So, it supposedly can pick up things we may not be able to see with the naked eye and display them in the stick figure looking images that a Kinect does." I turned the tablet side towards them. "It's not charged yet, but if it was, you'd see the screen broken up into six areas. The large part of the screen is the actual footage. What the camera is seeing. But then there are also smaller windows displaying a variety of other metered readings."

"So, this will come in handy for your team?" Elizabeth asked.

"Oh, most definitely." I responded. "And while the jury is still out as to whether or not this thing does what it says it does, the viewers love this kind of technology."

"Good." Tony said. "Now quid pro quo."

I simply stared at him waiting for him to expand on his feeble attempt at a dated movie reference.

"We do something for you…" He motioned with his hands. "You do something for us?"

"Yes, I know what it means. I did see the movie." I said disgustedly. "I was hoping you'd actually elaborate on what you wanted in return?"

"I believe we've discussed in the past Jerry toning things down a bit." Elizabeth tried to word delicately as I nodded. "The clothing, the gestures."

"Some of the comments." Tony added. "And we'd more than discussed it. We demanded it, and it never got taken care of."

"So, you want me to turn him straight?" I laughed. "I'll make sure to get right on that."

"He doesn't fit in with the network mold." Tony glared.

"The network image is very conservative, and he's made no effort to change." Elizabeth added.

"It's not as easy as all that." I defended Jerry. "I can't just tell him to change his whole personality."

Fact of the matter was, I'd never even discussed it with Jerry. Who was I to tell him to change who he is because a few of our holier than thou sponsors were uncomfortable having a gay man on the show?

"I'll talk to him again and see what we can come up with." I said trying to appease them for now, knowing full well the discussion would never actually take place.

"It's too late for that." Tony responded harshly. "We gave you the entire season last year to take of this and it never happened."

Elizabeth nodded in agreement.

"So, what are you saying? We're filming in two days. We would need time to transition in a replacement if it comes to that."

"We've already arranged that." Tony handed me a folder.

"What is this?" I opened the folder and began to skim through it. "Um, Anthony, he seems to have the same last name as you?"

"Yes, he's my nephew. You have a problem with that?"

"So many I wouldn't even know where to begin." I glanced briefly at the resume. "Lovely, what does he know about paranormal investigation?"

"What does he need to know about a fake show?" Tony sneered. "Just have him do what Jerry did. Watch the cameras!"

"There's a little more to it than that. Jerry helps Brandon edit, arranges the scenes, and pretty much directs the entire live operation."

"All of which William will learn in time with the help of Christy and the others." Tony spoke confidently.

"We're all a little too busy to play wet nurse for your nephew who thinks he'd like a career in television." My frustration was turning to anger. "Maybe you can get Billy a spot on one of the cooking shows?"

"Jerry is either off the show, or the shows off the air!" Tony demanded. "The network has cut the last check they ever will for him."

"I'm sorry it came to this." Elizabeth moved closer to me with a somewhat genuine look of sorrow on her face, while Tony stood there with a smug grin on his face that I so wanted to remove with my fist.

I moved across the room to the bar and poured myself a drink. I drank it fast, and poured myself another and carried it with as I walked back across the room to them.

"William will be there Wednesday. Make it work or find yourself a new career." Tony said while brushing past me.

"Anything else?" I asked.

"We're serious." Tony said. "Either Jerry's gone, or you're all gone."

I nodded and walked them to the door while sipping on my drink. I opened the door and motioned for them to exit.

"Wish I could say it was a pleasure to see you." I said as they exited, and I quickly slammed the door behind them.

I walked back across the living room to the bar, finished my drink and slammed the glass down on the counter. There was no way we were getting rid of Jerry. But I also didn't want to lose everything I'd worked to build. I poured myself a much larger drink and walked out back to sit on the dock. Nice thing about living on the water I could almost always calm myself down by walking out here and letting nature take over.

Living on Tybee Island was like the best of both worlds for me. Tybee Island was about fifteen minutes from Savannah, which for a ghost hunter was pretty convenient, seeing as half of Savannah seems to be haunted. Our entire first season was shot within two hours of my house. The old Charleston jail was the farthest we had to go that year. Quite a contrast from season two where we either had to fly to locations or spend a full day driving.

The other bonus to Tybee Island was water. I'd always loved the water. I'm not even that much of a fisherman or boating enthusiast, but there's always been something about the water I've been drawn to. I'd found myself a small house on a canal that leads to the ocean. Sitting on my dock, other than my neighbors on the sides, the view was all canal and marshlands. Being saltwater, we even saw the occasional dolphin or manatee come through our canal. As relaxing as it sounds, it didn't seem to be calming me down this time though.

I stood at the edge of the dock and looked down at my reflection in the water, waiting to see who was going to take a drink first, my reflection or me? Oddly enough it was a tie. I guess we both have a drinking problem.

As I sat down on the dock and let my feet hang off, I could see Theresa walking down the yard. While I normally enjoyed seeing her, this wasn't the time.

"I should have poured a larger glass." I muttered under my breath.

"I think that glass looks plenty large."

How the hell did she hear that from there? I must have been using my bar voice already.

"I've got to get a lock for that gate." I mustered up an obviously phony smile. After the conversation I just had, the last thing I wanted was more pressure.

"You know that wouldn't keep me out, right?" She laughed and came onto the dock, sitting down beside me. "I saw the evil twins were here."

"Hence the larger glass." I lifted my drink in the air to show her.

"You're not really blaming your morning drink on them, are you?" She smiled. "Remember who you're talking to."

"I wasn't blaming the drink on them, smart ass." I replied. "Just the fact I poured a larger glass than usual!"

She laughed as I took a sip and put the glass down on the dock.

"They want us to get rid of Jerry." As I forced the words out, they left a foul taste in my mouth that even the alcohol didn't seem to be able to wash away.

"I was worried it was something like that." She said. "I was worried all last season they might do it then."

"I never really thought they were that serious, I guess. I mean who really gives a damn about a person's sexual orientation?" As I spoke, I could feel myself getting worked up again. "He's great at his job and he's a good person. What else matters?"

"It's all political. The right person, saw the wrong thing, and they're making a fuss." She replied. "What are you going to do?"

"I don't know. I need to think on it." I took another sip of my drink.

"Think on it or drink on it?"

"Is there a difference when it comes to me?" I smiled. "I know I'm not getting rid of Jerry because of some uptight prudes."

"And you're willing to lose the show?"

"You know how many times I've started over in my life?" I laughed. "Who cares if I do it one more time."

"You know for a hundred bucks I know someone that will take them out." She joked.

"You've definitely been around me for too long. You're even starting to think like me."

"Well, except for the fact that I say it as a joke, and you've probably given it some realistic consideration." She added.

"Not like it would be a great loss to humanity." I took another sip of my drink and looked out across the water. "And as an added bonus, we get Billy on our crew."

"Who's Billy?"

"Tony's nephew." I said while taking another swallow of my drink.

"Oh god. William Vega?" She said with disgust.

"You know him?"

"Yes, and you would too if you ever bothered to attend any of the networks promotional events."

"I think the idea behind a promotional event is to get people to like the network programs." I smiled. "I'm pretty sure Charles Manson would make a better promotional figure than I would."

"Can't argue that, but you're a giant step above William Vega."

"How so?"

"Picture a spoiled, self-absorbed country club candy ass who can barely tie his own shoes without help."

"Lovely."

"I am going to leave you to your thoughts." She said as she stood up. "No matter how homicidal they may be."

As she began to walk off the dock, I finished my drink and got up to follow her.

"So why did you come back over?"

"I think we've been putting off a fairly serious talk because it never seems to be the right time." She sighed. "And now suddenly I don't think this is the right time either. You have enough on your plate."

I nodded, now feeling almost fortunate Tony and Elizabeth had stopped by. I at least dodged the divorce discussion one more time. She let herself out the gate while I took a deep breath. I started to make my way back to the house figuring I should still look over the Wakefield inn paperwork a little more thoroughly.

After making a quick stop in the living room to refill my glass, I headed to the office and began laying out the paperwork in chronological order. As I did, I began looking at the dates more closely. As I tried to space them by decade, I noticed a large gap from the beginning of the nineteen hundred's all the way to the nineteen forties. I looked through the folder again to make sure I hadn't left anything behind. I took out four post it notes and labeled them for each decade and stuck them in the gap of the paperwork.

I began to look over the incidents that were there, starting at the beginning with the Wakefield's. I opened my laptop and began searching the internet. Christy's research was spot on. I could find nothing further on the Wakefield's time at the inn.. So, I began reading further into Isadora Gallo's fateful visit, and the more recent cases that we had only skimmed over.

Nineteen fifty-eight, David and Kelly Palmer, checked into the Wakefield. Newlywed couple on their honeymoon. What should have been the couple's happiest day turned out to be anything but. By the end of the night, both were dead. Palmer, a pediatrician at St Mary's Hospital in Pennsylvania, shot his bride and then himself in their hotel room just hours after they exchanged vows.

Interviewed wedding guests noticed nothing irregular between the couple throughout the ceremony and reception and even remarked that they had never seen two people more in love. After the reception, the happy couple made their way up to their room. At roughly three in the morning, employees and guests awoke to the sound of gun shots.

When the police arrived on the scene, they were met at the door by the owner of the inn and were led to the couple's room. Inside they found Kelly Palmer shot once in the head, and David Palmer also shot in the head, gun still in hand.

Nineteen sixty-seven, Elizabeth Andrews, a guest at the Inn, suffered a severe allergic reaction to shellfish and died before they could reach the hospital. Doctors at the hospital confirmed that Elizabeth died from anaphylaxis after eating some type of shellfish that caused a violent and deadly allergic reaction.

The Wakefield Inn staff were interviewed, and pointed out that not only did they see her have the chicken that night for dinner, but there was no shellfish of any kind on the menu that week. Police investigating the property confirmed there was no seafood of any kind in the kitchen.

Nineteen seventy-six, John Ringling, staying at the inn while in town for business, was found starved to death. Ringling was a psychologist staying at the inn while attending a nearby convention. Oddly, he chose to stay at the inn, instead of the hotel attached to the convention center. Friends of Ringling said he chose to stay there specifically because of the haunted past. Ringling was known by his friends to be a bit of an amateur paranormal enthusiast, and would often stay at hotels with checkered pasts while traveling on business. The police had made a note of a briefcase in the room containing what they believed were paranormal tools and a Ouija board. But upon checking all evidence in back at the police station, this briefcase was missing.

After examination, the coroner deduced he had a form of paralysis in his legs, which prevented him from leaving his room. But it doesn't explain how a seemingly healthy man had starved to death in twenty-four hours. The staff were interviewed, and many remember seeing Ringling eating in the dining room the previous night. Not to mention he had a fully stocked mini fridge at the time of his death, which he could have dragged himself to even without the use of his legs.

Nineteen eighty-five, Jennifer Thomas was found drowned, face down in a tub of water no more than twelve inches deep. The medical examiner found traces of alcohol in her system, but not enough that would have caused her to pass out or lose control.

Thomas, in town to visit relatives for the holidays, chose to stay at the inn instead of with her family due to her allergy to their cats. The family contacted the inn when she didn't show up and couldn't be reached by phone. The medical examiner placed the time of death at eleven pm the previous evening, even though several staff members swear to seeing her in the hallway the following morning between five and six am.

Nineteen ninety-four, Thomas Spalding falls to his death from the roof. Spalding, a successful attorney, had just been promoted to partner in his firm the week before. When officers arrived on the scene, Spalding's body was found in the garden on the south side of the Inn, and the roof access door was still locked. An autopsy found that he died of multiple injuries typically seen from jumping from that height, the medical examiner's office said. His death was ruled a suicide. The only staff members with keys to access the roof were questioned and all had alibis for the whereabouts at the time of the accident. And all had their copy of the roof access key with them at all times.

60

Two thousand and three, Kathy Taylor was found hanged in her room. Taylor, a recent college graduate, was staying at the inn while in town for a job interview. When the staff entered her room to clean, they found her hanging by a bed sheet from the exposed beam in the corner of the room. Police were called and the case would be ruled a suicide, even though the sheet used was not from the bed, but an antique that would later be established as the same exact manufacturer as the sheet used by Abigail Wakefield to hang herself nearly a century earlier. A manufacturer that had not been in business for over sixty years.

There was room for interpretation or discrepancies in every one of these cases. The more intriguing aspect to me was the gap of forty years where there was no paperwork or history of any kind. Even taking the time to google Wakefield Inn for every individual year turned up zero hits. No records of any kind. It was as if it didn't exist for that stretch of time.

After combing the internet for what seemed like hours, I finally gave up. For one reason or another, the Wakefield itself was a ghost for those decades. Either under renovation, or closed down altogether, there were no records to be found. Whatever the case, I certainly wasn't going to get any further on this today.

CHAPTER 5

The next morning, we all gathered for our little refresher course on the equipment and terms. You'd be amazed at what some of us can forget in a single offseason. As I entered my office, all of our equipment was spread out on the desk and table. Jerry and Christy were testing equipment, while Brandon was looking at the computer and Theresa was going over notes.

"Where's Bobby?" I asked.

"He called. He's running a little late." Christy smiled. "He said it was fine to start without him."

I shook my head.

"Does he not realize the reason we're going over the equipment is for him to finally learn what everything is?" I ran my hands through my hair and sighed. "We all know most of this stuff already."

I walked over to the table and picked up an EMF meter.

"This will be our most watched episode ever. We don't need Bobby saying, 'I used the blinky thing to see if there is any PMS activity' like he did in Louisiana!"

"That was pretty funny." Brandon laughed.

"Made me laugh." Theresa shook her head and smiled.

"If we are going to break into the top two, we need to step things up this season." I continued. "All of us."

"I don't know." Jerry interjected. "I hate to say it, but I think a lot of people tune in just to watch him fumble through this stuff."

"I was thinking the same thing." Added Christy. "As much as

people like the paranormal side of the show, half of them just like watching you and Bobby get sillier as the night goes on and you have a few too many drinks."

"I'm not going to argue that." I conceded. "But I think he still needs to know the equipment, if for no other reason, so he can discuss it intelligently with us when the cameras aren't rolling.

Maybe I was expecting too much from a show called Spirits with Spirits? Observing feedback from our Twitter following, Instagram, and Facebook page, most of our supporters were following us for the amusement aspect of the show. Maybe trying to take us in more of a legitimate direction was a bad idea? But I felt our current format was never going to allow us to move up, and I truly believed we had had the potential to be a better show than the others. We just needed to find our niche.

"Not to put a damper on our investigation." Brandon changed the subject. "Anyone else noticing a disturbing pattern in all of the occurrences at the inn?"

We all shook our heads.

"I was reading through the copies of the reports Christy made for me, and there's a definite pattern to these documented events." Brandon walked over to the bulletin board. "Isadora Gallo nineteen forty-nine, The Palmers nineteen fifty-eight, Elizabeth Andrews nineteen sixty-seven, John Ringling nineteen seventy-six, Jennifer Thomas nineteen eighty-five, Thomas Spalding nineteen ninety-four, and Kathy Taylor two thousand and three."

We continued to stare at him waiting for more.

"Every nine years!" Brandon shook his head. "Did you all fail math class?"

"I'm sorry I thought we were actually listening for some useful information." I began to look at the dates to confirm what he had said, but didn't really see the relevance of what I just considered to be a coincidence.

"More importantly." He continued. "Am I the only one bothered by the fact that we a now going in two thousand and twelve? Coincidently nine, yes you heard correctly, nine years after the last documented instance."

"Let's not get too worked up until we can have a second party confirm all stories and dates." I said, then turned to Jerry. "Jerry, you still know anyone at the Tribune that could pull these up and verify for us?"

"I looked them all up and verified them myself last night." He explained. "All the dates and articles Christy pulled are correct."

"I was hoping we could get someone at the Tribune to verify. They have access to quite a bit that we don't."

"I used their system." He added. "I logged in remotely."

"You haven't worked there for years." Christy looked at Jerry. "How have they not pulled your remote access by now?"

"Oh, they pulled that the day I left." He smiled. "But before I left, I uploaded a Trojan into the system and left myself an opening so I can slip in the back door anytime I need to."

"Bravo!" I smiled and applauded his effort while Christy gave him a pat on the shoulder.

"Bravo?" Brandon question. "Am I the only one that has an issue with hearing Jerry use the terms 'Trojan' and 'slip in the back door' in the same sentence?"

"I guess we all hear what we want to hear." I laughed and shook my head. "I'm starting to think you may have some issues."

"I've been telling you all that for years." Jerry interjected. "Boy needs therapy."

As I was about to respond, I heard the front door open. As

65

Bobby walked into the office, the room got very quiet. Bobby looked around.

"What?" He asked.

"Nothing." I put the EMF meter back on the table. "Just Brandon being Brandon."

Brandon shrugged and kept looking at the bulletin board.

"I think we can get started now that the guest of honor is here." I glared at Bobby.

I grabbed one of our video cameras off the desk and held it up and looked at Bobby. "Who can tell me what this is?"

"Duh, it's a video camera." He responded as I could only shake my head.

"It is in fact an infrared video camera with night vision." I looked at Bobby. "Which is an important feature, why?"

Bobby scratched his head and grabbed the video camera from me.

"Night vision is import." I continued. "Because we tend to shoot most of our program in the dark."

"Really?" He asked as he looked at it closer.

"Yes." I nodded.

"I thought it was infrared and full spectrum?" He began pushing buttons on the camera. "So that it can pick up both ultra-violet and infrared, the parts of the spectrum we can't see with the naked eye?"

I stood stunned for a brief moment, then had to look over at Christy who nodded in confirmation.

"Yes, it is full spectrum as well." She confirmed.

Bobby started browsing around the desk and picked up a digital recorder.

"Digital recorder." He held it up for all to see. "For recording EVP's, electronic voice phenomenon. When recording, it will often pick up responses in the dead space, or white noise as we in the paranormal field like to call it."

He handed it to Brandon and grabbed the EMF meter and the EM pump off the desk.

"EMF meter." He paused. "For detecting spikes in electromagnetic energy, which is said to detect quote unquote signs of paranormal activity."

He put it back on the desk while holding up the EM pump.

"Electromagnetic pump. This creates oscillating magnetic fields. Which can draw spirits in, much like a siren, by helping boost their electromagnetic energy."

He put it back down on the desk and walked over to the table, grabbing a few more items.

"Devices for detecting changes in heat." He held up the thermal imager and the remote infrared thermometer. "Thermal imager takes pictures and videos to show the contrast in temperature for all objects in frame. The remote infrared thermometer can take temperature readings at a distance by pointing it at an object and pulling the trigger."

He pointed it at Christy's blouse and pulled the trigger. A small red dot appeared on her chest.

"A little on the cold side!" He laughed as he put the items back on the table while Christy shook her head.

"MEL meter." As he grabbed it off the table. "Can read both changes in ambient temperature and changes in electromagnetic field."

"The trusty REM pod." He grabbed a small round object with lights on the top from the table. "This has a proximity sensor and a temperature sensor. Any changes to either, will make the lights flash."

He turned it on and ran his hand over the top to demonstrate how the lights were activated. He put this back down on the table and continued.

"Laser grid scope." He pressed a button on an object that looked much like a pen, and wherever he pointed it, the room lit up with a green grid of light. "This can highlight subtle visual disturbances in its field of reference."

"The spirit box." He put the laser grid back and the table and moved back over to the desk and picked up a small black box. "Scans radio frequencies for white noise. If you listen closely, you can sometimes make out words."

"And last, but not least." He picked up another small object from the desk. "The Ovilus. Converts environmental readings from temperature and electromagnetic fields into words."

He shook his head and put it back onto the table. "Not sure why we have that one."

"Because it goes over well with the fans." I tried to justify the use of a tool I really wasn't all that sure of myself.

More importantly, the rest of the room sat in a stunned silence. The guy that referred to most of the equipment as the blinky things, seemed to be hiding his light under a bushel.

"How long have you known what all this stuff does?" I asked as Bobby shrugged his arms.

"Since I was about twelve, give or take a couple of years." He smirked. "You do know I graduated from MIT?"

"But we have to constantly remind you what everything is called and how it works?" Christy interjected. "While the cameras are rolling."

"That's my schtick." Bobby shrugged his shoulders. "I'm an

actor! Everyone else on the team can talk the talk, walk the walk, and sound like professors and whatnot. I'm the average Joe of the team. I think people respond to that. They can relate to me."

I certainly can't argue that, as his Twitter account has more followers than the rest of ours combined. Even if it is ninety percent female followers.

"Damn, you're a pretty good actor." Christy said. "I really thought you were clueless."

"Just give me the Oscar right now." He smiled and laughed as Brandon stepped up and grabbed the Ovilus out of his hand.

"So why do none of you like this thing?"

"It's okay in my opinion. But it's preprogrammed with only two thousand words to choose from, it's hard to put much credibility into it." Christy interjected. "Words like demon, death, and help come out because they only put words in relevant to ghost hunting. I'd like to see a database of the complete English language in there."

"Then it might spit out the word pizza." Brandon smiled.

"Not if it's really doing what it says it does." Christy replied.

"Unless the spirit is actually wanting pizza?" Bobby chimed in.

"Ah, there's the Bobby we all know and love." I smiled as my world seemed to be drifting back to the orbit I was comfortable in.

"Seriously, what if we had asked, what do you like to eat?" Bobby asked. "And we got the response, pizza."

"Unless of course it's Jerry's ghost." Brandon added. "Then we'd get the response, cock!"

Even Jerry began to laugh at that.

"Don't knock it til you try it, sweetie." Jerry said as effeminately as he possibly could.

"If you and I were the last two humans on the planet?" Brandon said. "It still wouldn't happen."

"That's a scary thought. Stuck with you and your Cheetos breath until the end of time." Jerry shuddered. "That'd be enough to turn me straight!"

Brandon breathed into his hand, then sniffed his hand.

"Do I really have Cheetos breath?" He asked me in a hushed tone. I could only shake my head as we were, as usual, getting horribly off track.

"So, what can you tell me about this?" I picked our latest piece of gear up from the table and handed it to Bobby in an attempt to get the group back on track.

"The SLS camera?" He took it from me and flipped on the power. "I've seen it used a lot. I'm pretty sure I know how to use it."

I'm glad he thinks he knows how to use it. Unfortunately, I was hoping he'd explain it to me without me having to come right out and ask.

"Me too, I think. I've seen it used a lot on other shows, but there were no instructions with it." I said sheepishly. "I was kind of hoping for a tutorial just in case I haven't seen all the functions."

The others obviously found amusement in this.

"How many of you know how it works?" I demanded as most of them shook their heads. "Well then maybe we all need a little tutorial on it."

"Look, it's pretty basic. It works pretty much just like you've seen on television." Bobby turned it so the screen faced the rest of us. "This main screen is your main monitor. It will show you whatever is in your viewing screen and if any anomalies pop up."

He directed it towards Jerry. At first Jerry's shadowy image illuminated green, then a stick figure was imposed on him.

"So, it will distinguish human forms such as Jerry's and outline them for us." Bobby continued. "The cool part is when you get a human form in the screen and none of us are actually in the frame."

I had to admit, even for a non-tech guy, I found this new piece of equipment pretty intriguing.

"Then to the right side of the screen are some other meters, right? Like EMF, static, etcetera?" I tried to ad lib from what I had seen of its use on television.

"Actually, it's temperature, distance, ambient light." Bobby pointed along the top of the screen. Then moved his hand to the lower right of the screen. "Then it also has a current audio input visualization and another screen that shows the audio over time."

"Why would both be needed?" Christy asked.

"I suppose the audio over time shows more contrast if something is glaringly different than the rest of the field."

Getting taught how to use equipment from Bobby. Pretty sure this is one of the signs of the apocalypse. Just waiting for his head to split open and out pop a soul eating demon.

"Thank you for the run down on our new gadget." The words were much harder to spit out than I would have thought. "I'd seen it in use before, but never actually had a chance to work one."

Bobby's grin widened, almost reaching ear to ear.

"What?"

"That had to be amazingly hard, almost painful I'm guessing?" Bobby laughed while I shook my head in disgust.

"You have no idea."

71

Theresa seemed to be enjoying it more than anyone. Not sure why she was surprised. My lack of technical prowess should not have been new to her. All the time pieces in my life, whether on the stove, in the car, or wherever, were only correct six months out of the year, due to the fact I could never reset them during daylight savings time.

"So as far as loading up tomorrow." I continued. "Can we all meet here around nine in the morning? That gives us a couple hours to load up, then we have a four-hour drive, and still get to the inn by three."

"That works." Jerry voiced as everyone else nodded in unison and began milling about the room.

As they began filing out the door, Theresa seemed to slow down just enough to remain in the house after the others had exited.

"You decided against talking to the others about the network and Jerry?"

"It wasn't the right time." I ran my hands through my hair. "I still haven't thought through how to spin this to our advantage."

"Not sure you can gain an advantage on the network. They pretty much hold all the cards. I think your odds are something like a million to one."

"So, you're saying there's a chance?" I smiled.

"I'm saying you might as well be playing Russian Roulette with an automatic."

"Jeez, you're supposed to be the optimist." I shook my head and looked towards the bar.

"Seriously?" Theresa frowned. "You can't even hold out until I'm gone?"

"Like you're ever really gone? I see you more now that we're separated than I did when we were together."

"You make that sound like a bad thing?" She smiled and began heading towards the door. "Don't worry, I can take a hint."

"I didn't mean it like that." I followed her to the door.

"I'm just pulling your chain. Don't worry about it." She opened the door. "I'll let you collect your thoughts. I know how you get the night before an investigation."

I smiled and nodded as she walked down the front steps. I found it very hard to close the door behind her. I took a breath, watched her for a moment as she disappeared down the driveway, then reluctantly closed the door. It's a strange feeling to continually be saying goodbye to someone, when you want nothing more than for them to stay. Seems to be my struggle lately. How to I change the past or myself, and make it possible for her to stay with me? This house hasn't felt the same since she moved out. My bed is now just a place to lay my head when I can no longer fight the urge to keep my eyes open.

CHAPTER 6

As I opened the drawer to the desk to retrieve my box of rechargeable batteries, I saw one of our original shirts in the back of the drawer. I pulled it out and brushed it off, then held it up to look admire it.

"Voodoo Blue paranormal tours, Savannah, Georgia." I read the front, then flipped it around. "The most fun you can have without a condom!"

I laughed out loud as I read the back. I had almost forgotten about these. Pretty sure Brandon came up with our early slogan. I miss the simplicity of those days. For the most part just scraping by doing haunted tours through the town so we could afford to do our own investigations. But we were in charge. No network executives telling us where to investigate and how to run things.

Odd to think about how many times our lives come down to dumb luck or simple chance. Meeting Theresa because Brandon had been a jackass and pulled the fire alarm in our hotel. Getting our show off the ground from a chance meeting during a ghost tour.

Elizabeth had been in Savannah on vacation with her husband. Seeing as Savannah has the reputation for being the most haunted city in the country, sooner or later everyone ends up taking a haunted tour. I had hit it off with her and her husband during the tour and ended up having drinks with them once the tour had finished up. After giving them my two cents on what was wrong with every current ghost show currently on the air, one thing led to another, and six months later we had a chance to film a pilot episode for the network.

Not sure how we ever made it past the pilot episode, though. It was a disaster. The network had sprung to get us the Waverly Hills Asylum for a four-night stretch. Just the six of us. We had never undertaken a location of that size before. We didn't have video cables long enough to run to all the locations we wanted. In my opinion, the four-camera set up we were used to using wouldn't even have been enough for a location that massive. We ended up having to use all the stationary cameras on the same level as the monitoring center, and go with each of us using a camcorder with night vision lights for moving to the upper floors.

Everything that could possibly go wrong, did go wrong. The show's lead investigators were originally going to be Brandon and me. Jerry and Christy were our assistant investigators, mostly responsible for handling the equipment while Brandon and I handled most of the speaking. Theresa and Bobby were going to man the control center and handle all the communications between groups. This was the first investigation we had that was in a facility large enough to split up like this.

Four hours into night one and we realized it was a train wreck. Team one consisting of Brandon and Christy was a disaster. Neither of them felt comfortable enough talking on camera to keep the dialogue rolling. That was until Brandon got his first few drinks in, then we couldn't shut him up. More importantly he seemed to have some alcohol-induced form of Turrets. About the only useable footage we could salvage from their first four hours was an off-color joke he made about Christy's wonderful orbs. To this day, still my favorite quote from that episode.

Team two consisting of myself and Jerry didn't fare much better. While I don't consider myself a homophobe, it was a little unnerving walking around in the dark with Jerry, who as it turned out in these larger spaces, was not very fond of the dark and kept trying to hang on to me. He had never had this problem in the past when we'd investigated hotel rooms and bars, but of course we were mostly confined to sitting in one spot at these locations as one large group. Something about the asylum though completely unnerved him and left him clinging to me so badly I could barely focus on the investigation.

By the end of our first night, we would be lucky to salvage five minutes of usable footage. Night two changes had to be made if we were going to have any hopes of salvaging this investigation and more importantly our possible television show. Team one would now consist of Bobby and Christy. Team two would consist of Theresa and myself, and Brandon and Jerry would man the control center. This line up, as it turned out, would serve us very well.

Bobby and Christy worked very well together. Bobby was very outgoing, so had no problem handling the lion's share of the talking. Christy knew more about the equipment and researched the locations so thoroughly, she could lead Bobby to the right spots and make sure he was asking the right questions.

Theresa and I worked equally well together. It became very apparent during editing that I was the skeptic, and she was the believer. The fact we were also husband and wife played very well also as our dialogue quite often morphed into some nagging or bickering any married couple watching could easily relate to. I think our classic quote from that first episode was us being lost somewhere in the basement, and when I wouldn't call the control center to try and figure out where we were, she blurted out 'because heaven forbid you ever ask for directions'. I still laugh when I see that clip.

Lastly, Brandon and Jerry actually made a pretty good team at the control center, once Brandon got past his fear of Jerry. Jerry was so tech savvy, he could navigate the equipment easily and ended up being quite masterful knowing just how to arrange the cameras and shoot the footage. Brandon handled the communication and kept us all aware of where everyone was to eliminate any possible contamination of the evidence we gathered and handled the final editing of the footage. Once we had a little more money to invest, we even started keeping a camera on them. Their awkward interaction made for some priceless moments.

As far as our drinking ritual? That was kind of a work in progress. Usually only Bobby, Brandon, and I would partake, leaving a non-drinker in each group for safety reasons. Then it all depended on how we filmed. We'd start with a drink during set up. Then a drink as we began the investigation. Then usually a drink every time from there on that we moved to a new location on the property. The final result was a show that had some pretty good paranormal evidence, but also had quite a bit of humorous moments thrown in.

By the time Jerry and Brandon had edited our Waverly Hills

footage from those four nights, I was very happy with the end result. The network, not so much. I believe the phrase they used to describe our pilot footage was 'Ghost Adventures meets Jackass'. But they didn't have a suitable replacement for the slot they had saved for our pilot episode, so they let it run.

And run it did. Within three days of airing, we were blowing up on Facebook, Twitter, Youtube, and just about every other media outlet. So much to the dismay of the network, they didn't really have much choice but to green light the first season. The rest is history. Ratings just good enough to hang onto our show, but never good enough to push us over the top.

I took a break from reminiscing long enough to look at our little hall of fame photos that covered the wall by the bar. We had someone take a photo of us at every location we've ever investigated. Of course, Bobby, Brandon and I almost always had a drink in our hand. I grabbed the tequila and poured myself a drink. Held it up to salute the photos.

"We had a good run!" I downed the shot and put the glass down on the bar, feeling a bit melancholy knowing that more than likely, this would all be coming to an end in the very near future. I patted Louie, who had joined me at the bar, on the top of the head.

"Just you and me tonight, buddy." I continued to pet him briefly, then made my way to the office.

Had I known this would be my last night with him, I would've made sure to give him a lot more attention than I did. But I went to the office to go over the equipment one last time.

The equipment was all laid out on the desk and the table. I turned the camcorders on and off to check battery levels, when the SLS camera caught my eye. I picked it up and turned it on to check the charge level. It was fully charged now. I unplugged it and began to press some of the buttons.

"Would've been nice to have a manual." I groaned as I relived having to be tutored by Bobby.

I tried to walk through the steps I had watched Bobby performed. I must have managed to hit the correct button, as the screen came to life. I began pointing it around the room to see how the display functioned. It was pretty much as I remembered it from seeing it on one of the other paranormal shows. Main screen shows any people or apparitions as stick figures. The smaller right side of the screen monitors sound, light, and temperature. I aimed it in Louie's direction. Sure enough he came up as a small little stick figure. Albeit a much thinner stick figure.

"Well, I'd say they were wrong when they said the camera adds twenty pounds." I said while scanning the camera around the room, and thankfully finding no other stick figures in my vicinity.

I turned off the SLS camera to conserve the battery and picked up the EMF meter. Not sure why I've always been fascinated with this, but I loved playing around with it. I turned it on and began walking around the room. This device could pick up changes in electromagnetic fields. Supposedly a sign of paranormal activity. It did, however, take me a few months to realize my kitchen wasn't haunted. You see microwaves and other electrical devices put out large electromagnetic readings, so when running, will set these off.

As I put it near the internet router, the lights flickered. I grabbed my drink and began walking around the rest of the house. As I moved through the living room, I watched it light up as I neared anything giving off large amounts of electromagnetic energy. I could do this for hours. As I made my way down the hall, I hesitated as I neared the end. As I approached the door at the end of the hall my amusement quickly faded. I slowly opened the door and stepped inside. The room itself was empty other than in the closet. Theresa and I had just used it for storage and rarely went in this room.

I walked over to the closet and looked inside; I smiled as I saw a familiar box on the top shelf. Chutes and Ladders. It had been ages since I had seen that. I reached up to pull it down, but as I did the EMF meter spiked. I was at first startled, until I realized I was close to the closet light, so I put the meter on the floor and went back to retrieve the game.

I set it on the floor and sat down next it, and the EMF meter once again began to spike. I grabbed the meter and moved it closer to the box. The closer to the box I moved it, the higher the reading it gave.

I quickly turned the meter off.

Most paranormal investigators avoid doing any real investigating in their own house for obvious reasons. Sometimes it's better to be blissfully ignorant. So even with all this equipment at my disposal, I never played with any of it other than the EMF meter. But tonight was different. The reaction the meter had to the game had piqued my curiosity.

I headed back to the office and looked over the equipment. Grabbing a digital recorder and a small speaker, I headed back to the room. I sat on the floor and set up the game, even putting a few pieces on the starting point. I set the digital recorder on the center of the board.

I took a deep breath and looked over at Louie. "This is a bad idea, isn't it?"

He licked his back side which I took to mean he thought it was a really bad idea. I ignored his advice and hit the record button.

"Is there someone here with me?" I asked.

As is customary, I left fifteen seconds between each question, to give time for responses.

"Do you like this game?" As I spoke, Louie now walked across the room and sprawled out on the game board.

"Do you like cats?" I stroked the top of Louie's head.

Louie stretched out and rolled over, covering the digital recorder. I dug the recorder out and placed it on the other side of the game board.

"You can have this one!" I said into the recorder.

I waited a little longer.

"Is there anything I can do for you?" I asked.

I never really had the patience for this kind of thing on my own. I hated how my voice sounded on recordings. Not to mention it felt odd talking to myself in a room. I know what you're thinking; but he apparently has no issue carrying on a conversation with my cat? I'm a complicated person.

"Okay, I think we're going to go to bed now. You have a good night." I waited a few seconds, then hit the stop button on the recorder.

I plugged the portable speaker into the headphone jack on the digital recorder and began playing it back.

"Is there someone here with me?" Played the recorder.

The next fifteen seconds were just static.

"Do you like this game?"

Once again, more static.

"Do you like cats?"

And the static continued. In a way it was a bit comforting. Not sure I really wanted to hear anything in my own house.

"You can have this one!"

Still no EVP.

"Sorry Louie." I consoled my trusty sidekick. "No takers."

"Is there anything I can do for you?"

Nothing but static.

"Okay, I think we're going to go to bed now. You have a good night."

Still static. As I reached to turn off the recorder a small blurb came out. I grabbed the recorder and rewound it. Turned up the speaker a little more and played it back again.

And there it was. Clear as day.

"Tissue." Mumbled the recorder.

Tissue?

Now you know why so many people are skeptical of what we do for a living. Ninety percent of the time, the words that get spit out have absolutely nothing to do with the situation or the questions we are asking. Which makes the other ten percent somewhat unreliable as sooner or later even a random word might fit into the context of what you were asking.

Of course, the more I thought about it, the more it made sense. Louie had been just licking his rear end. Maybe I was being instructed to grab him a tissue and handle his hygiene issue in a more respectable manner?

I played it back one more time. It definitely had a lot of static, but I'm still hearing tissue.

"Come on Louie, let's go clean this one up." I headed back to the office with Louie trotting behind me.

In the office I sat down at the desk and opened my laptop and opened my editing program. Most paranormal investigators use some type of software to help them clean up clips like this. I hooked the recorder up to my computer and dragged the sound file into my editing program. In this software I could amplify the voice I heard, and also reduce the background white noise. Which gives us a much cleaner EVP sample to listen to.

As I amplified it, I heard a hesitation in the middle of the word I didn't originally pick up on. I pulled some more of the white noise out to make the gap a little clearer. As I played the file back again, the recording no longer sounded like tissue.

82

I sat in silence for a moment and stared at the recorder.

Slowly I grabbed my glass and took a long drink, then cautiously hit the playback one more time. After cleaning up the file and amplifying it, the words were very clear. I took one more sip then played it back one last time.

"Miss you."

I stared at my computer screen for a moment, before saving the file. Then quickly shut the computer. I sat for a moment in silence, almost unable to move. This is exactly why one never conducts an investigation in their own home. I got up and made my way to the living room and headed straight for the bar. I pulled out the bottle of tequila, quickly refilled my glass, and downed the glass just as quickly. Louie climbed up on the bar and stared at me, almost gloating with an 'I told you so' look in his eyes.

"Yes, I know it was a stupid thing to do!" I told him as I poured myself a second glass. "These things aren't reliable. They can pick up transmissions from miles away."

I downed the second glass.

"It's probably nothing." I slid my glass down the bar, walked to the hallway and stared down at the door at the end. "It's probably picking up a cellular transmission from some lady a mile away pining away for her boyfriend on the other end of the line."

I moved back to the bar, only long enough to grab the entire bottle and made my way back to the room at the end of the hallway. As I entered the room, Louie was close behind me. We sat on the floor next to the game, I opened the bottle of tequila and took a big, long sip.

Then another.

And another.

As I kept drinking, I felt compelled to assemble the game and put the pieces out on the board. It had been years since I had actually played this game. Almost forgot it was even in the closet still. I wasn't even sure I was putting the pieces where they should be, but it didn't deter me. Once the game was set up as properly as I could manage, I took another sip from the bottle.

"You want me to go first?" I said to my newly acquired imaginary friend, who of course was unable to respond. "I'll take that as a yes."

I gave the spinner a flick with my finger.

"Ha, five!" I said triumphantly and moved my game piece forward five spaces. "Your turn."

I think I almost imagined the spinner would move. I've obviously been in this profession way too long. I laid back on the floor and stared at the ceiling. I wanted another drink, but it felt too good just laying here. After I stared at the ceiling for a moment, I quickly stood up and moved over to the light switch and turned the lights off. Went back to my spot, and laid back down staring at the ceiling.

It had been so long since I had been in this room at night, I had forgotten about the glow in the dark planets and stars I had painted on the ceiling. You can't see them with the lights on. But once you turned the lights out...

Voila!

I simply laid there staring at my own little Milky Way on the ceiling. Occasionally sitting up to take another drink. It was actually very relaxing. It was like laying in the grass at night and staring at the stars. All I needed was a small fan to simulate a breeze, and I would be set. I took another drink and was quickly startled as the EMF meter in my pocket started going off.

I pulled it out of my pocket and put it on the game board on my left.

It stopped.

As I picked it up to make sure I hadn't accidentally turned it off again, it started to light up again. I moved it to the right side of where I was laying and the lights pegged red. I smiled and turned the meter off. Took one last sip of tequila and laid back down. Oddly enough, the planets and stars seemed to be moving now.

Okay, I guess that might have been the tequila.

I made myself comfortable and closed my eyes. Opened them briefly to turn to my right and smiled.

"I miss you too."

CHAPTER 7

When I woke in the morning, I was still lying on the floor between the game and an empty bottle of tequila. My head felt like it was being used as a speed bag by Mike Tyson, or else I must have main lined LSD last night.

At least I think that's how I felt. Is main lining LSD a thing? Maybe it's main lining heroin? Don't know for sure, and as I've never actually been hit by Mike Tyson, I may be exaggerating that a little as well. As far as feeling like I had done drugs? I wouldn't actually know that either as I was never a big fan of the drugs. Which is odd as I seemed to be a huge fan of not being accountable for my actions while under the influence of alcohol.

I wasn't always like that. Yes, I have always enjoyed an end-of-night cocktail. But not to the extent of what I'd become in recent years. I was always in control, and I was always a good husband. And while I realize many of you will not believe me, I was a great parent.

You've all probably been wondering how a person gets as lost as someone like me obviously is. It's not hard to do. It's a pretty simple formula actually. You take a simple but flawed man, add the perfect wife, and add the perfect child. Build him a great life and make him believe he has achieved a life most can only dream of.

Then subtract one of the above.

In this case, my daughter.

It was a little over eleven months ago. Theresa and I had been married five years, we had one child that was three, our daughter Michelle. And we had one child that was a little over two years old.

Voodoo Blue Paranormal.

Theresa and I had a lock in at Pennhurst Asylum in Pennsylvania, which at the time was going to be our biggest investigation to date. It was the finale to the second season of Spirits with Spirits. Michelle had always traveled with us, and stayed in the hotel room with her aunt while we were at the lock in. Much like now, I am haunted by one thought.

What if I had just said no?

As I stared at the bottle of tequila on the coffee table, I didn't even have the strength to reach out and grab it. My mind began to wander back to a time I had tried all too hard to wash from my memory with the aid of liquor. In my mind I was reaching for the bottle, but my arms weren't cooperating. My salvation was out of reach and all at once those memories came rushing back.

They say memories can kill.

I don't argue that anymore...

I remember Theresa standing at the grave as the pastor finished up his closing remarks. Her parents and mine gave us tearful reassuring hugs, and then made their way to their cars. I hugged them while continuing to watch Theresa. One by one our friends and family gave their condolences and headed to their cars. The team was the last to leave. Eyes red from crying, one by one they embraced each of us. I thought Brandon was going to crack my ribs. As he released me, allowing me to breathe once again, he put his forehead against mine.

"Anything you need." He sobbed. "Anything."

I nodded and he made his way to his car.

Theresa and I were now alone. I walked over to the grave and knelt down. Theresa set some flowers by the grave.

"Three." I moaned while looking at her birth date and death date on the tombstone.

Theresa looked over at me.

"She was only three." I sobbed. "This can't be real."

I stood up and began walking around the grave. My sadness quickly turned to anger.

"Minister says at least we can take solace knowing she is with God!" I barked. "Really?"

Theresa tried to take my hand, but I pulled away.

"What kind of God takes a three-year-old child?" I threw the flower I was holding across the cemetery.

Theresa stood up and moved over to me.

"I need to get you out of here." She tried to pull me by the hand.

I pulled away again.

"You go." I motioned to the parking lot. "I'll catch up to you."

"Not a chance." Theresa shook her head.

I couldn't even begin to wrap my head around this. It couldn't be real. I kept thinking if I could just wake up, everything would be okay. I'd be fixing her breakfast, while she sat at the kitchen table watching me.

"This can't be happening." I was still trying to convince myself.

Theresa rushed to me and wrapped her arms around me.

"We'll get through this." She squeezed me. "I don't know how. But somehow we'll get through this."

"I don't think I will." I replied. "I can't"

"You can't talk like that." She pleaded.

I pulled away from her grasp and began pacing once again.

"I'm not like you." I shook my head. "I'm not strong, I've never been strong. I don't think I can make it through this."

"You will." She spoke softly. "We will."

"What if I don't want to? What if I don't want to make it through this?"

And I didn't make it. My life as I had come to know it was over. They should have probably just buried me that same day right next to her. I proceeded to drink myself into a coma on a daily basis and push away the only woman I ever loved. Here I was pulled back into the worst time of my life. That's what I get for being sober for a brief moment.

Startled by a loud crash outside the bedroom window, I jumped up from the floor quickly and regretted it immediately. My head began to sway like I was afloat in the ocean. This seemed to only aggravate the pounding in my head.

I quickly ran outside to see Brandon had removed a good four feet of my fence while trying to back the equipment van into my driveway. Brandon looked at me with a sheepish grin.

"I can fix that!" He grinned.

Not something I was ready to deal with before my morning coffee. I raised a finger to silence Brandon.

"Coffee." I insisted.

Brandon followed me inside while I began to rummage through the kitchen and prepare a pot of coffee. As it brewed, the smell took me away for a moment. It didn't take long for Brandon to bring me back.

"Hey, about the fence." He began to explain.

"Don't worry about the fence." I responded. "We'll fix it after we get back."

Brandon sat quietly while I began to pour the coffee. I brought the cups to the table and sat down with him. As I took a sip, Brandon continued to stare at me.

"What?" I asked.

"What?" He responded. "I've never seen you so calm over me destroying something of yours. You lose your shit when I get Cheetos dust on your things."

"That's because the only thing worse than your obsession with Cheetos, is your need to touch every afterwards with your gross orange hands." I stood up and went to grab the cream and sugar.

"That's worse than destroying your fence?" Brandon mused.

"Yes." I brought the cream and sugar back to the table and offered some to Brandon. "I had a long night. The fence seems like the least of my worries right now."

As I heard a second car pull in the driveway, I rose to look out the kitchen window.

"The gang's all here." I proclaimed. "And they managed to pull in the driveway without taking out a section of my fence."

Brandon shook his head and flipped me off.

"Rise and shine cupcakes!" Jerry gleamed and he entered the kitchen with a box of doughnuts. "Figured you two might need some sugar and real coffee."

"Inside voices, please." I demanded while searching through the cupboard for some aspirin.

"Someone a little hungover?" Jerry asked.

"More than a little." Upon finding the aspirin, I shook three into my hand, and headed to the sink.

I popped them in my mouth and held my mouth under the faucet to drink. Christy and Bobby entered. Each with a tray of coffee cups.

Theresa poked her head in the kitchen briefly, but something appeared to have caught her eye, and she disappeared back into the hallway. The others joined Brandon and I at the table and began distributing the coffee and doughnuts.

"So, what happened to the fence?" Christy asked.

"Ask Stevie Wonder here." I motioned to Brandon who simply flipped me off again and helped himself to a doughnut.

"We were kind of hoping you two would have all the heavy stuff loaded by the time we got here." Jerry tried to enunciate while chewing.

Theresa entered the doorway of the kitchen for a second time, this time intentionally getting my attention.

"Got a second?" She asked.

I nodded and reluctantly followed her as she exited the kitchen and began walking down the hallway. As I caught up to her, I could see she was heading to the end of the hall. She stopped just outside of the room and looked in. The game board and pieces were still on the floor, accompanied by an empty tequila bottle.

"Rough night?" She asked.

"You could say that." I responded while averting her eyes.

"Wanna talk about it?" She persisted.

"Not really." I started to retreat down the hallway. "Besides, you would never believe me."

"Try me." Theresa said as she caught up to me.

"Last night..." I paused as I saw Brandon come out of the kitchen.

"Everything good?" Brandon asked curiously.

"Yeah, just making sure we've got everything we need." I looked at Theresa then back to Brandon.

Brandon shook his head and made his way back to the kitchen. Theresa and I followed.

"This conversation isn't over." Theresa insisted.

"They never are, are they." I shrugged as we went back into the kitchen to join the others.

As we entered the kitchen, we found Bobby and Jerry at each other's throats, which was odd as I can't remember ever hearing the two of them upset with each other.

"You just don't have a fucking clue!" Bobby screamed.

"I don't have a clue?" Jerry stood up from the table. "Who's the pompous ass that lives in his own little fairy tale world?"

"Yes, my little fairy tale world." Bobby stood up and got in Jerry's face. "Which just happens to be where anyone with half a brain also resides."

Christy and Brandon were standing off to the side, not wanting to get in the middle of this. Theresa and I walked over to join them. I grabbed a cup of coffee and a doughnut and continued to enjoy the show.

"What the hell is going on?" I quietly asked Christy.

"Trust me. You don't want to know." She replied.

"Sucking dick must obviously decrease brain cells!" Bobby continued. "That's the only explanation that I can come up with."

"Or it's given me wisdom beyond that which you can even fathom!" Jerry retorted.

I knew I was going to regret it, but I made my way over to the two of them.

"Hey, guys..." I interjected quietly.

"What!" They both shouted in unison.

"We do have to get the gear loaded into the van." I continued. "Is this argument something you guys could let go for now, and pick up later?"

I looked to the others who were all nodding in agreement. "Seeing as we have work do to?"

Bobby and Jerry just turned and stared at me like I had asked them to give up their first born. I backed up slightly while they continued to glare. I was starting to regret getting in the middle of this. Without warning Bobby darted forward.

"Let's ask him?" He said to Jerry.

"Fine." Jerry pouted. "You'll see!"

As they both moved closer to me, I tried to take another step backwards, but ran into the kitchen counter.

"Okay..." Bobby looked me in the eye. "Star Wars or Star Trek?"

I was speechless while Bobby and Jerry both watched me like eager little school girls awaiting my response. It was all I could do to force out a single word.

"Seriously?"

"Yes!" Both shouted at me once again causing me to back into the counter.

"Both?" I answered as more of a question seeking approval than an actual answer. "I like both?"

"You can't say both!" Jerry demanded. "You have to choose one!"

Bobby nodded in agreement. I looked to the others for help. They simply shook their heads.

"You stepped in this all on your own." Brandon added.

"I like both." I stood my ground.

Bobby and Jerry both shook their heads.

"Pathetic." Jerry said.

"That's just sad." Bobby added. "Show some conviction."

"Even though I disagree with Bobby." Jerry put a hand on Bobby's shoulder. "I can respect him because he stands by his convictions."

Bobby nodded and put his hand on Jerry's shoulder.

"Me too." He turned to Jerry. "I respect the hell out of you."

Wow. Nice to see my ignorance can bring the two of them together and let them have their little moment of male bonding. If that's what you call it.

"Fine." I interrupted. "You want the truth?"

They both nodded.

"You can't handle the truth!" Brandon shouted from the other side of the room.

I tried not to laugh and break my train of thought. "The truth is..." I continued. "I have never seen either."

Judging by the expression on Bobby and Jerry's faces you would have thought I had just confessed to clubbing baby seals to death. A hush fell over the room. Bobby and Jerry looked at each other in shock and shook their heads.

"Tell me you're joking?" Bobby pleaded.

"No. I've never been a big fan of science fiction." I replied. "I always found it a bit on the boring side."

"You homo!" Jerry gasped as Bobby put a hand on his shoulder to calm him down.

"You must have had a horrible childhood." Bobby berated. "What did you do with yourself?"

"Um, I guess I played a lot of sports." I tried to justify. "Liked to fish a lot too."

They both shook their heads in disgust.

"I got laid quite a bit." I joked. "Something you two probably weren't really familiar with in high school?"

"We'll see who's laughing in the future when Jerry and I are prepared for the technological advances we'll start seeing any day now." Bobby lashed out. "And you'll be asking us how to work things!"

Jerry nodded in agreement with an oddly masculine swagger I'd never seen before.

"Dear God." I shook my head. "You're as bad as those people who think we will truly have a zombie apocalypse one day."

"Whoa, easy there." Christy chimed in from the back room. "Let's not get carried away. The zombie apocalypse totally has a chance of happening."

"Exactly!" Brandon's eyes lit up. "The way doctors are playing God. Someone is going to find a way to extend life."

"But it won't be of the same quality." Christy jumped back in. "We'll just be shells of what we used to be. Because while body functions may continue, our brains won't be as sharp!"

"Yes, so we will still have the basic desires, like eating." Brandon continued. "But we won't have the intellectual ability to determine what we eat, how to cook, etcetera."

I have apparently died and gone to nerd Hell.

Somehow, I have managed to put together a group of space nerds and zombie nerds without even realizing it. As I watched Brandon and Christy continue to bond over this ridiculous premise, I could simply shake my head. I looked at Theresa, who was also shaking her head, but finally smiling. Which I must admit, brought a long overdue smile to my face.

CHAPTER 8

There's nothing quite like the road trip to an investigation. Brandon and I always drove the equipment van, the others followed behind in Christy's car. Our van smelled like Cheetos and beef jerky. Their car smelled like women's perfume.

Mostly because of Jerry.

Our music of choice was eighties rock. Their music of choice was Alannis Morissette. That was when they weren't playing some irritating driving game. It wasn't hard to figure out why Brandon and I chose to be in the van. Too much time spent in the other car, and we might grow vaginas.

I took the first shift driving as I needed to be able to focus on something other than my EVP session from the night before. As I drove, Brandon went through some of the paperwork, trying to memorize the names and details. I was impressed he was actually doing a little research. That didn't last long.

"Do you think Abigail was hot?" Brandon asked while shuffling through the paperwork.

"You have issues." I tried to remain focused on the road.

"What you never think about a little ghost action?" Brandon grinned.

"I can honestly say no." I glared at him. "It has never crossed my mind."

"Think about it." He continued. "Marilyn Monroe, back from the dead, comes to visit you in bed?"

"So would she look like she did when she was alive, or would it be dead rotting zombie Marilyn coming back for a quickie?"

"Does it matter?"

"Uh, yes…I think it matters." I couldn't believe I was even allowing myself to be drawn into this conversation.

"Then you're not really a true Marilyn fan!"

"Excuse me?"

"A true Elvis would be happy to sleep with either young in shape Elvis or old out of shape Elvis."

"You're comparing apples to oranges!" I explained. "Large Elvis is not in the same category as dead rotting Marilyn!"

"Yeah, maybe." Brandon pondered. "But I'd still do her just to be able to say I had."

Resistance was futile.

"You never answered my question though. Do you think Abigail was hot?"

"For her day, probably." I nodded my head. "Why?"

"Was just wondering how hot a woman would have to be that someone is going to kill someone over her."

"I think you're missing the stronger argument."

"Which is?"

"In scientific terms?"

"Yes."

"He was bat shit crazy. Besides, love isn't usually based solely on looks." I said while Brandon nodded and laughed. I then realized who I was talking to. "In most cases."

"You have a lot to learn my friend."

I gave up for the moment and tried to concentrate on the road. As I drove, I tried to make a mental checklist of my pros and cons. Thinking if I could establish which of my cons were driving Theresa away, maybe I could make a conscious effort to eliminate them. Or at least, lessen their frequency.

Okay, number one, I'm messy. But it's hard to count that as a con, really. I've always thought tasks like making a bed were counterproductive. I mean, you're just going to use it again later that night, right? So by not making the bed, I'm really just giving myself an extra five minutes every day. And the rest of my house I clean when needed. Like holidays or when company comes over. It's not like Louie cares if it's clean. So I'm not really sure I can count this as a con.

Number two. I perhaps drink a little too much. That is most definitely a con that needs to be worked on. Although, I do have my own business, my own house and car. And all are paid for. So it's not like I'm not still a productive part of society, or my drinking is affecting my life negatively. And really, I really only drink tequila, which comes from the Agave plant. So when you look at it, it's almost like I'm drinking a vegetable. So I'm not totally convinced my drinking is a con either.

Number three. I hesitated as I thought long and hard for a number three. I don't think there is a number three. I'm not really sure I have any true flaws. You know the more I think about it, the more I think she should be trying to win me back.

"Why do you suppose there's this gap in paperwork from nineteen hundred through the nineteen thirties?" He kept flipping through papers.

"It's not like they had great record keeping back then." I grabbed one of the papers out of his hand and looked at it. "Even the nineteen..."

I threw the papers back at him.

"Jesus, do you have to get Cheetos residue on everything?" I checked my hands to make sure it wasn't on me.

"You know, you may be a germophobe." Brandon responded.

"It's not germophobic to despise having Cheetos residue on everything in my car."

Brandon turned towards me to debate, simultaneously putting his hand on the dashboard.

"Well, I think maybe it is." He countered.

I turned to look at him briefly and saw his hand on the dashboard.

"Get your hand off the dashboard!" I screamed.

As he pulled his hand away, there was an orange handprint on the dash that rivaled anything CSI could have dusted.

"See!" I pointed at the cheese dust handprint.

"That was there before." He argued.

It was no use arguing with Brandon. He was like one of those extreme medical cases where the body kept growing but the mind never matured. I could do a thesis on him if I didn't feel the need to wring his neck anytime I spent more than two hours with him.

Yet somehow, he's been my best friend for as long as I can remember? What does that say about me? Birds of a feather? Is that why Theresa left me? She wanted a relationship where she was a wife, not a babysitter? I keep telling myself if I can just show her that I've changed I might win her back. The only problem is the changing part. I don't really know that I want to.

I looked back over at Brandon who was still deeply engaged in his bag of Cheetos. He looked up briefly.

"What?" He tried to enunciate with a mouth full of Cheetos.

"At the rate I'm going I am going to die alone." I said while reaching for my water in the center console.

"You say that like it's a bad thing." Brandon smiled, grabbed my water and took the cap off for me, then handed me the bottle. "Who wants the hassle of being tied down?"

"Me!" I grabbed the water bottle and took a long drink.

I handed the bottle back to Brandon and let him put the cap back on.

"I'll see what I can do." He screwed the top back on. "I know a few nice girls."

"Ha, you?" I mocked. "Know nice girls?"

"One or two." He smiled back at me. "At least I figured they are nice. They wouldn't go out with me."

"Well, I guess that's a start."

"Then again, maybe that just means they're lesbians?" Brandon thought out loud.

"You're going to find this hard to believe." I offered. "But there are straight women that have morals and common sense."

"Yeah, but who wants to date them?" Brandon grinned while I shook my head. "Besides, if you recall, I did date Christy. Great looking, common sense, intelligent and morals!"

"And that lasted what?" I questioned. "One date?"

"I can't help it if some women just want to use me for my body."

"Yeah, I'm sure that was it."

I looked back in the rear-view mirror to see we'd lost the others. Which was nothing unusual. Brandon took notice and turned around to look.

"Well, they kept up a little longer this time, I'll give them that." He laughed. "Certainly, did better than when Jerry drives."

"Which reminds me, I need to bounce something off you." My mood shifted.

"What's that?"

"When Tony and Elizabeth stopped by to drop off the SLS camera, they also laid down an ultimatum."

"What do those useless suits want now?"

I took a breath. It seemed to me that it wasn't real if I didn't vocalize it. Brandon took note of my longer than usual silence and got a look of concern on his face.

"I don't care if it would help ratings or not." He said firmly. "I'm not doing the show in a mankini!"

As he chuckled, obviously amused with himself, my mind envisioned a place no one should ever be forced to visit.

"Ewwwww." I shuddered thinking of my friend in all his glory, tightly fitted in a lime green mankini. Which for some reason, my mind was envisioning a size or two too small. "And there goes any chance I'll be eating in the next day or two."

"You know it would boost ratings." He smiled.

"I wish that was all they wanted." I sighed. "As much as I am against cruel and unusual punishment directed towards what few viewers we have left, that's still far more doable than what they're asking."

Brandon's expression now went from amused to one of concern. I stared out at the road in front of me.

"Well?" Brandon grew impatient.

"They want Jerry gone." I replied. "If we don't get rid of Jerry, we're all done."

"Screw those uptight bastards." Brandon replied quickly. "We're a team. One for all, all for one is our motto."

"Actually, I think that is the Musketeers motto." I replied.

"Actually, theirs was something like M I C…" He defended dryly. "K E Y…"

"M O U S E?" I volunteered reluctantly, having a hard time figuring out if he was joking, or if he was really confusing the Three Musketeers with the Mouseketeers.

"Or something to that effect?" He said. "Point being, we're a family. I'd rather have the show go under than to let those pricks tell us to get rid of one of our own!"

I have to admit I was more than a bit surprised at his passionate response. While I don't consider Brandon a homophobe, he and Jerry had always had an awkward relationship. I figured Brandon would have had the easiest time with this news. Knowing Brandon's stance was to keep Jerry at all cost made the decision a slam dunk. Everyone else on the team would surely feel the same. This must have made me feel good enough to unknowingly let a smile sneak out.

"Don't get me wrong or anything. I'm still not saying that sword swallowing is a proper lifestyle choice." Brandon said, quickly bringing me back to reality. "But if anyone is going to mess with that little cock gobbler, it's going to be me."

"And he's back." I smiled in Brandon's direction. My world had returned to normal. While I enjoyed Brandon's rare and very brief moments of depth, I knew if they lasted too long it may put the entire universe out of whack and throw the earth off its axis. Everything and everyone has a purpose. It's never good to upset the delicate balance for too long.

"They have a replacement coming out tomorrow to train in." I continued. "William Vega, Anthony's nephew."

"Oh god, I hate that little bastard!"

"You've met him?"

"Yes, he's always at those stupid promotional parties." Brandon rolled his eyes. "You know, the ones you skip?"

"So does he have any chance with fitting in with our team?"

"No way. He's a smug little country club douche. Emphasis on the douche."

I found myself smiling and I'm not really sure why. This was obviously going to end in disaster. But it sure was shaping up to be an entertaining disaster. As we pulled up to the Wakefield I could feel the hair on the back of my neck stand up. I shivered uncontrollably.

"I just got the creepiest vibe when I got out of the car." Brandon shared as he closed his car door.

"Right there with ya." I responded. "Too late to turn back and go home?"

Before Brandon could answer the front door opened. Out walked the innkeeper.

"Holy crap." Brandon whispered. "The crypt keeper!"

I tried not to laugh, but he was right. This guy was creepy. If you can picture what Fred Astaire would have looked like after being on meth for ten years, that pretty much summed this guy up. He was like an even unhealthier looking version of Riff Raff from Rocky Horror Picture Show.

"Hello!" I tried to be cordial. "Angus? I believe we spoke on the phone?"

The old man walked down to meet us and extended his hand.

"Yes, nice to meet you. How was your drive?" He said in a rough, breathy voice.

"It was good. Not much traffic." I replied while shaking his hand.

"Never is this time of year." Angus growled. "The town is almost as dead as our inn."

He extended his hand to Brandon.

"Well hopefully we can help you change that." I assured him.

I wanted nothing more than to get this conversation over. This guy was creeping me out. Brandon shook his hand and as they released from their handshake, Angus looked at his hand. Then looked up at Brandon and proceeded to wipe Cheetos dust onto his jeans as he turned and walked up to the inn.

I glared at Brandon.

"What?" He responded innocently.

"Follow me." Angus said. "I'll show you around."

Brandon and I caught up to Angus as he entered the inn. He hesitated at the doorway and looked back.

"Will there be more of you?" He asked.

"Yes." I responded. "They're just behind us."

Angus shook his head and proceeded to lead us into the entryway. It was magnificent. Beautiful oak railed staircase going up the center, then splitting off to the right and left to the second floor. I could see to my right was the dining room. A bit outdated, but still very nice. And to my left, a sitting area with some very nice antique couches and a beautiful fireplace.

"This is beautiful." Brandon said.

"Thank you." Angus turned to us. "It is getting harder and harder to keep it up without steady business."

"I'm sure it will turn around." I assured him.

"We've had to let most of the full-time staff go." He continued. "Mostly part timers and seasonal help now."

As he continued walking to the front desk, I marveled at the beautiful marble tile floor, and the fountain to the left of the desk. As I peered into the fountain, I could see it was stocked with some fairly large koi fish.

"Would you like us to feed them while we are here?" I offered.

"No, they'll be okay." He muttered. "Fat little bastards."

I looked at Brandon. I could tell he was trying hard to bite his tongue. Angus was most definitely a charmer. Even if we manage to drum up some business for this place, I'm pretty sure Angus will find a way to scare them off.

"All the room keys are here." Angus gestured to the key slots behind the desk. "The inn is closed for the week, so you'll have the place to yourselves. Take whatever rooms you want."

"Perfect." I said.

"Although…" He paused. "I would avoid room twelve at all costs."

Brandon and I looked at each other, obviously concerned at this bit of knowledge dropped in our lap. I cautiously spoke up. "What's wrong with room twelve?"

Angus leaned in very close to us, looked around the room as if he was worried someone might hear him, then smiled. "Absolutely nothing. I'm just fuckin with ya."

Brandon and I both breathed a sigh of relief as he chuckled.

"Here is a map of the place." He slid it across the desk. "Just in case you need it."

As I folded the map and put it in my coat, he came out from behind the desk.

"Follow me and I'll show you what you need to know about the kitchen."

Angus led us through the dining room, and past the bar, into the kitchen. The kitchen had seen better days obviously.

"With the inn being closed for the week, we don't really have a lot here." He opened one of the cupboards. "Just the basics. But there's a grocery store about five miles down the road you can stock up at."

"I saw that." Brandon motioned to me. "We passed it on the way here."

"They don't have a great selection." Angus added. "But they at least have the essentials."

"Like meats and stuff?" Questioned Brandon.

"Like booze." Angus replied. "Which you'll need if you plan on spending the entire week here."

Angus reached into his pocket and pulled out a small metal flask. Unscrewed the top and took a swig. He reached out to offer Brandon and I a sip. I could see the dirty rusty opening at the top was still wet with Angus' saliva.

"No, I'm good, thank you." I quickly rejected his offer.

"Yeah, me too." Brandon shook his head.

Angus put the top back on the flask and returned it to his pocket as he headed back to the front door, he paused briefly to hand us the keys. He looked around the lobby with a suspicious stare. Then looked back at us. "You sure about this?"

"We'll be fine." Brandon took the keys out of his hand.

"We're professionals." I added.

Angus paused and looked back at us.

"Professional what?" He asked mockingly and chuckled as he made his way down to his car.

We stood in the doorway and watched him get into his car and drive off. Brandon and I headed down to the van and started unloading equipment. As we began carrying the cases up to the inn, I couldn't help but wonder what was taking the others. I wanted to get stuff set up and still have time to go get supplies before nightfall.

"Do you think they're lost?" I asked Brandon.

"With GPS?" Brandon shook his head. "Even they couldn't manage that. Jerry probably had to stop and change his pad."

I dropped a case on the front steps as I began laughing.

"Seriously?" I asked. "While I'm carrying the heaviest case?"

As we got the last of the cases up the front stairs, the others pulled into the parking lot.

"Perfect timing." I shook my head with a groan.

As we walked down to the parking lot to meet the car, Jerry exited the car smiling. "We timed that right!"

"What took so long?" Brandon asked with more than a hint of irritation in his voice.

Christy opened the trunk to reveal several grocery bags. Theresa appeared near the back of the car.

"Someone has to plan ahead." Theresa smiled.

"Did you think we were spending a week here without groceries." Christy said. "We figured we should stock up on essentials."

110

"I'll be the judge of that." Brandon pushed past me and began looking through the bags. "I see meats, bread, cheese, water...

As he finished looking through the last bag, he looked and me and shook his head. Then glared at the others.

"Essentials my ass! You do realize the show is called Spirits with Spirits?" He shook his head. "The only reason we are even surviving is people love watching our investigations as the night progresses and Sebastian and Bobby inevitably have too many drinks!"

"Not everyone loves watching that." Theresa glared in my direction.

"We were talking on the ride here." Jerry stepped forward. "We would like to try and make this a little bit more serious show."

The other all nodded.

"We're good enough." Jerry continued. "We don't have to rely on the drunken schtick anymore."

"I agree." Bobby took over. "I think we can use that every now and then. But we all agree we should at least try and take this in a more serious direction."

"So let me get this right." I stepped in front of Brandon. "After that history of this place you read to us, I'm supposed to stay here sober?"

"You'll survive." Christy said as I shook my head. "And weren't you the one saying you wanted to take the show in a more serious direction?"

"Yeah, but not cold turkey!"

"You'll be fine." Jerry walked over to me and tried his best to console me. "I brought weed."

The others all shook their heads.

"I'm kidding." Jerry reassured them.

Brandon and I could only look at each other for sympathy.

"This sucks." I said to Brandon.

"How about I go back and get a couple of bottles of tequila on the condition you guys only have a drink each morning after we've finished shooting for the night?" Christy tried her best to moderate. "To help you sleep during the day."

I looked to Brandon who was still pouting. Eventually we both nodded. I stuck my hand out.

"But give me the keys." I pleaded. "If we're going to be limited, we should at least get to pick out our own."

Christy reluctantly handed me the keys.

"I'm serious." She added. "Moderation!"

Brandon and I looked at each other with confusion.

"Geez." Brandon turned to me. "She acts like we have no self-control."

"The nerve of some people." I smiled.

Brandon and I jumped in the car and quickly made our way out of the driveway. As we drove down the highway, Brandon began looking through Christy's glove compartment.

"What the hell are you doing?"

"Just looking." Brandon said while pulling out a map.

"Well don't!"

Brandon put the map away and pulled out a small travel bag. I quickly grabbed the bag out of his hand and stuffed it back in the glove compartment. "Can you behave for ten minutes?"

"Probably not."

As we pulled up to the small grocery store attached to the gas station, I couldn't help but chuckle.

"Bret's Pump N Munch?" I shook my head.

"Nice." Brandon added. "Not sure I want to eat or drink anything that comes from this place."

As we exited the car, a few old timers sitting on the front porch of the building looked our way with curiosity. As we got closer, they each spit out some tobacco on the ground.

"Howdy all." I said cordially in what I assumed to be their native tongue.

The old timers both nodded, as I held the door open for Brandon and we entered the store. This place smelled like old cheese and tuna, and not in a good way. We immediately turned to each other.

"Let's make this fast." Brandon grimaced as he spoke.

"No doubt." I assured him.

We made our way to the liquor aisle. Which consisted of a four-foot section of shelving with hard liquor and an eight-foot cooler with beer and wine coolers. The store clerk watched us curiously while we considered our meager options. Basically, one selection of each type of liquor, from the cheapest manufacturer possible.

"I'm assuming you keep the good stuff in the back room?" Brandon shouted to the clerk.

The clerk scowled at Brandon and shook his head.

"Could you not start shit?" I pleaded. "This is the kind of town they'll either make chili out of us or turn us into their bitches."

"You do got a perty mouth!" Brandon said in his best hillbilly dialect.

I ignored him and grabbed two big bottles of the tequila. As we started to walk to the counter, Brandon hesitated.

"Wait a second." He went back to the liquor. "They'll be monitoring the two large bottles."

He began filling a shopping tote with a couple of dozen of the airplane sized liquor bottles in any variation they carried.

"You are wise beyond your years, my friend." I smiled at him as we brought our purchases up to the counter.

The clerk began ringing everything up as we emptied the shopping tote. Brandon grabbed a couple of small bags of Cheetos form the rack next to the counter and added them to the pile.

"Really?" I asked.

"One cannot live on alcohol alone."

I shook my head as I handed the clerk my credit card.

"Sixty-eight dollars and forty-seven cents." He said while swiping my card.

He slid the receipt across the counter for me to sign while he bagged our purchases.

"Thank you." Brandon said while he grabbed the bag off the counter and headed towards the door.

The clerk nodded as I followed Brandon out to find the two old men outside had left. As we made our way to the car, Brandon stopped me as I opened the door.

"Here." He began stuffing small bottles of alcohol into all my pockets. "We have to keep these hidden."

As we entered the inn, the others were all in the lobby still, deciding who was taking which room. They immediately stopped the discussion and looked our way as I pulled the two bottles of tequila out of the bag and put them on the table. The others looked cautiously. Jerry walked over to Brandon and looked him up and down.

"Empty your pockets." He asked.

"What?" Brandon said nervously.

Jerry patted down Brandon's coat pockets which resulted in a jingling sound. The other all looked at him. Brandon reluctantly removed all of the miniature bottles while Jerry gathered them in a bag. They all proceed to look at me.

"I'm offended that you think I would even consider that." I tried to sound indignant.

Jerry walked over and patted my pockets, but my pockets made no sound, which surprised them all. Especially Brandon. I proceeded to pull all my pockets inside out to show them I was not hiding anything. As Brandon stared at me the others picked up the discussion on room choices. Brandon walked over to me and looked me up and down.

"Large planter to the left of the outside stairs." I whispered to him.

"You are my Yoda." He whispered while smiling.

As he rejoined the conversation about rooms, I hesitated for a moment. I guess feeling a little guilty about lying to the group. But I quickly justified my decision with thought of a Hemingway quote 'drinking is just a way of ending the day'. I would have to say I agree.

CHAPTER 9

We began setting up for the investigation. To the casual observer, one would think there is not much involved. But there is much to consider when thinking through camera location, lighting, and so on. I began to unpack the cases for the control center in the lobby. Lobbies are always a good choice for setting up the control center as most locations will have action on upper floors and basements. This way you're not running extremely long sections of cable to any of the locations.

"Would certainly be nice to have a drink right now." I mused as I put the DVR recorder and the flat screen television on a table at the outer edge of the room. Theresa simply shook her head.

"Need I remind you of our investigation of the Harrow House?" Christy interjected.

Bobby and I looked at each other and grinned.

"You and Bobby doing shots of Patron during set up." Christy continued. "And the DVR never got turned on. A whole first night wasted with no filming."

"Like we're the only ones capable of hitting the record button?" Bobby insinuated as I nodded in agreement.

"In all fairness to Christy." Jerry added. "Bobby did say he had started recording."

"I don't remember saying that." Bobby pushed his way past Jerry and made his way towards me and leaned closer and whispered to me. "Of course, I really don't remember anything from that night."

I tried not to laugh as I hooked up the DVR to the monitor. As I turned the power on to both the DVR and the monitor, the screen illuminated, showing eight different boxes on the screen. One for each

117

camera that would eventually be connected to it. Brandon started pulling the cameras out of the travel case while Jerry grabbed the first roll of video cable.

"Well Maestro." I looked to Jerry. "How do you want to shoot this?"

"I think we have three cameras upstairs, two cameras on this level, and three cameras in the basement." He pulled out a sheet of notebook paper that had some scribbling on it. "Upstairs we have a camera in Abigail's room. Another camera shooting down the hallway. And the third camera shooting down the stairs."

We all nodded.

"On this floor, we're going to go with one camera shooting the restaurant and bar area." He motioned to the room next to us, then spun gracefully and pointed to the other side of the lobby. "And the other..."

"Was that a pirouette?" Brandon interrupted.

"Excuse me?" Jerry replied.

"That little spin move you just did." Brandon explained.

"You mean when I turned to look across the room?" Jerry dismissed. "We call that turning. Now where was I?"

"There was a little 'hop' in there." Bobby added.

"And you did raise your arm." Christy also chimed in. "But it was graceful."

Theresa rolled her eyes and signaled to me to keep things moving along.

"Anyway..." I interrupted. "Jerry, you were saying about the camera placement?"

"I'm torn between one at the far end of the lobby." He walked over to show where it would be. "Or putting that one in the kitchen."

"I'd vote kitchen." Theresa stated.

"I'm leaning towards kitchen." I added. "I think it's rare we get anything in the same area we are monitoring from other than you and Brandon playing footsie."

The others all nodded as well, while Brandon gave me a dismissive glare.

"Makes sense." Jerry continued. "We'll have it at this end of the kitchen shooting across the room, so we also get the top of the basement stairs."

He grabbed one of the cameras from the case.

"Basement I think we go with one in the back of the wine cellar pointing towards to entrance, so we cover most of that whole room." He continued. "Then in the main room, where we assume Arthur got buried beneath the foundation, I think we have it in the southeast corner pointed towards the stairs. That way we get pretty much the whole room, plus the bottom of the stairwell."

"And the last camera?" Christy asked.

"That storage room that's down there." Jerry pulled out some photos of the basement area and pointed at one in particular. "I want a shot of that wall where some of the bricks are crumbling. If nothing else, it will make for some good footage for the intro. If we get nothing after the first night, we can always rethink that camera."

We all nodded in agreement and began unpacking the rest of the gear. I grabbed three tripods and three cameras and began heading upstairs. Brandon moved three of the video cable rolls to the left side of the table and began unwinding the first, while following behind me stopping briefly at the desk to grab the key to Abigail's room. Brandon and I had this pretty much down to a science. We could get all eight cameras set up and wired in a little over an hour. Which left the other

119

details like making sure all equipment is charged, all memory cards are empty, and all lights are functioning to the others.

As we got to the top of the stairs, we made our way down to Abigail's room. Brandon hesitated at the door.

"You ready for this?" He smiled.

"Open the damn door." I groaned.

Although we were both joking, as Brandon turned the key in the lock and slowly pushed the door open, I couldn't help but notice that neither one of us rushed to go in. I politely motioned that Brandon could enter first.

"Thanks." He shook his head while cautiously making his way into the room. "Back corner, facing the door you think?"

I nodded and followed him to the back corner of the room, making sure to leave the door to the hallway open. I unfolded the tripod and attached the camera. Brandon handed me the video cable and I attached it to the camera, at which point the lights on the camera lit up. We positioned the camera shooting towards the door, which would catch most of the room as well. We quickly exited the room, but Brandon hesitated in the hallway as he reached for the doorknob.

"Open or closed?" He asked. "Open we could also catch a little of the hallway in the frame?"

He stepped away from the door to get an idea how far out the camera would pick up.

"I think either way." I explained. "No one is staying in this room, so if we..."

Without warning the door slammed shut. Brandon and I looked at each other and took off down the hall and to the stairs. As we made our way down the stairs, we could see the other others laughing hysterically.

"Sorry about that." Bobby laughed. "When I opened and closed the front door, the air pressure must have made that door slam shut."

The others were all still trying to catch their breath and compose themselves.

"But if it makes you feel any better." Jerry chuckled. "We got it on tape!"

"Assholes." I turned toward Brandon and muttered under my breath, scowling as I began to make my trek back up the stairs with Brandon close behind. "We're going to go finish setting up the upstairs cameras if you all are done messing around."

As we got to the top of the stairs, Brandon unfolded the last two tripods, placing one at the top of the stairs and one at the near end of the hallway. I attached one of the cameras to the tripod at the stairs and pointed it down the stairs.

"How's this look?" I yelled downstairs as I plugged in the video cable.

"Point it down about another five degrees." Shouted Jerry from downstairs.

I adjusted the camera as instructed.

"Perfect!" Yelled Jerry.

As I attached the camera to the tripod at the end of the hallway, I positioned it so it would shoot the entire length of the hallway. The power light came on as I attached the video cable.

"How's this one looking?" Brandon shouted downstairs as he stuck his crotch in front of the camera.

I shook my head and tried not to laugh as he began to gyrate like Elvis. Not young, sexy Elvis mind you. More like large older Elvis.

"Hard to see anything." Shouted Christy from downstairs. "Does this camera have a zoom or magnification setting?"

I looked at Brandon, who was now speechless and sheepishly moved out from in front of the camera.

"Perfect!" Yelled Jerry.

Brandon moved back in front of the camera and flipped it off. I patted Brandon on the shoulder as I made my way to the stairs.

"Come on slugger." I motioned to him as I headed down the stairs.

As we got to the bottom, the others were trying to contain their laughter. We made our way to the observation table.

"Next time I'm going to pull it out!" Brandon scolded. "Then we'll see who has the last laugh!"

"Can't wait!" Jerry replied excitedly.

Everyone burst out laughing while Brandon shook his head and looked at me.

"I can't win!" Brandon exasperated.

"Come on." I grabbed his arm. "Help me grab the stuff for the basement."

As we began to grab the cameras, cables and tripods for the basement footage, Bobby grabbed a camera out of the case.

"You want me to set up the two cameras on this floor while you guys do the basement." Bobby inquired.

"That would be great." I said. "Just make sure the wide-angle camera is the one you use for the lobby."

"Will do."

As I struggled grabbing one of the cable rolls with the cameras in my hand, Theresa looked at me and shook her head.

"Need me to lift the heavy stuff?" She mocked.

I simply looked at her and shook my head.

"What?" She asked as Brandon and I made our way through the dining room to the kitchen.

As we got to the basement stairs, Brandon tried to balance the three tripods and two rolls of cable he was carrying so he could hit the light switch.

The light flickered on, then off. Then flickered back on.

"Nice." Brandon looked back at me. "Even the lighting here is creepy."

I followed Brandon as he made his way down the narrow stairs. As we got to the bottom of the stairs, we put the equipment down and took a deep breath as we looked at each other.

"I got a really weird feeling as I got to the bottom of the stairs." He put his hand to his chest. "It's harder to breath down here."

"I'm not feeling any different." I looked at him. "It might be moldy? I can handle the set up down here. Why don't you head back up?"

"No, I'll be fine." He reached into his pocket and pulled out his asthma inhaler, shook it, and took a puff. "I don't think it's mold. I just got a really creepy vibe down here."

I watched Brandon and made sure the inhaler was helping. He seemed to start breathing better after a minute. As we began looking around the room, I had to admit it did have a horrible vibe to it. I've been in a lot of supposedly haunted places, but this is the only one that's given me a bad feeling while it was still light outside.

"Good thing the guests aren't allowed down here." Brandon wiped a layer of dust off a crate of dinnerware. "I can't imagine they'd feel good about eating food from a kitchen twenty steps up from a cellar that looks like it hasn't been cleaned since the eighteen-hundreds."

Brandon unfolded a tripod and brought it to the back corner along with an end of the video cable. I brought a camera over and quickly mounted it to the tripod and attached the cable. We faced it towards the stairs so it could catch most of bulk of the room and the bottom of the stairs. We heard footsteps running above us.

"Don't move it!" Christy shouted down the stairs. "It's pointed perfectly right now!"

"Okay." Brandon shouted back up the stairs. "Stay there and let us know on the other two."

I grabbed a tripod and a camera and headed into the wine cellar. Brandon began to unwind another video cable and ran one end up to Christy, then followed me into the wine cellar with the other end. I positioned the tripod in the back of the wine cellar and mounted the camera shooting towards the entrance. Brandon handed me the video cable and went to stand in the doorway. I hooked up the cable and gave him the thumbs up.

"How's that?" He shouted to Christy.

There was a slight pause.

"To the left about four degrees." She shouted down.

I adjusted the camera angle slightly and looked towards the entrance.

"That's good!" Christy shouted down the stairs.

Brandon grabbed a bottle out of one of the racks and dusted it off.

"I guess we really didn't need to hit the liquor store." He smiled.

"I'm pretty sure knowing the name of the show is 'Spirits with Spirits', they've inventoried every drop of booze in the place." I replied. "Maybe even the whole town!"

"Seriously?" Brandon shook his head. "I don't think Angus or the staff has cleaned down here in a decade, let alone inventoried."

He put the bottle back in the rack and we both made our way back into the main room, stopping briefly to grab the last camera and tripod. As I grabbed what I needed, Brandon once again ran one end of the last video cable up to Christy. Then returned to follow me into the storage room with the other end.

This place looked like one of those optical illusions where the room got smaller the farther you went in. But it was no illusion. It looks as though the ceiling may have been collapsing at one point, and now seemed to be patched together with massive vertical beams wedged between the floor and the ceiling and some extra bricks stacked up on the sides on the back side.

"You sure about this?" Brandon looked at me cautiously.

"Let's set this up fast and get out of here." I assured him.

I put the tripod and the camera as far back in the room as I could safely and pointed it towards the entrance. Brandon handed me the cable and I quickly hooked it up to the camera. Brandon went to the entrance of the room.

"Raise it up just a hair!" Christy yelled down to us.

I moved it up slightly.

"Perfect!" Christy yelled back down.

Brandon and I made our way back to the other side of the room. As I neared the entrance, something caught my eye on the wall. One brick in the wall that was noticeable out of place. I hesitated.

"What are you doing?" Brandon asked as I focused on the wall..

"Hang on." I said while walked over to examine the brick.

Brandon came back in the room and joined me at the wall. The

125

brick was crumbling but still had most of the mortar in place. Other than this one brick, where the mortar was completely removed, but the brick was still in place. I began working it back and forth to try and work it free. Theresa entered the room behind us as Brandon pulled my hand away from the wall.

"Are you insane?" He shouted. "That may be the one brick holding this place up."

"It's already separated." I assured him. "You can see that."

I went back to working the brick back and forth to slowly begin sliding it out.

"Don't." Theresa warned.

I hesitated for a moment, then pulled the brick out of the wall.

Along with the brick came a gust of cold, musty air that sent me back on my ass. Brandon quickly came to my aid and helped me off the floor. Theresa shook her head but looked concerned.

"I told you not to pull it out!" She scolded. "Are you ever going to listen to me?"

I ignored her and tried to dust myself off. I grabbed my flashlight off the ground and moved back over to the wall. I shined the light inside the hole made by the missing brick and moved the beam around. There wasn't much room to look, but from what I could see it looked like more storage. A bunch of plastic totes.

"What's in there?" Brandon asked.

"Looks like just another storage area." I responded. "I can see some totes in there."

Brandon grabbed the light out of my hands and looked in the wall himself.

"Why the hell would you wall up part of your storage area?" He

126

asked.

"Angus probably put his first wife in there." I grinned at Theresa, who simply shook her head.

"Angus probably buried half a dozen wives back there." Brandon added while grinning. "Or guests of the inn."

"They probably didn't have much choice when this area started to collapse." I continued. "They probably had to move fast to keep it from coming down and didn't worry about whatever was in there. Probably just boxes of cleaning supplies."

Brandon nodded his head, while Theresa shook hers, obviously not reassured by my hypothesis. Brandon moved away from the wall and started towards the doorway.

"At any rate." He added. "I think we've spent enough time down here. Are we good to go?"

I nodded as Theresa and I followed him to the main room of the cellar and began to make our way back up the stairs. We made our way up to the kitchen. I hesitated as I looked at some cases of liquor stacked up in the corner.

"What?" Brandon asked as he stopped in the doorway.

"Why keep all these boxes up here, when you have a completely empty storage room downstairs?" I questioned.

"You said it yourself." Brandon explained. "That room is unsafe. If it comes down, do you want it to crush a couple thousand dollars' worth of booze?"

I nodded in agreement but walked over to the stack of liquor boxes.

"I have to go take a piss." Brandon excused himself. "Meet you in the lobby?"

I nodded as Brandon made his exit. Theresa walked over to join me at the boxes as I opened one up. I felt a little disoriented for a moment and had to take a step back.

"What is it?" She asked as she looked in the box. "More liquor?"

"Yeah, just liquor." I hesitated and looked back in the box briefly.

"What is it?" Theresa prodded me to continue, obviously seeing that I was a bit shaken.

"When I first opened it." I continued. "I could've sworn I saw jewelry, watches and other stuff."

"You okay?"

"Yeah, fine." I nodded. "Just my eyes playing tricks on me, I guess."

I closed the box back up and Theresa and I headed out to the lobby, were we met up with the others and Brandon just returning from the bathroom.

"What happened down there?" Christy asked having obviously been watching the monitors.

"Sebastian was trying to kill us." Brandon joked.

"Just a section of the wall that didn't look natural." I explained. "Looks to have been built to help support the failing load bearing walls down in that room."

"Yeah, so Sebastian takes a brick out of the already unsecure wall." Brandon laughed.

"We survived just fine, didn't we?" I defended my actions.

"Other than the rush of musty air coming out of there that knocked you on your ass." Brandon added.

"We were wondering what made you back up so fast." Jerry questioned. "We thought maybe you saw something."

"Just boxes. Nothing exciting."

"Yeah, looked like cleaning supplies." Brandon added.

"So, we good to go?" I asked.

"Yes. Everybody want to take an hour or two to get cleaned up and rest a bit?' Jerry stood up from the console. "Meet back down here at eight to start?"

"That works." I looked down at my jeans, dirty from the spill I had taken in the wine cellar. "I don't want to film in these."

We all began our ascent up the stairs. As we got to the top, we each made our way to our separate rooms to get cleaned up. As the others each entered their rooms, Theresa paused with me as I unlocked my door. She glanced inside the room as I opened the door. I motioned inside my room.

"See, no mini bar!" I announced. "Aren't you proud of me?"

"Yeah." She smiled and shook her head. "I'd be even prouder if it weren't for the planter out on the steps with the mini bottles of booze stashed in it."

"You missed your calling." I laughed. "You should have been a detective."

"Yes, because it takes a genius to know you and Brandon will inevitably find a way to have a drink."

"You make us sound like addicts?"

There was an awkward silence. She began to walk down the hallway as I poked my head out the door.

"Tell me you don't miss this?" I motioned my hand back and

forth between us.

"There is so much about you I miss." She paused in the hallway, then frowned. "Watching you drink yourself to death is not one of them."

She headed off down the hallway shaking her head. I returned to my room with my proverbial tail between my legs. I wasn't drinking myself to death. I knew I could quit at any time. But I enjoyed it. If you enjoy something, why stop? Life is short enough as it is. I could step out in the street next week and get hit by a bus. So why not enjoy life while you can? But if she needed proof. I would avoid drinking tonight. Like I said, I can stop at any time.

I began pulling out my clothes for the night. This was always one of the more difficult aspects of the show. Picking the appropriate attire for the shoot. It seemed to always take forever. Do I go for the pair of jeans and the black shirt? Or do I go for the pair of jeans and the dark grey shirt? I was never good at these difficult decisions. After careful consideration I opted for the jeans and the dark grey shirt.

I laid them out on the bed and made my way into the bathroom. As I took off my shirt and threw it on the floor, I looked in the mirror. I definitely needed a tan. And maybe a week in the gym. Okay more like a year. I slipped off my jeans and my boxes and threw them on the floor as well. My glance once again drifted towards the mirror. I looked down, then quickly looked back up at my face in the mirror.

"It's cold in here!" I justified to myself, not wanting to start the night off on a confidence killer.

I reached inside the shower and turned the water on, half expecting blood to come out of it. But alas, it was nice and clear. As I stepped inside, I gripped the shower head and moved forward to put my head under the water. I stood for a moment enjoying the warm water run over me. This was pretty much a pre-shoot ritual for me, my last few minutes of relaxation before I end up crawling around on dirty floors and talking to myself for eight hours. I grabbed the soap and began cleaning up. As I regrettably turned off the shower, I paused briefly to stare down at the drain and watch the last of the soap suds find their way down. I stepped out and grabbed a towel.

"Shit, it really is cold in here." I toweled myself off drying desperately to warm myself up. "Angus must have turned the heat down for the week."

I went back into the bedroom and threw on the boxers and jeans I had laid out on the bed, before returning to the bathroom to apply a little deodorant. I retrieved the dark grey shirt from the bed and threw it on, then returned to look in the bathroom mirror.

As I brushed my teeth, I continued to stare in the mirror. I looked at myself up and down. I spit out a mouthful of toothpaste.

"Dammit!" I declared. "The black shirt will look better."

With toothbrush still in mouth, I quickly changed into the black shirt. Which in all honesty was but a fraction of a shade darker than the dark grey shirt. I returned to the bathroom, finished brushing my teeth, and reviewed myself in the mirror.

"Much better."

As I left the bathroom I was greeted with a knock on my door. I opened the door to find Jerry standing in the hallway.

"You got a second?"

"Of course." I stepped aside and motioned for him to come in. "Come on in."

He moved across the room and leaned against the dresser. He was obviously uncomfortable, which was odd for him.

"Brandon told me about the network and the change they want." He ran his hands through his hair. "Why didn't you tell me?"

"Because it's a non-issue." I moved over to him. "We're a team. You go; we all go."

"But you should have at least discussed it with me. I'm not sure I want to be the reason you all lose your show?"

"Our show, jackass." I moved across the room and grabbed two small bottles of tequila I had hidden in the top drawer of the dresser. "Our show!"

"So, you're willing to lose all you've worked for?" He shook his head.

"If it comes to that, yes. Family is more important than job." I opened both bottles and handed one to him along with a hotel room glass.

"We just need to make sure this episode we give them is so phenomenal they have no choice but to air it." I said while pouring my bottle into a glass. "So, you see, there is nothing to worry about. And we'll figure out what to do with the putz they send us tomorrow. I'm pretty sure we can make it so he doesn't last the week."

I raised my glass and he touched his bottle to it, then we both drank. I know what you're thinking. I had just made a promise that I wouldn't drink tonight, and now here I am drinking. But I also wasn't expecting to have this conversation with Jerry right now. Unfortunately, Brandon had to open his mouth and put me in this position. So I'm sure Theresa will understand.

"You wearing that shirt for the filming?" Jerry looked me up and down.

"Yeah, what do you think?"

"It's okay." He said while looking at the dark grey shirt on the bed I had just taken off. "But the dark grey one would play better with your eyes on camera."

"Dammit! I knew I should go with my first instinct!"

I quickly pulled off my shirt, grabbed the dark grey shirt from the bed, and slipped it on.

132

"Better?" I asked Jerry.

"Much better."

He made his way to the door and let himself out.

CHAPTER 10

After everyone had freshened up, we met by the DVR monitor to finalize our game plan. Brandon and Jerry always stayed at the table monitoring the cameras and supervising. That usually left a team of Bobby teamed up with Christy, and me teamed up with Theresa.

Can you say awkward? These had always been the pairings in the past, but now that Theresa and I were separated, this would definitely be an interesting investigation.

"So why don't we have Bobby and Christy start on the second floor." Jerry directed, then turned to me. "You good starting out with the basement?"

"Works for me." I replied.

"Me too." Added Bobby.

"I need a thermal imager, a digital recorder, and one of the camcorders to start off with." I grabbed the needed equipment off the table.

"I think we're starting off with the same set up, plus a rem pod." Christy added.

"And Brandon and I..." Added Jerry. "Will just take the anal beads and vanilla lube."

As we all had a good laugh at Brandon's expense, all he could manage was a shake of his head.

"Please don't leave me."

"You'll be fine." Bobby assured him. "I think."

Bobby and Christy headed towards the stairs. As I made my way

135

through the restaurant to access the basement with Theresa right behind me, I hesitated as I passed the bar.

"Don't even think about it." She snarled.

Kind of creepy that she knows me so well, she knew what thought was going to pop into my head before it even popped into my head. I grinned and shook my head.

"How the hell do you know I wasn't thinking about grabbing a bottle of water?" It was pretty hard for me to sound indignant given our past.

Theresa stared at me. "Good idea. Why don't you grab us each a water."

"I don't want one now." I pouted.

"That's what I thought." She turned and continued walking to the basement stairs.

As we got to the stairs and started down, I turned on my flashlight, and shined it down into the dark abyss awaiting below. I passed by her on the left side of the stairs. "Let me go first."

"Ma hero." She said in her best southern accent.

"No, just making sure if a demon sneaks up from behind it gets you, not me." I chuckled.

Making our way to the basement took a little more effort than anticipated. The railing on the stair was broken, and even a few of the steps had boards missing. I took Theresa's hand as we got to the bottom and helped her down the stairs.

"Maybe we should have done this with the lights on." I breathed a sigh of relief as we got to solid ground.

"That'd take all the fun out it." She responded. "Where's your sense of adventure?"

As we moved to the center of the main room, I turned on the video camera and began surveying the room. It always amazed me how much the camera could pick up in total darkness as long as it had infrared lighting. The infrared lighting, or night vision as it is also called, gave us the ability to record video in complete darkness without having to have any lights on.

Fairly ordinary as cellars and basements go. Dusty and a bit damp. Several storage crates piled up on the far side of the room. Behind us a wall devoted to newer wine racking. Seemed to be an overflow from the wine cellar in the next room. I made my way over to the wine rack, pulled out a bottle and dusted it off.

"Let's try a short burst EVP session in this room." I grabbed a couple of the crates and moved them over to the center. Theresa followed me to the center of the room and sat down. I turned on the recorder and placed it between us, then turned out the flashlight.

"My name is Sebastian. Can you tell us your name?" I paused and looked around the room.

"Can you tell us how old you are?" As I gave a few moments for response Theresa nudged me and pointed out the lights on my K2 meter were going off.

"Is this you making the lights on this box light up?" I slid the K2 meter further out in front of me.

As I paused the lights on the meter continued to flicker on and off.

"Do you want us to leave?" I asked.

"Are we communicating with Arthur Stratton?" As soon as I finished my question, the lights on the meter pegged.

"Are you buried beneath this room?" As I spoke, the lights on the meter turned off.

137

Seconds later we heard what sounded like footsteps heading into the room next to this one. I turned on my flashlight and turned off the digital recorder. We stood up and went in the direction of the footsteps. I fumbled for the radio attached to my belt.

"Guys, where are you all?" I spoke into the radio. "I have movement down here."

"You're alone down there." Jerry's voice came across the radio. "Brandon and I haven't moved a bit, and Bobby and Christy are still upstairs."

"Oh, this will be our most interesting investigation yet!" I looked at Theresa and mocked.

"You are without a doubt, the worst ghost hunter ever." She teased. "This is what you're supposed to live for."

"I guess I still prefer my most of my spirits to come from a bottle."

As we made our way into the wine cellar, I suddenly felt chilled as a rush of cold air seemed to pass through the room.

"Tell me you feel that?" I rubbed my hands up and down my arms.

"What?"

"A rush of cold air just came through here." I shook my head. "How could you not have felt that?"

I moved over to the wall where I had pulled the brick out earlier and began shining my light in there again. I could make out some boxes of what looked to be paint cans, cleaning supplies, and miscellaneous junk. I began cautiously moving another brick in the wall back and forth trying to loosen it.

"What are you doing?"

"I'm just trying to see how firmly some of these bricks are in place."

"Well knock it off!" She barked and backed up. "This room is not that stable!"

I ignored her and continued to work at the brick. After a little wiggling back and forth, it finally came free. Theresa shook her head in disapproval. I looked back at her for a moment, then turned back to the wall and began working on a third brick. This one also came out rather easily after a little bit of work. I shined my light back into the room now that I had a larger hole for viewing. With my expanded field of vison, I could now see additional boxes at the far side of the room. Unlike the boxes of chemicals, these looked to be sealed. "There's more boxes at the far end of the room."

"Great. More boxes." She said. "That's certainly worth having the ceiling cave in on us."

I began wiggling one last brick back and forth.

"Are you listening to me?"

"Last one, I swear!" As I worked it free, I now had a decent sized opening in the shape of a stretched out plus sign. One brick on top, two from the middle, and one more from the bottom. I shined the flashlight in again to try and get a better look at the boxes. Theresa was switching off between watching me and keeping an eye on the ceiling. I grabbed the radio once again.

"Hey Bobby, are you there?" I whispered into the radio. "Come in."

"Yeah, what do you need?" He whispered in response.

"You used to work construction, right? You ever do any brick work?"

"A ton. Why?"

"The bricks in the wine cellar wall are extremely loose. Wondering how hard it would be to remove about twenty of them, then put them back?"

"Not tough at all. Just need to match the mortar we use to what the existing mortar looks like."

I could feel Theresa glaring at me without even having to turn around and look at her.

"Good. Tomorrow you and I are driving into town to pick up whatever we'll need."

"Works for me."

I returned the radio to my belt.

"Are you insane?" Theresa scolded. "Twenty bricks? The wall might come down."

"We'll be careful." I tried to assure her. "I want to see what's in those other boxes."

"Don't you think if it was anything important, they would have moved them before they sealed the wall?" Theresa was quickly growing more concerned about the stability of the room.

"Who knows? I would have thought they would have moved the boxes of chemicals before they sealed the wall as well."

She continued to shake her head.

"Keep complaining and when it comes time to seal the wall back up, I may draw on my Poe influence and put you on the other side."

"Go for it." She smiled. "I'd haunt you for eternity."

"You keep talking to me like I'm the one that believes in all this shit?" I scoffed. "That would be you."

"Oh, come on." She walked over to me. "And all the weird stuff that's been going on here? You're still a skeptic?"

"We can't all live in the magical world of rainbows and unicorns now, can we?" I said while continuing to look at the bricks. "I've seen or heard nothing yet that can't be explained one way or another."

"You know, if you try hard enough, everything we find can be explained." She said as she came closer and began examining the bricks. "That doesn't necessarily mean that's the right explanation."

"And thus, proving why we make such a good team." I grinned. "Who knows, maybe one day, one of us will actually be able to prove our side to the other."

"And I'll be there smiling when you have to concede that I was right all along." She grinned. "Unlike you, I actually believe in what we're doing."

"And you're convinced beyond a doubt that EVP's are ghosts trying to talk to you?" I held up the recorder.

"Not all, some are just radio interference. But some are actually spirits trying to communicate." She frowned. "You should try listening more often."

"We do make an odd team, you and I." I laughed. "You and your faith and me and my facts."

As we paused for our lighter moment, it was cut short when we heard movement in the next room.

"What the fu…" I turned sharply towards the noise and cautiously began to make my way to the other room.

"What did you hear?" Theresa asked.

"You didn't hear that?" I turned back to her. "It sounded like something getting dragged across the floor in the main room."

I poked my head into the room and shined my flashlight around. There were no marks on the ground and our equipment appeared untouched. But there was still something that felt different about the room. I pulled my EMF meter back out of my vest and turned it on. The lights immediately pegged into the red.

"That's interesting." I pointed the meter around the room.

"I'm sure there's a logical explanation for it." Theresa smiled at me. "It surely can't be paranormal."

"Smart ass." I shook my head as I began to move around the room.

As I neared the outer edges of the room, the meter would quiet down. But each time I crossed the center of the room, the lights would peg again. I finally began to focus my activity on just the center of the room. I knelt down and put the EMF meter on the ground, and pulled out my digital recorder. Theresa stayed at the outer edge of the room and watched me from a distance. I pressed the record button on the digital recorder and placed it on the floor in front of me.

"Hello. My name is Sebastian." I spoke to the recorder. "Can you tell me your name?"

I gave a slight pause to allow time for a response.

"Are you Arthur Stratton?"

"Was that you that interrupted our first session moments ago?"

"Was that you that was walking in the next room?"

I turned the recorder off and plugged it into the portable speaker. I set the speaker down in front of me and started the playback.

"My name is Sebastian. Can you tell us your name?"

"Can you tell us how old you are?"

"Is this you making the lights on this box light up?"

"Do you want us to leave?"

"Are we communicating with Arthur Stratton?"

"Are you buried beneath this room?"

I heard the click of the recorder marking where we had turned it off to go check on the footsteps we heard before continuing.

"Hello. My name is Sebastian. Can you tell me your name?"

"Are you Arthur Stratton?"

As I heard something other than my voice on the recording, I grabbed the recorder and replayed that segment.

"Are you Arthur Stratton?" The recorder echoed my question.

"No." Spoke a very clear second voice, obviously not mine or Theresa's. I let the playback continue.

"Was that you that interrupted our first session moments ago?"

"Yes." Replied the same voice as before in a haunting, monotonous drone.

"Was that you that was walking in the next room?" I let the recorder continue on to my final question.

"Get out." Replied the voice in an even more raspy, breathy tone. Theresa and I looked at each other as I played the last segment one more time to confirm. There was no mistaking the voice on the recorder and its responses.

"Those were definitely class A EVP's." Theresa said, and I had to agree.

A class A EVP is one where you are definitely getting an intelligent response to a question that has been asked. Not a random word

143

or sentence, but a direct answer. Before I had a chance to play it again, I was interrupted by Brandon coming across the radio.

"Hey, can you hear me?"

I grabbed the radio out of my pocket.

"Yeah, what's up?"

"You need to come up here and look at the video we just got." Brandon hesitated. "I think there's something down there with you."

I looked at Theresa and we both turned to head up the stairs. As we made our way to the lobby, we could see Bobby and Christy had found their way down to the lobby as well and were all staring at the screen. As I got closer I could see what they were looking at. The basement camera had caught footage of two different anomalies. One that seemed to move about the room then disappear into the floor, and another that seemed to move towards me.

"Can you replay that section?"

Jerry went back to the start of the video. There were definitely some shadowy figures there, but filmed with night vision it's hard to tell if they were something paranormal, or just dark spots from the pixelation of the camera.

"That's good. Let's mark those spots and look at them again in the morning with fresh eyes." As I spoke the others nodded in agreement. I looked at the clock on the wall. It was close to two a.m. We don't normally call it until at least 4 a.m., but travel and set up usually wears on us a bit on the first night. So we decided to knock off a little early tonight. The others began to make their way up the stairs. Brandon stayed downstairs and poured himself a drink.

"Good stuff." He raised his glass.

"Let's not get ahead of ourselves." I said. "Let's see how the footage looks when we're not all looking through tired eyes."

I could see Theresa walking up the stairs, and as she turned the corner at the top, I grabbed Brandon's glass and helped myself to a sip.

"See you in the morning." I handed his glass back, nearly empty, and proceeded to make my way up the stairs.

The others had all made it into their rooms for the night, but Theresa was still in the hallway. She looked at me and grinned. "You can't explain that footage away with camera malfunction or pixelization."

"Wasn't planning on it." I defended. "I just want to make sure before we get too excited."

"Be happy, this was a good first night for an investigation." She shook her head and moved closer to me. "We need this to be a good investigation."

"I know." I sighed realizing everything was riding on this.

"Don't let your need for logical explanation keep you from seeing what's right in front of you."

I forced out a grin for her sake. "I've been doing this too long to get worked up over a few EVP's or a shadow on a screen."

"I know you can hear me." She grabbed me by the chin and made me look her in the eye. "But you never listen to me."

I smiled as she continued. Not because I liked being talked down to like a five-year-old, but because at this point, I was willing to settle for whatever physical contact she made with me.

"If you hear nothing else I ever say to you, hear this. It's okay to be happy. You've gotten so used to thinking you have to punish yourself, you don't ever let yourself enjoy anything anymore." As the grin faded from my face, she released my chin, allowing me to lower my gaze to the floor. "The past is the past. You've earned the right to be happy every now and then."

CHAPTER 11

In the morning, I sat in the lobby with a cup of coffee. Still trying to wrap my head around things and make sense of last night. I was usually pretty good at debunking events, but this had me off balance. Brandon and Christy entered with their coffee as well and sat across from me. We all just stared silently for a moment.

"Any ideas?" Brandon asked.

"I actually do have one." I responded. "I say we pack up and leave."

Brandon smiled and Christy laughed. I don't think they realized I was being serious. I moved over to the table with the DVR set up and sat down. I played the clip back from last night hoping maybe it looked different after getting some sleep. Brandon and Christy also moved over and stood behind me.

"Pretty damn cool, huh?" He reached over me and replayed the video again.

"It's got to be some sort of malfunction." I think I was trying to convince myself more than the others at this point.

There was no logical explanation for the shadowy figure that moved from one side of the basement to the other, then disappeared into the floor. It couldn't have been a shadow. It didn't look like any camera malfunction I'd ever seen. Then a second one seemed to follow me across the room, actually turning with me when I turned and then it changed direction.

"I don't know. Every other aspect of the video looks perfect." Christy added. "If it had gone in one direction, then disappeared, I could see it being just a shadow maybe."

"Precisely." Brandon replayed the video one more time staring intently at the screen.

"But one went across the room, then turned back and went the opposite direction and disappeared into the floor." Christy concluded then turned to look at me. "While the other seemed to go towards you."

As much as I wanted to, I couldn't argue with her. I'd never seen anything like it.

"And do I need to point out, that spot in the floor where the shadow eventually disappeared is pretty close to where we figure Arthur Stratton is presumed to have been buried?" Brandon raised a brow and grinned.

"No, you don't need to point that out. That just makes it all the more disturbing in my opinion." I replied.

"You may be the worst paranormal investigator ever." Brandon mused. "You're supposed to want this kind of evidence."

As the others entered the lobby Brandon turned to them and smiled excitedly.

"Someone tell this guy last night was a success." He laughed while shaking his head. "He's acting like this is the worst thing ever."

Bobby cued up the video yet again.

"He's right Sebastian." Bobby continued to watch the video. "This video is going to put us on the map. Maybe even bump us up to number three in the ratings."

"How can you not be happy about this?" Jerry asked. "This is exactly what we were hoping for."

"I am happy." I glanced over at Theresa in the back of the room to show her my exaggerated smile. "See, happy!"

The others looked at me oddly while I turned my attention back to the monitor. "But doesn't this make anyone else a little nervous?"

"You may be in the wrong line of work." Theresa joked at my expense.

I shook my head and replayed the video again.

"And before we jump to the paranormal." I continued. "Can someone do some digging online and see if maybe there's a video related malfunction that could have caused this."

As I watched the video end once again, I continued to think there had to be something we were missing.

"I would hate for us to put this in the show, and have someone point out a week later that this is a common occurrence either due to lighting or memory cards." I hesitated and looked at our equipment. "...cameras, or anything that might have caused this."

The others nodded. As they all dispersed, I nervously followed Christy across the lobby.

"I think that's great footage for only being our first night." She said.

"I agree." I replied trying to casually break into a more delicate conversation. "You know..."

I hesitated, as I was never very good playing the role of the boss. I had always felt more like one of the group than the leader. You'd think after seeing a video of what might very well be an actual spirit, dealing with a human would be a piece of cake. But no, I'm starting to think I might prefer communicating with the dead more than the living.

"What is it?" Christy asked.

"I'm glad to see you and Brandon getting along again." I tried to venture in delicately. "I really am."

"We've always gotten along, haven't we? What are you trying to get at?"

"As you know, I was aware the last time you two dated."

"Dated?" She laughed. "It was more like a fling. I had just broken up with Michael, and I needed to have some fun for a change."

"Some fun?"

"You know what I mean. I get tired of being the goody two shoes. I just wanted to be a little careless for once."

"Believe me, I get that. No one knows careless like me." I smiled. "But the last time you guys tried this, it crushed him."

"I'm not sure I'm following you?" She replied.

"He's my best friend." I continued. "And you're like a sister to me."

"And that means what exactly?" She smiled nervously.

"I just don't want anyone to get hurt." I smiled at her as I put my hand on her shoulder.

"What has Brandon said to you?" She asked while staring at my hand on her shoulder.

"Nothing. He hasn't said a word. I wanted to talk to you first." I said as I removed my hand from her shoulder.

"Then why would you assume..." She began to reply.

I raised one finger to silence her and motioned for her to turn around. I had her look over her shoulder in the large ornate mirror in the lobby. Reluctantly she did as I instructed.

"Well?" I asked as I pointed in the mirror.

It was hard to deny the large orange Cheetos handprint on the ass of her pants. I tried my hardest not to laugh.

"Jesus Christ!" She shook her head. "Would it kill him to wash his goddam hands?"

I think that was the first time I ever heard her swear. She began rigorously brushing off the back of her pants. Once she was satisfied all evidence had been removed, she once again engaged with me.

"Did anyone else see that?"

"I don't think so." I assured her.

"Good. I don't need to be taking crap from Bobby or Jerry on this. This is so embarrassing."

"So is this…" I hesitated. "Something more than a fling?"

"I know it's stupid, but we just click in a weird sort of way." She said. "I can't explain it. We're complete opposites and most of the time he irritates the crap out of me."

She hesitated.

"But when we're not in the group, and it's just us…" She smiled. "He's so very different. Kind of sweet."

"Kind of sweet?" I muzzled my laughter for her sake. "Hard to picture with Brandon."

"I know, right!"

"For the record." I smiled. "It makes me happy."

She looked at me curiously.

"Being alone sucks." I added. "Life is too short to not have someone special to wake up with."

She gave a half-hearted attempt at a smile. I could sense she was feeling a little bit sorry for me and my situation.

"Even if that someone is a slob?" She laughed trying to, once again, lighten the mood.

"Even if." I smiled as she shook her head.

"Remember, not a word." She raised a finger, before making her way back to the others.

"My lips are sealed." I said as I watched her walk away.

Of course, my thoughts immediately drifted back to Theresa, who was now watching me from across the room. I hope she didn't think I was hitting on Christy. She has that look in her eyes she gets when I've done something wrong. A look I know all too well. I figured I'd better nip this in the bud or there'd be hell to pay later. As I strolled across the lobby, I was unfortunately intercepted by Jerry.

"So, is this turning into a couples retreat?" Jerry said while pretending to act offended.

"Not sure I follow you?" I tried my best to play dumb. Which usually didn't take a lot of effort.

"Give me a little credit. Cheetos handprint on her ass, and a talk from the boss shortly thereafter." Jerry laughed. "Not hard to figure out."

"I trust you'll keep this quiet?" I smiled.

"From who? Bobby was the one that pointed it out to me." He shook his head. "So, everyone knows already."

"Shit. Well for Christy's sake just act like you don't know. She feels a bit awkward about it."

"I don't blame her. If I lowered my standards far enough to date Brandon, I wouldn't want anyone to know."

"Behave yourself."

"So, am I to assume I can invite my boyfriend to the next investigation?" Jerry laughed. "Seeing as love is in the air and all."

"By all means." I laughed. "I'd love to meet him."

Jerry laughed and glanced over his shoulder to make sure Christy was out of earshot.

"They make an odd couple, don't you think?" He grimaced. "She's so perky and pleasant."

"And he's kind of a jackass?" I interjected.

"Exactly." Jerry laughed. "And old."

"Whoa, easy there." I cut him off. "He and I are the same age!"

"I know that. But he acts his age, you don't."

I was trying to figure out if this was in fact a compliment in Jerry's strange little world, because I took it to mean I was a bit immature. It must have been obvious to Jerry I wasn't following his reasoning.

"He acts like my father." Jerry continued. "You act like my peer. He's come pretty far, but he's still a big fat homophobe. Whereas I think you got past it in the first month of working with me."

"If I'm being totally honest, I think it took closer to two months." I smiled and put a hand on Jerry's shoulder.

"Well, whatever." Jerry laughed and continued. "The point is you think like a young person, and he will always have a little hesitation when it comes to anyone that isn't like him."

I nodded in agreement, and certainly couldn't argue Jerry's assessment. I've been on enough flights with Brandon to see that his alcohol consumption on a plane is directly affected by how many people of middle eastern descent are also on the plane. One flight we had a pilot that looked slightly middle eastern. He drank so much, Theresa and I had to damn near carry him off the plane when we landed. I chuckled a little to myself.

"What?" Jerry asked as I chuckled.

"I just realized how correct you are. He is definitely a work in progress." I confessed. "But who knows. Maybe Christy can turn that lump of coal into a diamond?"

"I'm not holding my breath." Jerry laughed as he walked away and rejoined the others.

It would have been nice to have a moment of relaxation at some point, but as luck would have it, William came through the door of the inn and an awkward hush fell over the room. The silence was making my head hurt. William was wearing a pair of khaki shorts, brown loafers, and what looked to be some type of golf sweater vest thing. The rest of us were in jeans and t shirts.

"Sorry buddy." Brandon broke the silence. "The hot yoga studio is in town."

As everyone tried in vain to contain their laughter, even I had to smile. To some degree I truly envied Brandon for not having a filter. If something popped into his mind, there was a good chance he was going to share it with the room. I cautiously made my way towards William, who had a smug little grin on his face I wanted to wipe off with my fist. But I chose to be an adult and extended my hand. After all, if I'm going to sabotage his week, I needed him to at least trust a few of us.

"I'm Sebastian." As we shook the others began to come closer. "I'm sure you recognize the others from the show."

"William." He said coldly as he shook my hand.

They all nodded, but no one else chose to offer him their hand. I led everyone back over to the monitoring table.

"You'll be training here. Just watch what Jerry does, and you should be fine. Jerry is the best in the business at this."

"Shouldn't be too tough." William replied, then turned and gave a disapproving look towards Jerry. "I mean, if someone like him can do it."

"Someone like me?" Jerry stepped forward, but Brandon soon cut him off.

"Tell me, Billy." Brandon interrupted. "What does a smug little inbred asshole like you do for fun when you're not sucking off your uncle?"

William ignored Brandon for the time being but I could already tell, these two were fire and gasoline.

"Billy, if you're going to work with us, you're going to show the team respect." I motioned towards Jerry. "The entire team."

"My name is William." He turned to me, then looked sharply at Brandon. "You wanna talk about showing respect?"

"That was in response to your comment to Jerry. You show us respect, we'll show you respect." Even as I spoke, I realized the chances of getting Brandon to go easy on him were about a hundred to one.

He looked briefly at the monitor, then moved over to the table with the equipment and picked up the SLS camera.

"How long until I am in front of the camera?"

"Excuse me?" Bobby moved forward. I put a hand on Bobby's arm and pulled him back a little.

"I think there's been a little miscommunication." I stepped back in front of Bobby. "Bobby and I have always handled the hosting of the show. That aspect won't be changing."

"I think my uncle will be having some say on that." William said with a matter-of-fact tone. "I'm pretty sure the network values his input over anyone else's."

"I think your uncle has had a little too much input into the rear end of a sheep." As Brandon stepped into William's face, I had to ease him back yet again.

"I guess we know who's next to be off the show." William quipped with an irritating little smile that reminded me of the brat in the front of the classroom that always turned everyone in.

"Let's all take a break and get ready for filming tonight." I was trying my best to diffuse the situation. "Meet back down here at eight to start. William, you can grab any of the rooms that are left. Keys are all behind the desk."

"I have a room across town at the Hilton. I would never stay in a shit hole like this."

"Just make sure you're back by eight, then." I shook my head. This was going to be impossible. Ten minutes in and I already wanted to choke the life out of him. There was no way we would make it a week together.

As he exited the inn, the others shook their head and Brandon came closer. "We're not really going to let that ass have any say in this are we?"

"No, of course not." I shook my head. "But we need to play it cool until we can figure out how best to handle this. I don't need you intentionally stirring things up."

"I don't stir things up." Brandon shrugged.

I couldn't tell if that was his attempt at dry humor, or if he truly doesn't realize when he's being an ass to people. At any rate, I had too many other things to worry about to get drawn into one of Brandon's aimless conversations.

"You know for fifty bucks I know people that will break his legs." Bobby offered.

"For twenty bucks I know people that will take his virginity." Jerry offered. "And not in a pleasant way."

"As tempting as both of those offers are, I think we need to

156

handle this delicately." I started to make my way to the stairs, then paused. "Everyone take some time to clear their heads and relax, then we can meet back down here for a bite to eat."

I walked up the stairs feeling absolutely drained. The sound of the others continuing on their conversation about William was growing faint as I neared the top of the stairs. As much as I felt I should be down there and involved in their discussion, I just needed some down time. All the little balls I had managed to juggle and keep in the air, seemed like they were about to come crashing down around me.

Although I clung to the faint hope of salvaging our show, I was quickly beginning to realize it was more likely this would be the end. All the clever little scenarios I had played out in my head were falling apart. I don't know which was more exhausting, the thought of trying to hold this all together, or the thought of letting it go and having to start all over again. I stood in the hallway outside my door with my key in hand. But I almost felt too tired to extend my arm and put the key in the slot. I stared hoping maybe I could just open the door telepathically.

"It puts the key in the door." Theresa said after having obviously been watching me for a little while. I was too tired to even smile. "Wow. You have had a bad week."

"You could say that." I cocked my head slowly to the side to look at her. She came down the hall and grabbed the key from my hand and opened my door for me. I slowly walked into the room and collapsed on the bed, while she watched from the doorway. I rose slightly to look at the bottle of tequila on my nightstand, but decided it wasn't worth the energy it would take to retrieve and laid back down.

"Wow, you must really be tired." Theresa gasped from the doorway. I could only nod my head. "Get some rest. I'll wake you in an hour. You'll feel better."

"I certainly couldn't feel any worse." I struggled to raise my hand and wave goodbye as she disappeared from my doorway.

CHAPTER 12

I don't even remember dozing off, but after waking I did feel a little bit better. I was still convinced this would end in disaster, but at least had convinced myself to make our last show a great one. As I prepared for our second night of investigating, I was still thinking about the previous night's footage. Without a doubt the best footage we'd ever obtained, and for the first time I was actually hoping it was in fact a spirit. If we're going down, we're going down in style.

I grabbed two of the small bottles of tequila out of the top drawer and poured them into a glass. Yes, I realize it's pathetic that my courage was usually found at the bottom of a glass. But I couldn't get those shadowy figures out of my head. Not because they scared me, but because if those figures were real, then that EVP response I got in my house might be just as real.

I brought my drink into the bathroom. Took a long hard look at myself in the mirror. My five o'clock shadow probably needed a little grooming, but it's been a while since friends and family have trusted me with a razor. Luckily, they let me keep an electric trimmer with my toiletries. I don't think they've caught on to the fact that I could easily achieve the same results by taking the electric trimmer or the hair dryer in the bathtub with me.

I glanced briefly at the hair dryer, then at the tub and chuckled. "Nah, I got shit to do."

I plugged in the electric trimmer and gave it a quick run across my face. The vibrations of the trimmer felt good running across my face. I ran some water through my hair and brushed my teeth. Smelled my arm pit and quickly decided some deodorant was in order. I normally don't use cologne on an investigation, as most paranormal experts say it may deter the spirits, but spending nights with Theresa has made me a little self-conscious. I want to make sure she knows any rancid musty smell is coming from the building and not me.

After applying a little cologne, I exited the bathroom and looked at the clothes I had laid out on the bed. Jeans, black shirt, and sneakers. That was the nice thing about my wardrobe, simplicity at its finest, even if it did take me an hour to decide between two shirts.

I joined up with the others downstairs in the dining room. They had sandwich fixings sprawled out on the bar and were having a snack at the large round table in the corner. I walked over to the bar, grabbed a plate, and started making myself a sandwich. I picked up a piece of what looked to be roast beef and smelled it.

"We're not really sure either." Jerry grimaced. "We think it may be roast beef."

"Or human." Bobby added. "The little grocery store didn't have a wide selection and the guy behind the counter was a little on the creepy side."

I put it down on my bread and slathered mayonnaise over it hoping that might drown out the taste of whatever mystery meat it truly was. I threw a piece of lettuce on, then closed the sandwich, walked over to the table and put my plate next to Brandon. Looking at the table, everybody was equipped with a bottled water.

"There's a stocked fridge in the kitchen if you want a water." Christy said.

I nodded and made my way into the kitchen. As I opened the refrigerator door, the wine rack caught my attention. I moved over to it and pulled out a bottle of red wine. I figured if I was going to be forced to eat gas station food, I should at least have something decent to wash it down with. And besides, red wine is supposedly good for you. So, this was pretty much the same as drinking a glass of milk as far as I was concerned.

I rummaged through the drawers until I found a wine opener. Opened the bottle and poured myself a glass. I held the glass under my nose briefly to take in the aroma. Then took a sip.

Heaven.

What is it people say? The world's problems may truly be unsolvable, but with the right liquor, it won't matter anymore. Okay, maybe that's just what I say. But you have to admit, I make a pretty strong argument. I finished the glass and poured myself another.

"Nice." Theresa scowled.

Startled, I quickly turned around to see she had followed me into the kitchen.

"One glass." I defended. "To help make that indigestible meal go down."

"One glass? That's funny, because I thought I smelled tequila on your breath when you first came into the dining room?"

I grinned sheepishly.

"Look, I'm just a little creeped out." I explained. "Trying to take the edge off."

She shook her head and left the kitchen. I grabbed the bottle and my glass and made my way back to the dining room. The others quickly noticed the glass and bottle in my hand.

"What the hell?" Jerry gasped as he ran over to the bar to grab himself a wine glass.

"Grab me one too!" Shouted Bobby.

"Make that three!" Brandon added.

Christy and Theresa simply shook their heads in disgust.

"So, this great idea to do a show without alcohol is history?" Christy said in a condescending tone.

"We'll leave the booze off camera." Bobby said. "But a bottle of wine split four ways isn't going to kill anyone."

"Famous last words." Christy added. "Remind us of that later when Brandon or Sebastian have had so much one of them trips down a flight of stairs."

"You make us sound like alcoholics." I smiled and stood up from the table with my glass of wine in hand. "A toast."

The boys all lifted their wine glasses. Christy grabbed her bottle of water. But Theresa, obviously still unhappy about the addition of alcohol to the investigation simply glared at me.

"We could have worked in small stuffy cubicles, with crappy bosses…" I began.

"Well, we don't have the small stuffy cubicles anyway." Bobby interrupted and everyone laughed.

"Ha ha." I directed Bobby's way as I continued. "But we get paid to take vacations in some of the more unique inn's across the country."

They all nodded.

"We don't wake to alarms. We go to sleep when we want. And we can even have a drink or two while we work." I smiled, as everyone was nodding in agreement with the exception of Theresa.

"It's just…" I had to pause for a moment while I searched for the right words. "If this does end up being our last season."

I hesitated for a moment. Saying it out loud like that seemed to suddenly put things in harsh perspective. There's an impending finality looming, knowing there's a strong chance we will lose it all.

"If this does end up being our last season." I continued. "I want you all to know how much you all mean to me, and how much I've loved working with you!"

162

I raised my glass as did the others, and we all drank. Even Theresa had managed to finally force out a smile. There was a long awkward silence, until Bobby could no longer remain silent.

"Get him a glass of tequila. This sappy version of Sebastian is scaring me." Bobby blurted out while the others laughed.

I smiled and sat back down at the table and took a bite of my sandwich.

"Jesus." I groaned. "I think this might be human."

"It is odd we haven't seen William back yet?" Bobby laughed while everyone hesitated long enough to look at the meat, pause eating, then at Brandon.

"Even I wouldn't stoop so low as to use his meat for sandwiches." Brandon defended. "I prefer my human to taste a little less stuffy."

"Scares me you think you know what human would taste like." Jerry responded.

"There's a gay joke there somewhere, but I just haven't had enough to drink to think of it." Brandon laughed.

We ignored Brandon and continued eating. As we finished eating, Jerry collected the dishes and brought them to the kitchen. We each finished our glasses of wine as Jerry returned to the dining room.

"So, you'll take the upstairs tonight?" Jerry looked at me, then to Bobby and Christy. "And they'll take the basement."

Bobby and Christy nodded. I hesitated.

"You sure you guys want the basement?" I asked.

"We'll be fine." Christy assured me.

"Yeah, unlike you, we actually look forward to getting evidence that proves our chosen profession isn't a waste of time." Bobby smiled.

"You won't be laughing when the basement floor opens up and Arthur Stratton's zombie eats your brains."

"I would kill to get a zombie on film!" Exclaimed Christy.

Everyone stared in Christy's direction.

"Was that out loud?" She said sheepishly while we all nodded.

As we all made or way back out to the lobby to collect our gear, I poured what was left in the wine bottle into my glass, once again drawing a glare of disapproval from Theresa. Growing tired of her disapproving glances, I intentionally raised the glass to her and drank it in defiance. She too then headed out to the lobby while shaking her head. I smiled smugly at my bold act of defiance. Knowing full well I would most likely apologize to her within an hour. But I could still enjoy my moment for now.

In the lobby we all began to gear up. We all took the same sets ups we used the previous night. As a paranormal investigator you end up with a set of tools you feel the most comfortable with. So, while there may be a vast array of tools at our disposal, we always seem to gravitate to the ones we've grown accustomed to.

"Why don't you guys take the SLS camera tonight." I grabbed it from the table and handed it to Bobby. "I think we need to get some footage of it in use, and seeing as you seem to be the most familiar with it."

"Yeah, no problem." Bobby took it from me, powered it on and scanned the room with it.

Just as we were about to disperse, William made it back to the inn. I looked at the clock on the wall.

"Eight o'clock means eight o'clock." I glared. "Not eight twenty-three."

William looked at the expensive looking watch on his wrist.

"Twenty minutes, big deal." He said. "Will the fake ghosts be mad we're late?"

"Why the hell are you even here if you don't believe any of this?" Brandon's chair slid across the room as he stood up fast and moved towards William. I cut him off midway and tried to calm him down.

"Not worth it man. He's just a candy ass that needed daddy to get him a job because he's too worthless to be able to get one himself." I said then turned towards William. "We are all about to leave to do our job, which will leave you here with a guy that wants to pummel your head in. I suggest you shut your mouth and take notes as this is the last time I will step in front of him and save your pathetic ass."

The smug smile finally faded from William's face as he nodded and made his way over to the table. He pulled up a chair and positioned it so Jerry was between Brandon and himself, and began watching the monitors.

Bobby and Christy hesitantly made their way to the basement, while Theresa and I headed up the stairs and made our way into Abigail's room. We figured that would be as good a starting point as any.

"What are the odds we make it through the night without Brandon taking a swing at him?" Theresa asked me.

"I wouldn't put money on it, and as you know, I'll bet on just about anything."

I pulled out my digital recorder, set it on the bed and started recording.

"My name is Sebastian." I started off. "Is there anyone here with me?"

"Abigail, are you still here?"

"Abigail, do you know if Arthur is still here?"

Not even two minutes into our session and we heard a scream

coming from downstairs. My first thought was Brandon was already pummeling William, which I admit did briefly bring a smile to my face. We scrambled downstairs as fast as we could. There was no one on the main level anymore, so we continued through to the kitchen and to the basement stairs. By the time Theresa and I arrived at the cellar, we could see Bobby laying at the bottom of the stairs motionless. I ran down the stairs and knelt down by Brandon who was already checking Bobby over.

"What the hell happened?"

"He came upstairs to grab a fresh set of batteries, and a moment later we heard Christy scream." Jerry explained as I turned to Christy.

"Our batteries were fully charged. I checked them myself before we came down." She was obviously very shaken up. "He went up to get another set, but on his way back down he tripped and fell down the stairs."

"Bobby." I checked his pulse. "He's got a pulse, thank God."

"I don't have reception down here." Christy moaned. "I'm going upstairs to call for help."

"Go with her!" I motioned to Brandon who was already ahead of me and following her up the stairs.

I touched Bobby's forehead and tried to get him to come to, but he was out.

"Jesus, I'm on hold with nine one one!" Christy yelled down the stairs.

Almost as if Christy's shout had woken him, Bobby moved his head slightly.

"What the…" He said groggily, trying to lift his head.

"Not so fast." I held him in position. "You just fell down the stairs."

"My head is throbbing."

"How do you feel other than your head?"

"My ankle hurts a little. But mostly it's just my head."

"Anything yet?" I yelled up to Brandon and Christy.

"Still on hold." Brandon yelled down the stairs.

I started to help Bobby sit up.

"Jerry, give me a hand." I helped Bobby to his feet, so Jerry and I could guide him up the stairs. "I'm going to drive him into town to the hospital."

William had remained silent through all of this. Probably a good thing as it wouldn't have taken much for me to go off on someone right now. We helped Bobby up the stairs gingerly and made our way out to the lobby.

"While I take him into town, you guys want to go through the tape and see what happened?"

"Will do." Brandon took Jerry's place helping me with Bobby. "Jerry you want to cue it up. I'll help Sebastian get Bobby to the car."

Jerry nodded and took a seat in front of the monitors. Christy ran to catch up to Brandon and me as we headed out to the parking lot with Bobby.

"I'm coming with." Christy climbed in the back seat with Bobby as Brandon and I carefully loaded him in.

"Okay, keep him talking." I said as I jumped into the front seat and started the car, then turned to Brandon. "Where was William when this happened?"

"He was with Jerry and me. I know where you're going, but he didn't have anything to do with it."

"Call me if anything turns up on the tapes."

167

I peeled out of the parking lot and headed for town. Nice thing about shooting in small towns, you never have to go far for anything. It wasn't but ten minutes when we were pulling up to the emergency room. As I screeched to a stop in front of the door, I drew the attention of two paramedics who came over to assist us.

"Get him checked in." I nodded to Christy. "I'll park the car."

As I entered the lobby, they had already taken Bobby back into an examination room, leaving Christy pacing the lobby. She looked over when she heard me open the door and rushed towards me.

"I know I had charged those batteries." She sobbed. "I am positive."

"I know you did. This wasn't your fault." I put an arm around her. "He's going to be fine."

As I did my best to reassure her, my phone beeped with an incoming text message. I pulled up a message from Jerry that simply read 'you need to see this' with a video attachment. Christy looked over my shoulder as I opened the video. We were stunned as we watched video. You could clearly make out Bobby at the top of the stairs, and clearly see the same dark image from the night before appear, just moments before Bobby is hurled forward down the stairs. We played the video one more time to verify what we were seeing.

"Well, he sure as hell didn't trip." I gasped.

As I put my phone away, a doctor emerged from the examining room. Christy and I both rushed towards him for an update.

"How is he? Is he going to…"

"He's fine." The doctor cut Christy off before she could become too frantic. "Sprained ankle and a mild concussion."

"Thank god." I finally breathed a sigh of relief.

"I gave him a sedative so he could rest. I'd like him to at least stay

168

until morning." The doctor looked at his watch. "I would think if all looks good he can go by noon tomorrow."

"Thank you." Christy shook the doctor's hand.

"Yes, thank you." I made my way over to the waiting area followed by Christy as the doctor once again disappeared into the back hallway.

CHAPTER 13

I sat at the edge of Bobby's hospital bed while he slept. There was an ominous feeling telling me it was time to pack up the gear and get out of that place before anyone else got hurt. A I stood up and began to pace the room as a male nurse entered the room.

"How's he doing?" He asked

"Still asleep." I responded. "He was..."

"I'm awake." Bobby rubbed the sleep out of his eyes. I moved over to the bed. The nurse went to his side as well.

"How's the pain sweetie?" He asked. "We can up your dosage if needed?"

"It's fine. My ankle is feeling more numb than anything." He answered while inspecting the wrap on his ankle.

"That's good to hear. Just buzz me if you need anything, darling." He gave him a pat on the shoulder than exited the room.

"Sweetie?" I smiled. "Darling?"

"Piss off." He smiled as he replied. "I can't help it if everyone loves me."

"You always said you wanted to do a nurse." I laughed.

"Prick!" He barked while looking at another wrap on his wrist. "You had to take me to the one hospital with a male nurse on duty?"

"Um, we were a little more worried about your ankle than your libido, jackass." I replied dumbfounded.

Christy entered the room and quickly moved over to the bed and grabbed his hand. "How are you doing?"

"I'm fine." He groaned. "Why the fuss? I have a sprained ankle and a mild concussion. Not the first time someone has fallen down a flight of stairs!"

Christy looked at me and began shaking her head and ran her hands over her face. "You haven't told him, have you?"

"He just woke up!" I threw my hands in the air. "I hadn't had a chance yet!"

We both looked to Bobby, who now had a very concerned look on his face. "Something you would like to share with the class?"

I once again began to pace the room. Not really sure how you tell your friend they didn't so much trip down the stairs by accident, but were more or less heaved down the stairs by a malevolent force. I guess you use the band-aid approach and just rip it off.

"We watched the footage of you falling down the stairs." Christy interjected. "You didn't fall down the stairs. You flew two feet off the stairs like you picked up and thrown down the stairs."

"You don't remember that?" I was finding it odd he wouldn't have felt something odd at the time. "You didn't feel that?"

Bobby simply shook his head and sighed. "It's all really still just one big blur."

"You're lucky you don't remember." I said as I turned to Christy. "I'm still freaked out after seeing it."

"You sure it wasn't just me losing my balance?" Bobby was obviously still trying to wrap his head around this.

I pulled out my phone and moved back over to the bed and cued the video up for Bobby to let him watch for himself.

"Jerry also went over the SLS camera footage." Added Christy.

"We didn't use the SLS." Bobby looked up briefly from the video

172

to look at Christy, but quickly returned his gaze to my phone so he wouldn't miss anything.

"You had turned it on when I handed it to you, and must have forgotten to turn it back off." I continued. "It was sitting on a shelf in the cellar."

"And?" Bobby asked still staring at the video.

"There were three figures on the footage when only you and Christy were in the cellar."

"And one of the figures followed you up the stairs when you went for batteries." Christy added.

I could tell by his expressions Bobby had reached the crucial moment of the video. His eyes grew wide and his head moved closer to the screen to strain for a closer look.

"Oh my God." He exclaimed.

"Yeah." I confirmed his disbelief while putting a hand on his shoulder.

"That was awesome!" He cheered while I had to rub a finger in my ear to make sure I was hearing him correctly.

"Awesome?"

"Yes, awesome!" Bobby exclaimed once again, proving my ears were fine, but my jaw was now suddenly on the floor. "We got it recorded!"

"Yes we did." Christy smiled.

"Yes, we got video of something hurling you down a flight of stairs and trying to kill you." I stuttered in disbelief. "This makes you happy, why?"

"This is why we do what we do, isn't it?" Bobby asked while

sitting up and looking for his clothing. "Am I cleared to get out of here?"

"Whoa, slow down. You're not going back there." I insisted, then turned to Christy. "Which brings me to the next subject. Are they all packing the gear up?" I asked.

"Not exactly." She squirmed nervously.

"What does 'not exactly' mean?" I asked.

"They want to continue." She stood up and began pacing. "They're excited about what we've gotten so far."

Bobby nodded and smiled.

"Have they not watched the tapes?" I was in utter disbelief that any of them actually wanted to continue.

"Of course they have." She stopped pacing and looked me in the eye. "They're not alone. I want to stay too. We've never gotten anything like this before."

"Yes, wonderful!" I shouted. "We have a real haunting, and said haunting seems to apparently want us dead!"

"Sebastian, this is a game changer." Bobby seemed to be equally puzzled as to why I wouldn't want to continue.

I looked at him, then to his ankle, and shook my head. "Of course it is. But that doesn't mean I'm willing to risk everyone's safety over a stupid television show."

"Don't you think that's for each of us to decide ourselves?" Christy said.

I could tell by the tone in her voice she was becoming frustrated at my reluctance. It's not that I wasn't thrilled we had gotten some hard evidence, but this isn't Casper that's apparently haunting this place. Arthur Stratton obviously holds one hell of a grudge. And who knows what he is capable of doing if we stay.

"You spoke with the others?" I looked at Christy. "And they all want to stay?"

She nodded, then looked to Bobby, who was also nodding strongly in agreement.

"We'll send you updates on your phone." I explained to Bobby. "Hopefully that will entertain you while you are here."

"Surely you jest." He demanded. "Screw that. I'm going back today."

Christy stood up and looked at me while I came back over to the side of the bed.

"You've got to be kidding me?" I hit the buzzer on the wall that calls the nurse. "After nearly getting killed last night?"

"You can barely walk!" Interjected Christy.

"I don't have to." He sat up on the edge of the bed. "Look, I'm not saying I need to do my usual role, but I can sit at the table with Jerry and monitor. With all that's going on, surely an extra pair of eyes on the monitors is a good idea."

Christy and I looked at each other. Neither of us remotely thinking this was a good idea with him being hobbled, if we should need to make a hasty exit for any reason.

"And Brandon can work the camera for you." He looked at Christy. "While you take over for me."

"I think it's a bad idea. Jerry is able to handle the monitors on his own, and he's got William there if he needs an errand to be run." I debated.

We paused our argument momentarily as the nurse entered the room.

"You rang dear?" He smiled at Bobby.

175

Bobby quickly shook his head.

"Uh no, actually he did." Bobby quickly pointed to me.

"Can you explain to him he should be staying here and taking it easy on his ankle today?" I explained to the nurse. "He's thinking he wants to get out of here and come back to work."

The nurse looked at me curiously, but had no response. I felt maybe I had not explained the situation very well.

"Bobby." I pointed to Bobby and purposely spoke much more slowly this time. "Is trying to get out of here, and come back to work today."

The nurse looked at me and shook his head. Christy put her head in her hands.

"I understood what you said the first time." The nurse now spoke deliberately slowly to mock me. "He has a sprained ankle, a bruised wrist, and a mild concussion."

He looked to the bed at Bobby who was moving his ankle and wrist around in an effort to show how unaffected he truly was.

"These are not life-threatening injuries, sweetie." The nurse looked back towards me. "He is free to go as soon as I find him a pair of crutches."

The nurse gave me a cross look, turned to Bobby and smiled, then quickly exited the room.

"Imagine that." Bobby gloated triumphantly.

"Fine, but if you're on pain meds, no booze tonight." I looked at Bobby, then to Christy. "Right?"

Christy nodded in agreement and smiled.

"What?" I asked curiously, thinking it was an odd choice of

moments to be smiling.

"Nothing." Christy shook her head. "Just thought it was cute hearing one of the Booze Brothers acting all motherly and lecturing someone else on booze."

"Booze Brothers?" I questioned.

"Um yeah, that's kind of our nickname for you and Brandon." Bobby then looked sharply at Christy. "Of course, not usually to your faces."

"Oops." Christy blushed.

"Wonderful." I shook my head.

"Oh, come on." Bobby added. "It's all in good fun."

"And you do have to admit; you and Brandon seem to partake a bit excessively?" Christy added meekly.

"Partake?" I asked.

"You know, indulge." Bobby explained.

"I know what partake means." I snapped. "But who the hell talks like that?"

We paused our conversation as the nurse came back in the room with a pair of crutches.

"Here you go." He handed them to Bobby then turned to me, once again speaking deliberately slowly. "Will there be anything else?"

"No, thanks." I shook my head. "We're good."

The nurse gave me a dirty look, then smiled at Christy and Bobby on his way out of the room. Christy turned as Bobby stood up and changed from his hospital gown back to his street clothes.

"I'm wearing boxers." Bobby laughed. "Not like you had to turn around."

"Boxers are still underwear." She replied. "If I was in my bra and panties, you'd turn around, right?"

"Hell no." He replied confidently, at which point Christy turned towards him with a stern glare, and Bobby's confidence faded. "I meant, yes. Yes, I would absolutely turn around."

Bobby meekly looked my way for help. I could simply shake my head. As Bobby finished dressing quickly, Christy handed him his crutches.

"I'm not even sure I need these."

"Take them anyway. The last thing we need is another trip to the emergency room." I demanded.

He slowly put the crutches under his arms and began walking with them.

"Happy?" He asked.

"Ecstatic." I said dryly and began leading them out into the hallway.

As we entered the hallway, our nurse was standing there with photos of Bobby and Christy he must have just printed off the show's website.

"Would you sign these for me?" He smiled as he handed each of them their respective photos.

"Of course." Christy grabbed the photo, quickly looked at his nametag, and read aloud while she signed. "To Victor, my favorite fan."

She handed the signed photo to Victor and handed the pen to Bobby.

"Anything special you'd like me to sign?"

"I suppose your phone number is out of the question?" Victor smiled and Bobby blushed.

"Maybe someday." Bobby smiled, then began signing while reciting. "To Victor, thank you for last night."

Victor giggled like a little schoolgirl as Bobby handed him the signed photo and the pen, then disappeared down the hallway. I had felt the urge to remind him that I too am on the show. To be honest, probably get more camera time than anybody. But I'm pretty sure he already knew that and was intentionally snubbing me. And people wonder why I rarely show up for the network events.

"That was very nice." Christy reached over and patted Bobby on the arm.

"It was nice." I smiled. "I would have probably written Brandon's phone number on it."

Christy shook her head while Bobby grinned.

"And this is why we don't let you handle public relations." He patted me on the shoulder and began hobbling down the hall on his crutches. Christy and I followed closely.

As we got to the parking lot, we saw Angus getting out of his car. Once he recognized me, he made his way over to us.

"What happened?" He asked gruffly.

"I wasn't watching where I was going." Bobby downplayed the accident. "Fell down the cellar stairs."

"As long as you didn't damage the stairs." Angus replied dryly.

"Um, no. Stairs are still fine." Bobby muttered while rolling his eyes.

"Is everything okay?" Christy asked while motioning to building, concerned that Angus was on his way into the hospital.

"Oh yeah, just have to get yearly exam so I can refill my prescriptions."

"That's good. Glad to hear." I patted him on the shoulder as he resumed his course towards the building. But then he paused and turned back to us.

"You know, I've been meaning to ask." He looked at me curiously. "What made you think to call me and ask to investigate the inn?"

"Sorry?" I was confused by his question, as I had not initiated the contact. "I was simply returning the voice mail I had gotten from the inn, asking us for our assistance."

"Oh, I didn't realize we had called you? Normally I handle all the business and vendor operations for the inn."

"Yes, Teddy had left us a message expressing interest in having us come out."

"Teddy?" Angus questioned.

"Yes. What does he do at the inn?"

Angus hesitated, looked at the ground a bit then looked back up at me. "Teddy is unfortunately no longer at the inn."

"Oh, sorry to hear that." I felt a bit awkward, then chuckled. "Hopefully him being let go didn't have anything to do with inviting us out to investigate."

My poorly timed joke was an attempt to lighten the mood a little. But Angus' awkward silence simply made things all that much more awkward. It felt like an eternity waiting for Angus to respond. Christy and Bobby both gave me uncomfortable glances. Finally, Angus looked up from the ground again.

"No, no, not at all. He's been gone for quite some time." His words sounding forced and disingenuous. "He had a difference of opinion with the owner."

"Oh, that happens." I nodded.

"I should get going. Don't want to miss my appointment."
Angus turned abruptly and made his way into the hospital.

"Can you say awkward?" Bobby shook his head and resumed his
course for the car.

We got Bobby situated in the back seat and threw his crutches in
the trunk, then made our way back to the inn. Seeing William's car still in
the parking lot was a bit disappointing. I had hoped last night's events
might have been enough to scare him off. No such luck.

As we entered the inn with Bobby, everyone rushed over to check
on him. Everyone that is, except William. He sat on his cell phone at the
other end of the lobby, looking at us occasionally out of the corner of his
eye.

"Glad to see you're still with us." Brandon patted him on the
shoulder and tried handing him one of the small liquor bottles.

"I don't think so." I intercepted the small bottle of tequila from
Brandon. "He's on pain meds."

I handed the bottle to Christy for safe keeping, then turned back
to Brandon. "Did you realize they have nicknamed us the Booze
Brothers?"

"Hah, I like that!" Brandon giggled. "I think I might have us
some shirts made."

The others all seem to find humor in this. I could merely shake
my head.

"Hey Jerry, if your current boyfriend doesn't work out, you may
want to check out the nurse I had." Bobby winked at Jerry.

"Cute?" Jerry inquired.

"Very." Christy jumped in. "And very sweet."

I had to laugh observing Brandon following the conversation. I hadn't seen a grimace on his face like this since he accidentally ordered the pay per view of Brokeback Mountain, thinking it was a good old John Wayne type western movie. Brandon looked at me with an expression someone might have after drinking a glass of old milk. He grabbed the tiny liquor bottle from Christy, unscrewed the top and downed it in one swallow. We all chuckled for a moment until William came over to our side of the room, at which point a hush fell over the group.

"Don't let me interrupt." He said smugly.

"I think we're finished." I said as the group began to disperse.

"Hold up, that was my uncle on the phone." William continued. "I told him about Bobby's accident, and he said this would be a good chance for me to take a turn in front of the camera."

"Christy is taking Bobby's place, and Brandon is assisting her." I said firmly. "You'll stay at the monitoring table with Bobby and Jerry.

"This wasn't really a suggestion." William countered. "Look, I know you want to keep your group intact. Maybe I can help with that."

"I'm listening."

"Get me some time in front of the camera and see how I do. If I do well, maybe I do a solo camera like you do, and we have three camera crews going forward."

"It's rare I go solo. We almost always try to stay teamed up." I explained.

"Well, my way we still need Jerry around." He looked at Jerry. "And if I tell my uncle we still need everyone, he'll listen to me."

"You can team up with Christy tonight." I hesitantly choked out the words. I didn't trust him in the least, but this might at least buy me some time. "Brandon can hang at the table with Bobby and Jerry."

182

"Why don't I tag along with you?" Brandon inquired.

"Maybe tomorrow night." I responded. "I feel like the teams we've been doing have been working out pretty well so far. Don't really want to change them up."

Brandon looked at me oddly but nodded.

CHAPTER 14

A smart person would have left by now. Not sure what that says about me, but it surely can't be good. But I just can't leave the others here. I feel responsible. I should have been more forceful. I realize they're adults and make their own decisions, but I don't believe they fully understand what they are dealing with here. I'm not even sure I understand what we're dealing with, and I was the one that brought them here.

I was sure of one thing, though. I was going to see what was behind that wall. I figured now, during the day, would be my best chance. Everyone still asleep resting up for tonight's activity. I made my way into the kitchen and grabbed a large knife and headed down to the basement. Upon reaching the bottom of the stairs I hesitated and looked around the room. This place was even creepy during the day. I hesitated as I heard a rustling sound coming from the far side of the room, near the entrance to the storage area. I cautiously made my way over and shined my light into the room. Seeing nothing out of the ordinary, I ventured in.

I took one quick look around to ease my nerves, then knelt down at the wall. Using the knife, I began to scrape away any mortar that wasn't already loose, so I could begin removing one brick at a time. These bricks came out far too easily. It made me question the overall integrity of this wall, or for that matter, the entire structure. Before long I had managed to remove a dozen or so bricks in the shape of a large diamond. Large enough to crawl through. I crawled though, and just when I had almost made it, another couple of bricks gave way and I found myself face planted on the dirty cellar floor.

"Dammit!" I rolled over on my back coughing up what I could only imagine was centuries old dirt and dust. I fumbled around in the dark for my flashlight and turned it back on. It flickered for a moment, then went out. I shook it until it illuminated once again. "Don't fail me now."

I made my way over to the boxes closest to me and started rummaging through them. There was quite a bit more in here than I originally thought. The paint cans I assumed to be old paint were actually filled with personal belongings. There were watches, jewelry, letters, and various other personal effects. What odd items to seal up behind a wall. They obviously had some sort of value, even if not monetary, I would imagine sentimental to someone.

"What the hell?" I muttered as I continued to look through the paint cans.

Each can had a label as well. With a name, a date, and contact information. As I shone my flashlight around the room looking for more, I caught a flash of a face. As I jumped back I fell over the stack of paint cans.

"Nice job." Theresa said trying not to laugh.

"How about a little warning?" I said as I stood up and tried to brush myself off. "Why would you sneak up on me like that?"

"Why on earth would you remove a section of that wall." She replied. "A wall that already looked like it was close to coming down."

"Well, it's fine isn't it?"

"For now." She moved closer and began looking through the paint cans as well. "What is all this?"

"Looks like personal effects of the hotel guests."

"Why would they end up down here?"

"Maybe the previous owners killed them and took their belongings?" I said sarcastically.

Theresa shook her head and looked at the junk stacked up against the wall.

"Or maybe they weren't hotel guests." She pointed to the side of

186

one of the boxes while I pointed my flashlight in that direction.

"Mooresville Sanitarium?" I shook my head as I read the box. I moved back over to the paint cans and began reading the dates on the labels. "Nineteen hundred and twenty-seven, nineteen hundred and eighteen."

I walked back over to the boxes.

"That's the gap in the paperwork we were missing." I opened one of the boxes. "From the early nineteen-hundreds through the nineteen thirties this place was a sanitarium."

"I don't think that's all it was." Theresa's gaze was fixated behind me.

As I turned to follow her eyes, I saw that this room was more of an L shape and in the back corner was a small alcove. As I shined my flashlight back into the alcove, I could now see the far back wall. It looked to be fitted with six cold chambers. I was starting to regret my decision to remove the bricks and open up this room. For those of you that didn't take Creepy 101 in college, a cold chamber is probably more clearly referred to as a morgue drawer. You know, the little sliding drawers in horror movies where all the dead people are.

I slowly made my way over to them. Followed cautiously by Theresa. I looked back at her as I neared the wall of drawers.

"Tell us Johnny, what do we have behind door number one!" I grabbed the handle of the door.

"What are you doing?" Theresa quickly grabbed my hand.

"I was going to look inside."

"What if there's something in there?"

"You think they'd close down a sanitarium slash morgue and leave the bodies in the drawers?" I smiled and shook my head, then returned my attention to the drawer.

As I slid open the drawer, I jumped back in shock. "Oh my God!"

"What?" Theresa shouted.

"An empty drawer!" I laughed and motioned for her to look in the drawer. She punched me in the arm as she passed me.

"Asshole." She muttered as she looked in the drawer.

I opened them up one by one and revealed all six were in fact empty.

"Disappointed?" Theresa asked.

"Kind of. Was hoping for a sack of money." I closed the last drawer. "Or a vintage bottle of bourbon."

Just as we were about to walk back over to the stack of boxes, we heard a thump coming from inside one of the drawers. We both stopped as I turned and shined my flashlight back at the drawers.

"Did you hear that?" I asked Theresa. She nodded as I put my hand on the handle of the first drawer. I pulled it open and shined my flashlight all the way to the back.

Nothing.

I did this for another four drawers and turned up nothing as well. As I grabbed the handle to the last drawer, Theresa leaned in closer. The handle on this one was in bad shape, and it didn't quite close all the way the last time I shut it. I opened the last drawer to reveal yet another empty drawer. I shook my head and began to close the drawer.

"Wait a second." Theresa grabbed my arm. "Open it back up."

As I slid it back open, she pointed to the back of the drawer.

"Shine your light in the back again." She said as I flashed my light in the back of the drawer. "There did you see that flash?"

I shined the light in the drawer once again. Theresa was right. The light was reflecting off something in the back corner. I tried to reach it, but it was back too far. I started to climb inside the drawer, but hesitated.

"Do not close this on me!"

"Give me some credit." She smiled. "If I was going to do that, I would have got you in one that closed all the way and locked."

I shook my head and continued to crawl into the drawer. It was cold. Colder than it should be. I can understand these must be somewhat insulated as a refrigerator would be. But this was something else entirely. At the back of the drawer was an old tin type. An old type of photograph from the late eighteen-hundreds, that was taken on a small metal plate.

"It's a photograph." I shouted out to her. "Just some old dude in a suit."

As I picked up the photo, I felt a strange charge of energy run through my body. My flashlight went out at the same time.

"Dammit."

"What's going on in there?"

"Flashlight died." I began shaking my flashlight but it refused to turn on.

Without warning the drawer slid shut, sealing me in the dark chamber.

"Dammit!" I shouted at Theresa. "Not funny! I just hit my head on the back of this drawer!"

"I didn't do anything!" She yelled to me. "It won't open!"

I frantically began kicking the inside of the door, but to no avail. It wouldn't budge. I was having a hard time believing Theresa wasn't leaning against the door holding it shut. I saw for myself the latch on this door was broken.

"Not funny anymore!" My voice was now a bit panicked.

"I can't open it!!" She yelled back.

"Go grab the knife I was using to remove the bricks. It's by the entrance." I yelled out to her. "See if you can pry it the door open."

As Theresa went to locate the knife, the door popped open on its own. I breathed a sigh of relief and quickly exited the drawer with the photo. As I stood outside the drawer dusting myself off, Theresa came back in with the knife.

"How'd you get it open?" She questioned.

"Magic." I said sarcastically. "As soon as you weren't leaning against it, it opened."

I looked at the latch which was still dangling to the side and obviously not in working order.

"You still think I did it?" She shook her head. "Remember, I'm the one who takes these investigations seriously!"

"Whatever." I was not buying her innocent act. I took the photo out of my pocket and began looking at it with my flashlight, which was now functioning again. Theresa leaned closer and looked at the photo with me. She then backed away.

"That's creepy."

"No kidding."

"No, I mean it's creepy how much that man resembles you." She grabbed the photo out of my hand and inspected it more thoroughly.

"What?" I took the photo back out of her hand. "I don't think so."

"Look at the eyes." She explained. "And the cheekbones."

"I don't see it."

"Look at the jawline!" She persisted.

"You're on a roll today." I carefully put the photo in my pocket, made my way back over to the other side of the room and began to focus once again on the stack of boxes.

"Lovely." I pulled one of the boxes down to the floor. "Sanitarium with its own mortuary. This place just keeps getting better and better."

I sat on the floor next to the box and began pulling files out. I paged through a couple of them and found nothing out of the ordinary. Medical records, receipts for personal belonging, psychiatric history, etcetera. All the things one would expect to find. At least what I assumed one would expect to find in an asylum. I myself wouldn't know as I have never been mentally unstable enough to be checked in to one. Not for their lack of trying mind you.

I don't know why, but it brought me back to a story my father used to tell me when I was young. Anytime I was caught acting up in school, I was guaranteed a lecture that somehow involved one of my ancestors. If I was caught skipping class, it was "you know Uncle Jack used to cut school all the time, now he makes three dollars an hour selling newspapers on the corner and can't afford food'. If I got caught with a girl it was 'you know Aunt Janet used to be promiscuous, now she goes by the name of Lola works on the street corner'. I always wondered if it was the same corner as Uncle Jack and if they knew each other?

At any rate, I knew it was all fabricated. Just made-up cautionary tales to try and keep me on the straight and narrow. But I always figured, if all of our ancestors really were that messed up, why fight it? It must after all run in the family.

But I digress.

At one point, somewhere between junior high and high school, my mother had caught me and my friends playing with a Ouija board. We were young and fascinated by Tarot cards, Ouija boards and anything else supernatural. So, my friends and I had saved up our money and all chipped in to go up to the local mall and buy a deck of Tarot cards and a Ouija board. We had a grand plan of using the Ouija board to unleash a demon and send it after our math teacher. Of course, it probably wouldn't have done any good, as I had been pretty sure he himself was a demon of some sort.

All I ended up unleashing was the wrath of my parents. In addition to being grounded for a month and getting extra weekly chores, I got the 'great grandfather Theodore' lecture. Apparently, this old coot was a dark bastard. Played with the Ouija board, Tarot cards, but also took it a step further and found his way into black magic, Satan worshiping, and just about anything else that my parents figured would make a great fictitious scary relative. The family disowned him and he pretty much disappeared. I guess moral of the story was don't do creepy stuff and you can still see your relatives on the holidays.

Obviously, this was one story that didn't do the trick as I ended up in the paranormal field. Which in my parent's eyes was one step away from devil worship. I think they had managed to come to terms with it though as I was still invited round for all the holidays. I was just introduced as 'he's an actor on a ghost show'. I think that was their coping mechanism. As long as I was just acting, it was all okay. I know deep down they are still holding out hope I'll be something more respectable when I grow up.

So here I sit in an old asylum thinking about my fictitious great grandfather. I'd offer a toast, but sadly I've left all my mini tequila bottles upstairs. I must have drifted off a bit, as I began to feel Theresa's eyes on me.

"What?" I asked.

"Why am I looking over all these papers by myself?" She responded.

192

"Because you're a much better reader than me." I smiled.

She looked at the stack of folders, then at the ones that were already spread across the floor.

"All these folders are dated between nineteen hundred and nineteen thirty." She looked me. "These are the missing years."

I glance back at the crate these were in, clearly labeled Mooresville Sanitarium and can only shake my head.

"The hits just keep on coming." I grab a folder. "The years that were unaccounted for, this place was a fucking asylum."

I begin paging through the folder in my hand. Jesus, as the words ran through my head, I could barely believe them.

"Oh my god, listen to this." I got Theresa's attention. "Horace Williams, male, age thirty-eight. Committed here after seven counts of kidnapping, torture, and murder. Not to mention cannibalism. Pieces of all seven victims were found in the freezer and a whole human head in the refrigerator."

I put the folder down.

"Cannibalism." I repeated. "Let that sink in for a moment."

"Hard to wrap my head around." She replied. "How does a person keep a human head in their refrigerator?"

"That I understand." I justified. "It's the other parts that I find disturbing."

She looks up from the papers.

"You understand the severed head in the refrigerator?" She shook her head. "I'd say I got away from you just in time."

"Oh, I totally get it." I shuffled through a few more papers. "Especially after you moved out."

She could only stare at me with a dumbfounded look on her face. She was obviously waiting for me to expand on this.

"I can't begin to tell you how many times I was home alone and wished I could get a little..."

"Do not finish that sentence." I could tell she was trying hard not to laugh.

"And you wonder why I left you?" She said as I shook my head.

"No, I completely understand actually." I responded. "My only question was why it took so long."

I continued to shuffle through the files.

"We have Thomas Heyden." I opened the file quickly and glanced through it. "Split personality, lovely."

"I know one of those." Theresa mused.

I quickly flipped her off and grabbed another file. "Edward Wurst." I continued. "Paranoid Schizophrenic? This is a who's who of the truly deranged."

"Let's bring this stuff upstairs and look at it up there." She pleaded.

I grabbed another folder. "Ted Smith." I flipped open the folder. "Jesus."

"What?" Theresa moved closer.

"This guy makes Dahmer look like a boy scout." I replied.

"Those guys named Smith are usually pretty messed up." She grinned.

"Why do you think we only use first names during the intro credits." I shook my head. "Sebastian Smith sounds like a guy that should have his own line of shampoos and conditioners."

As she had a good laugh at my expense, I started thumbing through the thick folder.

"Serial killer, killed several people." I continued. "Eventually declared sane and moved to Eastern State penitentiary and executed."

I kept paging through.

"This guy had a hard time finding a rhythm." I added. "One victim was dismembered. Another was drowned. There was a poisoning."

I threw the folder on the pile and grabbed another.

"Finally, a woman!" I declared. "Glad to see crazy crosses the gender lines."

I began paging through the folder.

"Ha, this lady killed three different husbands before they caught her." I chuckled. "She cut off their..."

"Wait!" Theresa interrupted. "Go back to that last folder."

"Why?" I questioned.

"Just do it." She demanded.

I grabbed the folder and opened it once again.

"What am I looking at?" I asked.

"Read all of the deaths to me."

"As you wish." I sighed and began flipping through the pages.

"He killed a woman and mutilated her body. Chopping it up into several pieces." I shook my head.

"Isadora Gallo, female, cut up into several pieces." Theresa

195

added.

I hesitated, then read on.

"Next was a man and woman, shot to death." I took a deep breath as I remembered the history.

"Honeymoon couple the Palmers, shot in the head." She said.

"There was a poisoning." I continued. "He slipped shellfish powder in a woman's food."

"Just like the woman at the inn." Theresa responded.

I kept paging through the file.

"Next victim..." I could barely keep reading. "He kept a man confined in a cage at his hunting cabin until he starved to death. Doctors figured it took two to three months for the man to die."

"John Ringling starved to death in 24 hours at the inn." She shook her head. "They are all matching up."

"Then we have a woman drowned in the lake at his cabin, his accountant thrown from the roof of his office, and his ex-wife found hanged in her new house." I took a breath.

"Same order as our research." Theresa added. "Woman drowned in tub, man fell from roof, woman hanged in room."

I stared at the next page of the folder. Theresa waited for me to continue.

"What?" She insisted.

"There were two more before he was caught." I said reluctantly.

"Well?" Theresa waited for an explanation.

"He threw a man down a flight of stairs. The man's neck was broken in the fall." I looked up at her briefly. "Sounds a little too familiar."

"But Bobby lived. Just got a sprained ankle." She assured me.

"But do you see how bad things could have been?"

"What was the other incident?"

"His ex-wife's new husband." I hesitated. "Was found impaled in their garage."

A hush fell over the room. Neither of us had words. Although I couldn't help feeling at least a little relieved that at least if events continue to follow the pattern, Christy and Theresa were at least safe, as the last death would have to be a male.

CHAPTER 15

It's hard to tell anymore, which are my more glaring mistakes, as the list seemed to grow by the minute. Taking on this investigation, bringing my ex-wife on said investigation, or agreeing to let William lead one of the teams tonight. With a little over half an hour to go before we start up for the night, the lobby was oddly quiet. Everyone still up in their rooms getting ready for filming I suppose waiting until the last possible minute to avoid more drama like we had this afternoon with William.

After the week I'd had, it was kind of nice having a chance to sit quietly and not have to deal with anyone. No mediation, no refereeing, just peace and quiet. I finally had the chance to argue with the voices in my head for a change, even though I know fully well they always win out in the end.

It's not like I mind the voices. Quite to the contrary, their ideas are often more lucid and pragmatic than my own. Which I why I tend to give into them eventually. Right now, they were telling me I should head back to my room for the remainder of my down time before the investigation started up again.

As I saw Theresa start to come down the stairs, I knew my moment of serenity was coming to an end, and the voices had in fact been right once again. She smiled at me across the room, and I politely smiled back.

"Oddly quiet down here?" She looked about the room.

"It was." Even as the words came out of my mouth, I couldn't believe I had let them slip. I really had not intended that to sound as rude as it must have. I tried to downplay it with a smile. "But now it's much better because I have you to talk to."

She glared as she walked across the room. I apparently hadn't made the save I was hoping for.

"Sorry, I really didn't mean for it to sound the way it did." I tried in vain to apologize. "It's just there's been so much bickering, I was just enjoying the silence, and you caught me off guard."

"You do realize you can ask me to leave at any time?"

"I don't want you to leave. I like having you around." I assured her as she took a spot next to me on the couch. "It can just be a little awkward at times."

"You don't think this is strange for me as well?"

"I know it is." I continued. "And I like our talks, I really do. But it keeps me on edge a bit because I know sooner or later, we're going to have the serious talk."

"I know. I purposely have been avoiding it because I know you have so many things on your mind, and I'm worried any more pressure will just send you over the edge." She took my hand in hers. "But the more we drag this out, the worse we make it. Don't you feel like you need some kind of closure?"

"Closure?" I stood up and began pacing about the room then turned back to her. "I'm still crazy about you. I don't want closure. I want us, back like we used to be. Every time the thought of divorce pops into my head, I can't help but hate myself for having let it even get this far."

She put her hands to her face as her eyes began to well up. I sat on the coffee table in front of her and took her hands in mine.

"I lost Michelle, I don't think I'll make it if I lose you too. I still love you. I always will. You're the last piece of my life that I'm even hanging around for."

"Oh god." She pulled her hands out of mine and put them back to her face to wipe a tear. Then touched them back to my face. "You're really not understanding any of this are you?"

"I understand completely. And yes, I know it was my fault."

"You can't possibly understand, or you wouldn't still be drinking."

"Has it ever occurred to you, if you and I were back together, maybe I wouldn't need to drink?" I pleaded.

"You're always going to find a reason to drink. Even if I came back to you, you might be happy for a month or two, but sooner or later you'd just find another reason to drink."

"I think you're wrong."

"Believe me, I wish I was. I would give anything to be able to fix what we had." She wiped a tear off my face that had managed to slip out. "You have to know by now that I will always love you."

I wish these words would have been enough to bring a smile to my face, but it was like the consolation prize. Yes, she loves me, but not enough to give me another chance. As we sat briefly in silence, I could feel a part of me dying. That last bit of me that was holding out the faintest of hope for my happy ending.

"We can't keep doing this." She pulled her hands back from my face and wiped another tear from her eye. "I think we need a break from each other. Being together is only going to make this harder to do. I'm going to sit things out tonight and let you and William handle it. Besides, I don't think I can stand to be around him for a whole night anyway."

"You going to man the table with the others?"

"No, I don't think so." She shook her head. "I really need some time to think."

"What am I supposed to tell everyone?"

"William's got everybody in such disarray, I doubt anyone will even notice if I take the night off."

I nodded, understanding that it would be best to let her have her space for the moment. I certainly hadn't intended to spring this on her or make her feel like she was backed into a corner. I had always figured us getting back together was an extremely long shot at best. But I certainly didn't want her to feel like we couldn't still play a part in each other's lives. Even if, God forbid, I was allocated to a permanent spot in the friend zone.

"Focus on tonight's filming. You need to get your head right. I'll come see you after so we can finish this talk." She smiled with a sorrowful vacant look in her eyes.

I nodded and watched her walk back up the stairs. Going to be a little hard focusing on the filming right now. Right now, my thoughts seemed to be about the last several months and how many times I could have done something to avoid this, and chose to do nothing. I looked at the bottle of tequila on the coffee table. As I reached for it, a flash went through my head that sent a chill down my spine. I could see myself clear as day, sitting on a bar stool, drunk as usual, dialing Theresa on the phone. It was vivid and seemed so familiar. And made me quickly realize, we had probably been through this conversation many times before, but I had just been too drunk to remember.

I started to wonder how many times I must have drunk dialed her in the middle of the night and pleaded with her to take me back, like I had just done sober. How many times was I so inconsiderate, that I woke her up because I couldn't sleep? How many times had I reminded her of exactly the reason she would never be able to be with me again? I stopped reaching for the bottle and sat back on the couch.

It's a rude awakening when you realize that maybe you're not the hero of the movie, but the villain. My story was not going to write a love song, but sadly it would pen a heart wrenching breakup song. It was painfully clear I wasn't a good husband. I wasn't even a good friend to her. The best thing I could possibly do for her would be to let her go and let her get on with her life. She's wasted enough time on me, hasn't she?

Noticing my laptop on the coffee table, I pulled it closer and opened the lid. As it powered on, I found the EVP file of Michelle and played it once. The computer voiced her message, and I sighed, trying to manage a smile. I played it one more time, not sure if I was punishing myself, or just trying to hold on to whatever sliver of my former life I could. Now that I've realized all of it would soon be gone.

Thank God for Christy's impeccable timing. She managed to pull me back to our present situation just in time.

"Hello?" She snapped her fingers. "Hello?"

"Hi." I said slowly as I slowly looked up at her.

"Good to have you back." She grinned. "Where were you?"

Not wanting to risk slipping back to that place, I quickly grabbed the bottle of tequila and looked for a glass. Damn, no glass in site. I took the top off the bottle and took a long, much needed drink.

Christy shook her head.

"Now what were you asking me?" I sighed between sips.

"Never mind, I know exactly where you were." She looked at the bottle. "You okay?"

I nodded.

"Not a place you should visit very often." She said.

"Believe me, I know. Unfortunately, it's the only place that'll have me anymore."

As she shook her head and frowned, and I resisted the urge to take another drink. I certainly wasn't looking for pity from anyone at this point.

"We still have work to do." She smiled. "How about if you try and stay focused?"

"I'm trying to get focused." I said. "How else am I to prepare for a night with William?"

She laughed and slid the bottle across the table out of my reach.

"I was looking through this folder and doing a little more research." She opened the folder and began flipping through some pages. "Ted Smith?"

She slid the folder across the table to me.

"Yeah?" I picked up the folder and looked at the page she had it opened to.

"Abigail's maiden name was Smith." She paused. "Son Theodore, or as the file calls him, Ted."

This was enough to bring me back quickly. My eyes opened wide as I sat up straight on the couch and studied the file.

"You can't be serious?"

"Afraid so."

"This is fantastic!" I exclaimed while Christy looked at me with a dismissive frown. "Well, obviously not fantastic for his victims, but this ties it all together. It explains why everything keeps coming back to this place."

"Careful, it almost sounds like you're leaning towards a paranormal explanation for what's happened."

"We've been assuming this was all due to Stanton, but it's all coming back to Abigail's son."

"Or both? Ted Smith is the son of Stanton."

I stood up and began pacing the room.

"You okay? This may be the first time I've seen you actually get excited about evidence?"

"I need to tell you something." I moved back closer to her. "I had something happen the night before we came here."

"What do you mean something?" She asked.

"I was testing some of the equipment the night before we loaded up. The EMF meter went off in Michelle's room. When I put it near the game." I tried not to mist up.

Christy immediately began to mist up while she smiled.

"Theresa used to tell me how she had to pick that game up off the floor every day." Christy reminisced. "You two loved playing that game, but never seemed to be able to put it away."

"But she was so good at putting it away." I grinned. "All the money got sorted back, the pieces all went where they should."

"I knew something was up when I saw that game on the floor again at your house, but I didn't want to say anything." She smiled. "Well, that and the empty tequila bottle which was also a strong clue."

I smiled and slid the laptop across the coffee table.

"I got an EVP." I said.

She was silent as I opened the file and hit play. As the recording revealed 'miss you', her misting turned to tears.

"Oh my god!" She gasped.

"Yeah." I responded.

"Have you shown the others?" She questioned.

"No. I was too freaked out." I shook my head. "I'm still too freaked out."

Christy played the recording one more time.

"I've been trying to tell myself it has to be just a random

transmission from a cell or something right?" I reasoned. "But given what we've seen here, it could be her?"

Christy nodded and laughed.

"What?"

"We're starting our third season of a paranormal show, and you're just now starting to believe?

"I believed in a lot of this stuff." I motioned around the room. "I just needed a little more viable evidence."

"Not to play devil's advocate, but this still isn't what most people would consider viable."

"I know, I'm not saying it is or isn't. I'm just saying it's a strong possibility." As I spoke the smile quickly faded from my face as another very real question began to sink in.

"Hey, what happened to the smile?" Christy voiced her concern as it must have become obvious that I was not as excited as a moment ago.

"Spirits need a reason to stay behind, right?"

"That's the general consensus." She nodded.

"If they were happy, they move on."

"Stop. You don't even know if…" Christy tried to console me.

"What possible reason would Michelle have for sticking around? What unfinished business could a child that age have?"

"What if it's not even her? Like you said, cell transmissions, or there is another possibility."

"Like what?" I asked.

"Did you ever think that it could have been…" As she spoke, Brandon walked up and interrupted the conversation, and we both became

206

silent.

"That's not good, you must have been talking about me." He laughed.

"No, we were just discussing the plan for tonight." I lied as I didn't feel like it was time to get into the EVP with Brandon. We had enough to worry about tonight with the current investigation and the addition of William. "I'm taking William with me tonight. Can you take Bobby's spot with Christy?"

"Sure, no problem." He grinned.

"You need to be able to carry on enough of the dialogue so we can get some decent footage." I explained then turned to Christy. "You're going to have to be a bit more vocal too. Bobby's a hard act to follow."

"Not a problem." Brandon boasted while Christy nodded. "We have done this before you know."

"Yeah, I remember. Look at those orbs! Oh wait, that's just Christy's…" I stopped myself short or replaying the whole incident.

"Best scene we ever had." Brandon chuckled. Our moment of levity was cut short as the rest of the group, including William, began to enter the lobby. We moved over and joined them by the monitor.

"Slight change for tonight." I looked at William. "Billy's coming with me. Brandon is going with Christy."

William nodded, while the others began to snicker.

"I'll get the editing equipment ready." Jerry laughed and turned to Brandon. "Try to leave us at least five minutes of clean material to work with."

"And try not to put any Cheetos prints on her." Bobby added. "That crap glows under the infrared lights."

The others laughed while Christy looked at me in horror, while I shook my head and tried to assure her, I hadn't said anything. She turned and glared at Brandon.

"What?" He shrugged.

"Enough, let's get ready." I couldn't tell if my lack of patience was due to my conversation with Theresa or the fact I had to babysit Billy. Probably a little bit of both. "Billy, why don't you pick out a few pieces of equipment you feel the most familiar with."

"I'd prefer it if you called me William when we're on camera." He said as he looked over the table of equipment.

"Well, I'd prefer it if you weren't even here. But I guess we're both shit out of luck." I started to grab the equipment I wanted off the table.

"Going to be an interesting night of filming." Jerry mused under his breath. "Who's taking upstairs, and who's taking the cellar."

"We've got upstairs!" William blurted out quickly.

"We've got cellar." I glared in his direction.

"The cellar is grungy and musty." William looked down at his nice slacks. "I really think…"

"We've got the cellar." I cut him off firmly as he shrugged and began to pout. "I guess you should dress for the job you have instead of the job you want."

I could see the others smirking out of the corner of my eye, but as tense as things were getting, nobody felt like chiming in. I grabbed the SLS camera and a digital recorder, while I slid a camcorder across the table to William.

"Here, even you should be able to work this."

He took the camcorder and began familiarizing himself with the buttons, while Brandon and Christy grabbed their items off the table.

Brandon motioned for me to follow him across the lobby. I reluctantly followed him.

"What?" I said as soon as we had gotten out of earshot of the others.

"You okay?" He asked. "Can't believe I'm about to say this, but I'm almost starting to feel sorry for Billy."

"I'm fine, just had an argument with Theresa." I felt like I had to vent to someone. "She's staying up in her room tonight. Apparently needs some space."

Brandon's expression changed from mild curiosity to serious concern.

"I need you off the booze tonight! I need you focused, and I need your head in the game." He lectured as I tried to dismiss him. He grabbed me by the collar and made me look at him. "Listen to me. Too much shit has been happening in this place for you to be walking around in your own little world anymore. I don't want you getting hurt because you're thinking about Theresa instead of paying attention to what you're doing. That cellar is dangerous!"

"I'm fine, dammit!" I pulled out of his grasp. "I can do this shit with my eyes closed!"

"Yeah, so I've noticed." He said condescendingly. "When we're done tonight, you and are having a long overdue talk."

"Take a number. My dance card is pretty full tonight with the long overdue talks." As I spoke, Brandon stormed off and rejoined Christy who had been watching us from across the lobby. They grabbed their gear and headed upstairs.

I found his condescending tone insulting. I had no problem separating my personal life from my business life. I waited a moment until I had cooled off, then made my way back to the others.

CHAPTER 16

I led William through the kitchen, and down the stairs into the cellar. I'm not going to lie to you, I did think about pushing him down the stairs for a brief moment. There I go, lying to you nice people again. It wasn't a brief moment. I've been thinking about pushing him down the stairs since the first moment I met him. To be honest, I've already thought of half a dozen ways I'd like to do him in. But sadly, we have video cameras covering all of the areas I'd like to off him.. Once at the bottom of the stairs I turned the video camera on and began filming.

"Okay Billy, let's see what you've got."

"It's William."

"I already explained to you; William is too stuffy for the show. It's either Billy or Willy."

He hesitated for a moment, then shook his head and began to walk to the center of the room while I continued to film.

"Night four at the Wakefield inn, and we've already gotten some very good evidence." He said smoothly. "But we're just getting warmed up. I have a feeling before the night is through, we will get quite a bit more. Maybe even more than we've bargained for."

As I followed him with the camera, I was more than a little disappointed. He was actually quite good at this. The smug little prick was pretty relaxed in front of the camera. He might be harder to sabotage than I thought.

"In the center of the room here is where we believe Arthur Stratton to be buried." He continued to the center of the room. "For those that aren't familiar with the back story, Arthur Stratton was originally a partner in the building of the hotel. But James Wakefield, had a thing for Arthur's wife Abigail, and during a jealous rage, beat Arthur to death and buried him beneath the foundation of the hotel."

He paced the center of the room.

"He lies buried beneath the very concrete we are currently standing on." He shined his light to the floor. "I can feel a presence here. It's not friendly. It's almost as if…"

William dropped quickly to his knees and grabbed the back of his neck.

"Shit! What is that?" He hung is head lower and began to moan, as I quickly moved closer to see if he was okay.

"What is it?"

"I could feel him! He put his hands around my throat and tried to choke me." He said as he looked into the camera and gasped. "Do I have any marks on my neck?"

As he leaned in to me, I could actually see hand prints and fingernail scrapes on his throat. I put the camera down and tried to steady him.

"Here, just sit down." I couldn't believe I was genuinely concerned for him.

"Why did you set the camera down?"

"You should see your neck." I explained as I tried to keep him calm.

"Dammit! That was perfect!" He stood up quickly and began pacing the room. "And you stopped filming?"

"You got attacked!"

"I didn't get attacked. I did it myself." He smiled as he matched up his fingers with the marks on his neck. "Now we have to reshoot it."

I was speechless, and yet had to give the idiot more credit as an actor than I wanted to.

"Let's start from the beginning where I come to the center of the room talking about Arthur Stratton." He picked up the camera and handed it to me. "And keep filming for god's sake!"

If he hadn't already put those marks on his neck, I was pretty sure I was about to put some of my own.

"What do you think you're doing?" I struggled with every ounce of self-control I had to keep from taking a swing at him.

"Duh, I'm filming the best show you guys have ever had."

"We don't work like that. We don't fake evidence or events."

"Oh, come on, I see the guys on the other network do it all the time!"

"We don't!"

"And that's why you guys are ranked last!" He shook his head and gloated. "And probably always will be."

I put the camera down and walked into the wine cellar in the next room. Partly to clear my head, but mostly because I felt I needed to put some distance between us or things would end badly for him.

I'm no saint by any stretch of the imagination, as is no one on my team, but the one thing we all vowed to each other when we started out was, we would sooner lose the show than fake the show. We would never turn this into a scripted paranormal show.

"Dammit!" I grabbed a bottle of wine out of the rack and seriously considered taking into the next room and clubbing him like a baby seal.

I returned the bottle to the rack and tried to calmly return to the main room. "Look, we're going to start over. Perform an EVP session, and narrate however you like, but don't fake it!"

William shook his head and pouted like a five-year-old, but he pulled out the digital recorder and appeared to be willing to cooperate. At least for the moment.

"We can edit the footage, and your intro last time was actually pretty good." It killed me to throw him a compliment, but I needed him to try it our way. "So just start in the center of the room with an EVP session, and Jerry will edit as needed."

"Fine." He nodded his head and slowly walked to the center of the room as I turned the video camera back on. "We're going to try an EVP session and see if we can communicate with Arthur Stratton."

I followed him to the center of the room with the camera, as he sat down on a crate in the center, and placed the digital recorder in front of himself.

"My name is William, what is your name?" He paused giving adequate time for a response. I could tell he was annoyed at having to play it straight. "Do we have Arthur Stratton with us here tonight?"

As he continued talking to the recorder, I started to drift back to my earlier conversation with Theresa. I can admit, there was a slight resemblance to Theodore Smith, but I am far better looking. If all these accidents were being created by residual energy from his murders, there were still two more to go. A broken neck and my personal favorite, death by impaling.

I drifted back to my current situation just in time to hear William wrap up his first on screen EVP session.

"Arthur, are you aware that James killed you and married Abigail?" He was trying to provoke a response from Arthur. "Arthur do you realize he raised your son?"

He was actually asking some very good questions trying to get a raise out of Arthur. As much as he claimed to have hated these types of shows, he must have had a slight interest in them to know to ask these types of questions.

"Well, do you know I also banged Abigail?" He grinned and motioned his hand in front of his crotch while gyrating.

"What the hell is wrong with you?" I continued filming but turned on my light for a brief moment. "I don't care if you provoke the spirits, but don't disrespect them."

"Disrespect them?" He laughed and shook his at me in a dismissive condescending way that almost made me take a swing at him. "Disrespect the non-existent spirits?"

"Yes."

"I'm telling you, the only way to save this show is to let me do it my way. In case you haven't figured this out yet, ghosts aren't real." He stood up. "If you want better ratings, we need to fake some of this."

"Not an option."

"Well then, I hope you're happy at the bottom of the ratings."

"Better than being frauds."

"Until my uncle gives you the boot and has me take over the show."

"Why do you even want to be a part of this show if you don't believe any of this?" As the words left my mouth I finally realized how I must appear, albeit to a lesser degree, to the others when I continually try to debunk any evidence we get. "I'm sure your uncle can get you a spot on Naked and Afraid or something."

"I told you, this turd of a show is merely a stepping stone. I have much bigger plans for my career."

"Don't you ever get tired of listening to yourself? I know I sure as hell do." I turned my attention back to the video camera.

"Play back the recording, see if we got anything." I turned the camera back on and focused on William listening to the EVP's.

The beginning didn't have much of anything, but after he had asked if we were talking to Arthur Stratton I heard something faint.

"Play that part back again, and turn it up a little."

He replayed the section and sure enough his question got a clear response.

"No." Replied the voice on the recording.

That was definitely a class A EVP, a direct response to a question being asked. We let the recording continue. There were no more voices until we got to the final question. William asking if he knew that he banged Abigail. It was here we got another very clear response.

"Already dead." The voice clearly said through the recorder.

I looked up William and smiled. "You see why we don't disrespect the spirits?"

"Oh, please." He laughed. "That could be radio interference from anywhere. Even if it was in response to my question, all it's saying is that Abigail is already dead. So, I couldn't have banged her."

"Or maybe he meant you're already dead?" I shook my head. "We have a theory the malevolent spirit here may not be Arthur, but in fact Theodore, Abigail's son."

William thought for a moment, clearly a little disturbed by my comment, then shook his head. "No, if anything it's referring to Abigail."

"Well, at any rate, two class A EVP's in your first out. Not a bad start." I chuckled. "Even if you do have a spirit that want's you dead cause you said you banged his mommy."

"Are you still rolling?" He asked as I nodded in the affirmative and turned my light off. "Watch this."

216

"I'm right here, tough guy!" He started pacing around the room with his arms up in the air. "I'm not afraid of you, you crusty old mama's boy!"

"Crusty old mama's boy?" I could only shake my head as what had started out as a fairly promising EVP session had now digressed to William prancing around the cellar like a peacock. "Are you almost done?"

"Just getting warmed up." He stopped long enough to look back at me. "You know why I can do this?"

"Please, educate me."

"Because none of this shit is real! People like you are never going to get it through your heads that all of this is explainable."

I was about to respond when the camera shut off. "Dammit!"

"What?" He stopped prancing long enough to come over and look at the camera.

"You broke the camera!" I responded as I pulled off the battery pack.

"I broke it? I wasn't even near it!"

"Yeah, but it chose to kill itself rather than continue to film you prancing around like an extra from West Side Story."

He grabbed the battery out of my hand. "Dead battery?"

"Brilliant deduction." I nodded.

"What would have been even more brilliant would have been to charge it fully before we started shooting."

"It was fully charged." I motioned to the battery in his hand. "Take that upstairs and give it to Jerry. He'll give you a replacement."

"Why me?"

217

"Because you were the one that was just prancing around the cellar like Richard Simmons. I figured you had some energy to burn."

William reluctantly took the battery and walked slowly up the stairs while I grabbed my radio.

"Jerry, I'm sending William up for another camera battery. Bobby and Christy having any luck upstairs?"

"They've had nothing." Jerry's voice came through the radio. "Not a peep. But I've got some footage for you to look at when you're ready to switch floors. Lots of shadowing I can't explain with you in the cellar."

"Not from William or myself?"

"No, it's at the wrong angle, and some of it moves when you and William are standing still."

"Okay, we're going to give it another hour down here before we switch." I responded. "We're getting some good EVP's down here. The little candy ass is turning out to be pretty good at riling these spirits up."

"I can hear you. I'm standing right next to Jerry." Responded William through the radio.

"Good. Get the battery and prance your way back down here. I want to do another session before things cool off."

As I sat in the cellar waiting for William to return, the temperature gauge on my mel meter began to drop steadily. It had dropped so suddenly, I could actually feel the change myself. I moved my hands up and down my arms in an effort to warm myself up a little.

"Theodore are you here?" I stood up and began to move around the center of the room. "My apologies for Billy's comments. He's not one of our team."

Not sure if it was my eyes playing tricks on me or not, but I could make out what looked to be a very large shadow moving across the room.

218

I grabbed my radio from my hip.

"Jerry, are you seeing anything on the monitor near me?"

"Yes, there is definitely a shadow figure moving around you."

"It's not my shadow?"

"Can't be. There's only one light source coming from the infrared camera, and I can see clearly where it's casting your shadow."

"Theodore, is there anything I can do to help you?" I turned my attention back to the cellar. "Why are you still here?"

"Are you talking to yourself?" William entered the top of the stairway and interrupted my questioning. "I've got the batteries."

As I heard William take his first few steps down the stairs, I felt what I can only describe as a swell of cold air move past me to the stairwell. I turned on my flashlight just in time to see William tumbling down the stairs. As he landed at the bottom, I heard a loud crack and watched as his head turned in such an unnatural position to his body, it felt too surreal to be actually happening.

"Jerry, get help!" I shouted up the stairs as I ran to try and help William.

The angle he was lying made me afraid to try and move him. I tried to put my finger to his neck to check for a pulse as I had seen people attempt on television, but I quickly pulled my hand away. Where there should have been a smooth area to check for an artery, I could feel a rough jagged protrusion. I could only imagine cartilage or bone from a broken neck.

The others quickly began filing down the stairs and turned the cellar lights on. As I saw him in full light, I knew it was pointless to check for a pulse. The angle his head was at, and the glazed lifelessness of his eyes told me all I needed to know. I backed away from the stairs as the others all reached the bottom. Theresa was the last to make her way down.

Jerry was the only one with enough courage to attempt trying to find a pulse. He turned from Williams' body to look at us, and simply shook his head. A collective gasp managed to find its way out of our mouths and fade across the room.

"This can't be happening." I pulled one of the crates over and sat in the center of the room.

"It was an accident." Brandon put a hand on my shoulder.

"I'm not so sure." I looked over at Jerry. "We were seeing a lot of anomalies moving back and forth down here. The temperature dropped a good ten degrees in less than a minute."

As we continued to stare in disbelief, we could hear the front door open and the sound of several footsteps above us.

"We're down here!" Bobby shouted up the stairs. "Through the kitchen and down to the cellar."

As two paramedics rushed down the stairs, they knelt at the bottom when they reach Williams body. One of the paramedics put a finger to William's neck for a moment, then shook his head. Confirming what the rest of us had already feared to be true.

They loaded Williams body onto a stretcher and carefully carried him up the stairs. The rest of us remained in the center of the cellar, speechless and almost unable to move. As the sheriff came down the cellar, I began to realize the ramifications of the situation and how this might look to someone from the outside.

"Who can tell me what happened?" The sheriff addressed the group.

"I think I can." I stepped forward. "We were in the middle of filming a television episode. We have a paranormal show, and the inn had asked us to do an investigation here. William and I were down here filming."

"William was the deceased?"

"William Vega." I nodded to the sheriff. "The camera died, and William went up for a new battery. When he was coming back down he must have tripped."

The sheriff began to walk around the room, then stopped in front of the camera.

"This camera that's pointed at the stairs, was it filming?"

"Yes, it was." I tried to be as cooperative as I could under the circumstances. "We can download the footage for you."

"We also had one running in the kitchen pointed towards the top of the stairs." Added Jerry. "I can put that footage on a drive for you as well."

The sheriff nodded and walked back over to me.

"I'm going to need you to accompany me and the footage to the station. I've got some more questions for you, and I'll need to take a formal statement."

"Of course, anything I can do to help." I looked to Jerry. "Jerry can have the footage downloaded in a matter of minutes."

Jerry went up the stairs ahead of us to begin transferring the footage onto a drive for us. As the sheriff began to lead me up the stairs, I looked back at the group to make sure they were okay. They gave me a reassuring nod as I turned and continued to follow the sheriff. As bad as I felt for William, I couldn't help being distracted by the thought, is this how our careers finally end?

CHAPTER 17

As I sat at a desk in the police station, I was overtaken by the smell of old coffee. I could see the pot across the room, and at least a cup, more often two, on every desk in the room. Oddly though, I could see no doughnuts in sight. Pity seeing as my stomach was grumbling horribly.

I began to hope that the video footage at least showed me well away from William at the time he fell. I thought about praying a bit, but as I've never been a particularly religious person, that might seem a bit shallow to the big guy. Maybe even give him the urge to screw me over a bit, just to teach me a lesson. I was truly hoping he wasn't a vindictive God. Shortly after Michelle's death, Theresa began to attend church. Not sure if it was to come to terms with our loss, or to pray for me and my inner demons. Either way, it didn't last more than a month or two. I figured she either found her way to move past the tragedy, or she realized no amount of praying was going to save me.

The sheriff returned to the room with two cups of coffee and the drive containing the footage. He sat across from me at the desk and slid me over one of the coffee cups. "Thought you could use this. Looks like you've had a hell of a night."

"Thank you." I smiled and nodded as he popped the drive in his computer.

"You're going to want to see this." He shook his head in disbelief as he watched the screen light up.

"Hopefully it shows none of my guys were anywhere around him when Billy fell?"

"It does. But I'm more interested in what was next to him when he fell." He began playback of the video for me. "Or quite possibly pushed."

As the video played through, it was nearly identical to the footage we had of Bobby's incident. The dark mist-like image moving up the stairs and positioning itself just behind William. Then appearing to thrust itself forward with enough force to push William down the stairs. Unfortunately, William did not fare as well as Bobby had. I let out a sigh as the video finished up and looked across the desk at the sheriff. We sat silently for a moment, neither of us wanting to the first to state the obvious for fear that maybe the other didn't see things the same way.

"Accidental death?" I finally broke the silence, not wanting to commit to what I had seen in the video.

"That's the way I saw it too." The sheriff nodded and took a sip of his coffee, then slowly looked up at me. "Even though we both know it wasn't."

I nervously took a sip of my coffee and took a moment to choose my words carefully. I hadn't been read my rights or anything, but I still wasn't convinced they didn't need some type of fall guy for this. The inn certainly didn't want to be sued, and even though we all signed wavers absolving the inn in case of an accident, I'm sure a good lawyer can get around those pretty easily.

"I've got to be honest with you, up until this investigation I was still pretty skeptical of the paranormal aspect of our show." I started the video once again. "But too much has happened at this place for me to ignore it. We had almost the exact same incident happen to one of our other team members, Bobby. But he at least walked away with only minor injuries."

"Yes, your tech guy has that video footage on here as well." He gave me an odd, puzzled look. "Didn't that make you think to pack up and get the hell out of there?"

"We did consider it. But when you've been doing this for as long as we have, and had minimal evidence at best, when something like this starts to produce undeniable footage." I took another sip of my coffee to give me a second to choose my words, so as not to sound completely uncaring. "We felt we had to try and follow through."

The sheriff nodded and seemed to accept my answer for the time being.

"Obviously we never thought anything like this was going to happen." I shook my head.

"And that's the only reason you stayed?" The sheriff seemed to still be expecting more of an explanation for some reason.

"Yes, of course. It's what we do for a living." I was caught a little off guard that this hadn't seem to satisfy him.

The sheriff pulled a familiar looking file folder out of his briefcase and put it on the desk.

"One of your assistants gave me this." He opened it, slid it across the desk, and smiled. "A Christy, I believe? Nice girl, attractive."

Wasn't sure I cared for the way he was grinning when he said attractive.

"Yes, we found that file in the cellar. It was behind a makeshift wall." At this point I was probably offering up more than I should. "Theodore Smith's victims coincide with the accidents that have been happening at the inn ever since. Every nine years."

"I was more interested in the fact that you both have the same last name." He took a small sip of his coffee.

"Smith?" I grinned. "Do you have any idea how common that name is?"

"Give me a little credit. Not all small-town sheriffs are inept." He pulled out another piece of paper. "Only problem is, when we run his name though the computer, we come up with his son Michael, who had a son named Jonathan."

"Still not sure where this is going?"

"Jonathan Smith? John Smith?" He asked in a slightly accusing tone.

"Yes, I get it. My father's name is John Smith. Probably almost as common as any other given name you put in front of Smith."

"Except for I'm guessing none of them named their son Sebastian?" He slid the computer printout he was holding across the desk to me.

I picked it up grinning at first, but the smile soon faded from my face as I followed my lineage down the page.

"This can't be correct." I started shaking my head in disbelief. "This is some kind of mistake?"

"Talked to the innkeeper, Angus." The sheriff continued. "Why did you ask him if you could investigate the inn?"

"I was just returning his phone call. The inn asked us to investigate."

"Not according to him. He said you made first contact."

"Somebody at the inn left us a message, when I called back, that's when I spoke to Angus."

"Who left the message?"

"I think it was a Teddy." I strained to try and remember more detail. "I don't remember the last name."

"Teddy?"

"If memory serves, yes."

"As in, short for Theodore?"

"No, it was…"

I suddenly began to recall how odd the message had actually

sounded. Like someone was talking through an old AM/FM radio. How it had taken me several playbacks just to decipher and write down all the data. This wasn't possible.

As I reached for my coffee, the sheriff obviously sensed the melt down that was occurring inside my head, and reached inside his desk drawer and pulled out a bottle of whiskey and two fresh cups. My mind raced as he filled both cups halfway. Before he had even managed to finish screwing the cap back on the bottle, I grabbed the glass closest to me and finished it off in one gulp. He hesitantly refilled my glass, then took a small sip of his own.

"Round these parts, we tend to sip this stuff." He grinned as he showed me how much was left in his glass.

"Yeah, well where I'm from, dead people don't usually make phone calls."

He smiled and took another small sip. I tried to be a good guest and follow his suggestion, taking an incredibly small sip of my own this time.

"You really had no idea, did you?" He appeared to be continuing his informal interrogation.

"I still don't know if I believe it." I put my glass down just long enough to pull the case file back over to me. "But it would explain why my crappy show was the one called in to investigate."

The daylight was beginning to make its way through the window, and yet I didn't feel the slightest bit tired. This was all way too much to process. At least sober, anyway.

"If you want, I can have a few deputies help you pack up when they drive you back to the inn?" The sheriff offered. "Probably best to get out in the daylight."

"We should be fine. It only takes us about an hour to tear everything down and pack up." I shook my head. "I have a feeling today we'll get it done in forty-five minutes."

"Thank you." I took the last sip of my drink, stood up and slid in my chair.

"Not sure you should be thanking me for the bomb I just dropped on you."

"It was bound to come out sooner or later. I truly do appreciate it."

"Well, in that case, I might as well get it all over at once." He frowned and pulled out his phone. "Kind of like a band aid."

"Let me guess, you got a call from my producer?"

"How'd you know?" He smiled.

"I've ignored about ten of his calls since I've been here." I smiled. "Did he have a message for me?"

"I'll leave out his colorful language, but to paraphrase, season three has been cancelled. You have all been let go." He took a small sip from his glass and set it back down on his desk. "I'm sorry to be the one delivering the news."

"Don't be. We were done long before he called. They have other ideas of what the crew should consist of, and I think our crew is perfect the way we are."

"Never caught your show." The sheriff shook his head. "But now I'm definitely going to have to check it out."

"In re-runs anyway." I smiled, the sheriff nodded. "Although with the footage we've got from the inn, I'm thinking it won't be that difficult to get another network to pick us up."

"Well, I wish you luck." The sheriff raised his cup, as did I. We both had one last drink, then I made my way outside to the deputy waiting to drive me back to the inn.

"All finished?" The deputy opened the passenger side door of the squad car as I walked down the front steps.

"I think for the time being. As we go through the week's footage, I'll send you guys anything pertinent that we find."

"Thank you." The deputy nodded. "We appreciate your cooperation."

I jumped in the passenger side of the squad car as the deputy made his way to the other side. As he started the car and sped off, I stared out the window and began to sort through my thoughts of what had just transpired. Maybe more of our life is predestined than we think. Is this the reason I was drawn to the paranormal?

We pulled up to the inn, and the deputy circled the car around the parking lot and stopped the squad car in front of the main entrance. "Here you are."

"Thank you." I opened the door and stepped out. "I appreciate it."

"You want me to stick around while you all pack things up?" He looked nervously out his window at the creepy old building and smiled. "I'd wait out here, of course."

"No, we'll be fine. Won't take us very long." I looked to the upper window of the inn for a moment, feeling that I was being watched. "I appreciate you though."

As I closed the car door and watched him speed off out of the driveway, my attention turned back towards the upper window of the inn, where the curtain was now moving back and forth.

"Screw this." I muttered to myself as I quickly made my way up the stairs.

On my way by, I looked in the large vase on the stairs and all of the miniature liquor bottles had been removed. I took this as a good sign that the group had been packing things up while I was at the station, and maybe we were already set to get out of here. But as I walked in the front door, I quickly realized we did not all share the same sense of urgency, as all the equipment was still set up and they were in the midst of discussing our final night of investigation.

"Seriously?"

"Hey, you're back!" Bobby quickly spun his chair around to greet me, but his smile faded when he saw my stern expression. "What's the matter?"

"You guys are actually considering staying the final night?" I was in absolute disbelief.

"You're not?" Brandon seemed to be shocked at my reluctance. "We have to finish this. This show is going to beat anything that's ever been done before."

"There is no 'show' anymore." I pulled out my cell and showed them the many missed calls and messages from Anthony. "We have all been officially fired as of nine this morning."

The quiet that fell over the room assured me I had managed to give them the last nudge they needed for packing it up and quitting while we're ahead. As usual, I gave myself far too much credit. They obviously had no intention of leaving.

"All the more reason to finish the week." Jerry stood up and began to walk towards me. "Network or no network, we've gotten great footage. If we really are out of a job, we need to finish filming, edit the footage, and shop it to a new network."

The others immediately began to nod. All except Theresa, who was shaking her head.

"It's just not worth the risk." She reminded me.

"Are you all forgetting there's one more murder in the Ted Smith

230

file?" I reminded the rest of the group.

"Yeah, but they have happened every nine years? How can we not finish this investigation?" Christy pleaded.

"Easy for you to say, last murder has to be a male." I grinned for the first time since this conversation started. "If we do this, we work in teams."

"Kind of a no brainer." Brandon laughed.

"No, I mean the buddy system! Anyone has to leave their filming location for anything." I continued. "Fresh batteries, bathroom break, etcetera, the other goes with."

Everyone except Theresa nodded in agreement. I could tell she still wasn't on board with this idea. Truth be told, neither was I, but I was sensing I was not going to be able to talk the rest of them out of this.

"Have any of you slept yet?" I tried to get my mind back to investigation mode.

"You're kidding, right?" Brandon spoke excitedly.

"We need to try and at least get a little rest. Doing tonight with no sleep is just asking for an accident of some kind." I began to head towards the stairs as the others reluctantly followed.

"I may never be able to sleep again." Jerry said as he reluctantly followed the others upstairs.

As we got to the top of the stairs, everyone was hesitant about splitting up and going to their own rooms.

"We all need to keep our doors propped open, so we can get into any room fast if needed." Bobby suggested.

"That's a good idea, let's do it. Although nothing has ever happened here before sundown, so we should at least be good for a short nap." I had hoped.

"Better safe than sorry." Brandon sighed and nodded.

As everyone headed to their rooms, I stood at the doorway to mine and made sure they all got into their rooms and followed Bobby's recommendation to keep their door propped open. I did the same with mine.

I laid on the bed and closed my eyes. Seeing as I had been up all night, I thought it would be easier to get some sleep, but my mind was racing with everything that has happened over the past twelve hours. I stared at the ceiling and debated whether or not to tell the group that I was related to Ted Smith. Was my presence here going to be putting them in more danger?

I sat up and looked across the room at the bottle of tequila on the dresser. That may be the only way I was going to get any sleep today. I stood up and made my way across the room to pour myself a small glass. Then poured a bit more until the glass was half full. As I sipped on my glass of tequila I moved back across the room and sat on the edge of the bed. I stared out in the hallway, which was unusually quiet. The others must have had no problem falling asleep.

As I started looking around my hotel room, my eyes were drawn to the cheap watercolor painting behind the headboard of the bed. A farm scene with an old Victorian farmhouse, with a white fence and a little blond girl riding her bike in front. It looked like one of those paintings you'd buy in a shopping mall. I began to focus on the little girl on the bike, I could almost hear the sound of the spokes spinning around the somewhat bent bike fender.

That was how it usually started. One image, one thought, one tiny detail that would remind me of Michelle. I took another long sip from my glass in hopes of pushing her back to the furthest recesses of my subconscious. A place that seemed to be safer for the both of us. But she was having none of it this time.

I laid back down on the bed and stared at the ceiling. It's futile to try and explain this feeling to someone that has never lost a child. The loneliness, the sorrow, the feeling of absolute emptiness. If there truly is a hell, I'm sure it can't be any worse than this. I'm sure it's been said a thousand times before, but it's true, no parent should ever outlive their child. It's unnatural.

I closed my eyes and a small part of me hoped it might be for the last time.

CHAPTER 18

I awoke in my room and tried to rub the sleep out of my eyes as I stumbled my way into the bathroom. I stared at myself in the bathroom mirror. Everyone kept telling me to move on, like that was a realistic option. Don't even think that was possible at this point. They said the past is the past and I needed to focus on the future. But what if the past is where I belong? What if the past represents the last time I was truly happy?

I splashed some water on my face. I certainly had seen better days. It would appear as though we did manage to catch a ghost on video, and the one thing I could say with utmost clarity is, it still looked more alive than me. I turned from the mirror and exited the bathroom.

"Shit!" I screamed.

Theresa sat on the bed, slightly amused at my panic.

"Wow, kind of jumpy." She smiled.

"Ever think about knocking?" I asked. "I damn near had a heart attack!"

"All the doors are open. Nothing to knock on."

"You can still knock on it and warn me."

"I was just making sure you were okay? Hadn't had a chance to talk to you since you got back from the police station. Was worried maybe they thought you had killed William?"

"No, luckily they can see in the video footage, there is no one near him at the time."

"I feel bad. I didn't like the guy, but he certainly didn't deserve to die." She frowned.

"Yeah, I hear you. But in all honesty, if it was a choice of him or one of our people, glad it was him."

"I'm surprised they didn't call this place a crime scene now and shut down the filming?"

"No, they got what they needed. They've got copies of our footage for the time being. But they said it was clearly an accident."

"They called it an accident?"

"I don't think they can write in pissed off paranormal entity for cause of death."

"Probably not I guess." She stood and began pacing the room. "So, you're really going to let everyone go through with the investigation tonight?"

"It looks like it, why?"

"We still need to have that talk."

"I'm listening."

"I'd rather do it when I can have your full attention, not just before an investigation." She looked at the bottle of tequila on the dresser, then back to me. "I'd like you clear headed."

"I haven't had any. Still a bit freaked out." I paused as I saw Christy standing in my doorway. I walked over to her as she stared at me curiously.

"You okay? I could hear you scream two rooms away." She looked past me into my room.

"I'm fine. Just had a bit of a scare."

"Who are you talking to?" She made her way past me into my room and looked around my room.

"I came out of the bathroom, and she was..." As I turned to look, Theresa was gone. "Wait a second."

I went into the bathroom and pulled back the shower curtain but found no one. I made my way back to the other room where Christy waited with a concerned look on her face.

"You okay?" She asked.

I shook my head.

"I must have been…" I looked around the room one last time. "Guess I'm getting a bit burnt out with our schedule this week."

She nodded as I walked her back to the door.

"I'm fine, I just need to start getting more sleep."

"I'm here if you need to talk." She put a hand on my shoulder. "About anything."

I nodded and closed the door behind her as she left.

"That was close." Theresa whispered as I froze in front of the door. I slowly turned around to see her sitting on the edge of the bed once again. I smiled and shook my head.

"That was clever." I looked quickly under the bed to see there was not enough space for her to have been under it. I had checked the bathroom and the closet. "I'll figure it out."

"You still don't get it do you?"

"Oh, I get it."

"Do you?" She laid back on the bed, and without warning she was gone.

I started frantically rubbing my eyes and even looked over at the bottle of tequila to make sure it was still at the same level. She emerged from the back, walked back across the room, and sat back on the edge of the bed.

"I didn't want to have this talk now." She motioned for me to come over to her. "But I think we have to."

I felt dizzy. I backed away from her and made my way across the room and sat down at the chair at the desk. I had a hard time speaking. I could simply stare at her sitting on the bed with a concerned look on her face.

"Are you okay?" She asked with a worried tone in her voice.

"I don't think so." I replied as I shook my head. "It's not possible. You're not…"

"You know this to be true. You know this in your heart of hearts. You just won't let yourself believe it."

Everything started to rush back upon me. I felt like I was drowning inside my head. I could see flashes and make out bits and pieces, but it was like a compilation movie made up of my thoughts. Just fragments. Nothing that I could actually piece together in any type of discernable sequence. I could see Theresa, I could see an ambulance. Then there were flashes of us on the phone and Brandon and I standing at a gravesite. It was just one big horrific blur coming at me in bright flashes of light and sound.

"Are you starting to understand how unhealthy this is?" She asked. "You need to let me go."

I lowered my face to my hands for a moment, then looked back up at her with red eyes.

"What if I can't?" I sighed.

I felt a tear begin to well up in my eye. As it pooled, it soon outgrew its location and made its way down my cheek. I lowered my head and began to watch the trail of tears, one by one, make their way down my cheek and fall quietly to my hands. As each tear created a growing pool in my palm, my head began to throb. Almost as if in time with the impact of the tears hitting my hand.

And then I remembered.

Alcoholism is one of the vilest of diseases. We may all dance around the issues surrounding it, and pretend it can be funny and entertaining, but in our hearts, we know it destroys everyone and everything it touches. When Michelle had passed away, alcohol became my coping mechanism for life. After all, it was better to be inebriated and happy, than sober and miserable. Who cared if it costs me my liver? Who cares if it even ended up costing me my life? As far as I was concerned, my life had ended the day I had put my daughter in the ground. And therein lies the problem with alcohol. Long before it takes your life, it takes your vision.

I could no longer see the reasons to go on. Could no longer see the things I should hold dear. I had a great wife and great friends that loved me no matter how much I tried to make myself unlovable. I had a career, that while many might not consider a success, still paid the bills and was never boring. I still had a life that a lot of people would have traded for. But I could no longer see it. Alcoholism gives us tunnel vision. It makes us focus on the part of our life that is impacting us the most at that particular time. We may think it's making us happy, when in fact all it's really doing is numbing us to the outside world and any pain we may be feeling at the moment.

Take me for example. After a few drinks I didn't have a care in world. I had gotten so good at blocking out the pain, two months ago I was ready to let myself go to sleep in a tub, rather than go on with the emptiness I knew as my life. It may be hard to imagine from the outside looking in, and hopefully you never have to experience it. But take my word for it, if your world becomes a dark enough place, alcohol is sometimes all it takes to start making all the wrong decisions. It's like the voice of a trusted friend telling you they can make all the pain go away, and you can be with those you love again if you just listen to what it has to say.

Now don't get me wrong. I am in no way condemning alcohol. Or for that matter, blaming alcohol. The weakness and the blame fall solely on me. Most people can have a drink, even two, and then stop. They can hit happy hour after work with their friends. They can have a cocktail at a family get together. They know what moderation is.

That wasn't me.

I remembered sitting at the end of the bar, talking the bartender's ear off. I'm pretty sure I told him my life story, from birth all the way through the death of my daughter. As I finished my drink and laid some cash down on the table for him, I reached for my keys that were sitting on the bar, but apparently not quite fast enough in my current condition. He managed to grab them before I could.

"I don't think so." The bartender shook his head while placing my keys safely in the register. "I've seen entire rugby teams drink less than you did tonight."

"Says the bartender who over served me." I retorted.

"Call for a ride or you'll be sleeping on that stool." He said smugly as he went to the other end of the bar to converse with other patrons. I could tell they were talking about me by the way they were shaking their heads and trying hard not to watch me.

My uncoordinated hands fumbled to retrieve my cell phone from my pocket. My bloodshot eyes tried to focus on the screen. I managed to focus on the screen long enough to call Brandon. Unfortunately, there was no answer. Looking at the clock on the wall and seeing that it was two in the morning, I shook my head but reluctantly dialed Theresa. After a ten-minute lecture on this being the very reason she had moved out, she finally agreed to come and pick me up.

I would never see her again.

As fate would have it, her car would be hit by a drunk running a red light, on her way to try and help another drunk. She died in the ambulance on the way to the hospital. Friends and family are quick to tell you it wasn't your fault. It was the drunk driver that ran the red light. You did the responsible thing and call for a ride.

But I knew who killed her.

There was no doubt in my mind. She was only out on the road that night because of me. You see that's the problem with alcoholics. While we are busy trying to self-destruct and inflict harm upon ourselves, it's actually quite rare that we actually do harm ourselves before we harm everyone else around us. My self-induced war now had a body count. But not the one it should have been.

I stood at her grave long after all our friends and family members had gone, trying to think of what I could say, how I could possibly apologize for being such a self-absorbed asshole. But there were no words strong enough. I sat next to the grave for hours until I came upon the only penance I could think of that would have meant anything to her.

I vowed to her I would never drink again.

After all, some good had to come out of this tragedy, right? So, for her, I would do whatever it took to get myself sober. My teary farewell at her grave became a declaration to give up the only thing in my life that has been constant for the last several months. I was convinced I was going to turn my life around. I could do this for her.

Stop me if you've heard this one before. One of my favorite old Russian fables.

A scorpion and a frog meet on the bank of a stream and the scorpion asks the frog to carry him across on its back. The frog looks at the scorpion and laughs.

"How do I know you won't sting me halfway across?" The frog questioned for obvious reasons.

"Because if I do, I will die too." Replied the scorpion. "I can't swim."

The frog is satisfied with the scorpion's response, and they set out on their journey. But in midstream, the scorpion stings the frog. The frog feels the onset of paralysis and starts to sink, knowing they both will drown, has but just enough time for one last question.

"Why?" Pleaded the frog.

"Because it's my nature." The scorpion replied coldly just before they both sank to their watery death.

One's nature is a hard thing to outrun. Pretty much impossible I found out. I made it almost three whole weeks after Theresa's funeral without a drink. Then I began to find easy excuses to begin again. After all, who could possibly blame me? I had buried the two people I loved most in the world in less than a year. Of course, I conveniently chose to forget that the most recent was my fault.

It looks like I've conveniently forgotten a lot of things lately.

"Hello?" Theresa's voice echoed as it broke my train of thought and brought me back to my hotel room. "You okay?"

I simply stared at her. She looked the exact same. She wasn't transparent, and she didn't float around the room. Not that I expected her to. Not really sure what I had expected. I honestly don't think I would have ever had this much contact with a spirit. Let alone, one I knew.

"You need to get your head right for tonight." She said.

"Head right?" I chuckled. "I'm sitting in a haunted room, in a haunted inn, having a conversation with my dead wife."

"Well as close to right as you can get it. I realize this may be an awful lot to process right now."

"You think?"

"I don't think sarcasm is going to help our situation." She said sharply.

"So, are you real? Or just in my imagination?"

"You mean am I proof that there really are ghosts, or have you just gone crazy?" She reworded my simple question.

242

"My wording was a little easier on my psyche."

"I am real. We…" She motioned around the room with her hands. "Ghosts…are real."

"Well at least my career choice isn't quite as pointless as my family has made it out to be." I spoke almost catatonically. "They'll be so proud."

She continued to pace, then stopped in front of me.

"But why are you here?" I asked as I looked up at her.

"What do you mean?"

"Why haven't you…" I fumbled for a delicate way to say this. "Why haven't you moved on?"

"From what they tell me." She suddenly got a very serious look on her face. "I can't move on until I know you'll be okay. That you have quit drinking and straightened your life out."

I sat shocked and speechless. My eyes grew wide and fixated on her as I arched my head forward. "What?"

"Sometimes I crack myself up." She chuckled. "I don't know why I am still here. It's not like they give you a handbook or a how-to video to watch."

She stood up and moved over to look at the tequila bottle on the dresser, and once again chuckled to herself.

"Can't move on until you quit drinking." She shook her head and laughed. "I'd be here forever."

I'm glad she was having a good laugh at my expense. Although, I guess I'm not in a position to protest, as I'm the reason she's here in the first place. This certainly did explain a lot.

"Can anyone else see you?"

"I don't think so." She shook her head. "But I'm pretty sure Brandon has caught on. Between him seeing you constantly talking to yourself, and always pouring one drink too many, he'd be stupid not to."

243

"Great." I stood up and took a breath.

"But look at the bright side, he probably just thinks you're crazy."

"Perfect." I walked over to the mirror and tried to compose myself, when I noticed her reflection. "I can see you in the mirror?"

"You really need to crack open a book every now and then." She waved her hand in front of the mirror. "I'm not a vampire."

"Yes, I know, I'm just a bit off right now."

She looked at me with an almost sympathetic look. Noticing the bottle of tequila on the dresser, she slid it towards me. I looked at the bottle, then looked at her. I picked up the bottle, unscrewed the top, walked into the bathroom, and poured it down the drain. I turned to see her standing in the doorway.

"Yeah, I know." I frowned as I exited the bathroom. "Too little too late."

She followed me back out as I sat on the edge of the bed.

"I'm not here to make you feel bad." She sat next to me on the bed. "Or make you feel guilty."

"Don't worry, you're not. I'm feeling that all on my own."

"I just want you to be okay. I want you to be able to move on."

"That may take a while." I stood up and began pulling out my outfit for the night, threw them on the bed, then turned back to her quickly. "So, the game, the night before we packed up?"

"Uh yeah." She smiled nervously. "I do miss you."

Part of me was sad that it hadn't been Michelle, the other part me was happy she wasn't stuck here.

"Michelle?" I asked cautiously, not sure of what answer I was hoping for.

"Like I said, there's not a handbook or anything." She smiled reassuringly. "But from what I've heard from others, young kids have no problem moving on quickly."

"That makes me feel a little better." I grabbed the jeans from the bed and was about to change, then hesitated and looked at Theresa.

"What? Like it's something I haven't seen a thousand times?"

"Seriously?"

"Fine, get dressed." She sighed.

And like that she was gone. I looked around the room nervously and began to unbutton the jeans I had on, then hesitated.

"Your still here, aren't you?"

"What do you think?" Responded her disembodied voice.

"You know what, screw it." I shook my head and threw the clean jeans back on the bed. "What I'm wearing is fine."

I grabbed my key off the dresser and went to open the door, then looked back around the room.

"This isn't funny." I slammed the door behind me and stormed off down the hall to the stairs.

So, this is how it all ends? My mind slowly slipping into the abyss of insanity. No fanfare, no fairy tale ending. It's going to be just me, sitting alone in an asylum somewhere, listening to my dead wife.

Welcome to hell.

CHAPTER 19

I sat in the corner of the room watching the EMF meter. I tried my best to block out her voice but it was like trying to block out the sun.

"You can't ignore me forever." She demanded. "We need to work through this."

"I'm trying to work here!" I finally looked up at her. "For the love of god!"

"Oh, that's right, sorry. You're trying to get evidence of paranormal activity aren't you?"

"That's what we…" I stopped in mid-sentence as I realize how stupid my argument now was.

"And here I am! Evidence achieved!" She mocked me. "Now can we talk?"

"Exactly how long are you going to be following me around?" I shook my head.

"Not really sure, to be honest. Don't exactly know what the goal is here."

"Weren't you the one that told me I need to move on?" I screamed.

"Ignoring me isn't moving on." She moved closer to me. "If I'm still here, you're still in trouble."

She sat on the floor next to me.

"You do realize this wasn't your fault." She said. "I made my choices."

I stood up and moved away from her, pacing the room. "And if had been there for you?"

"You were there for me." She moved across the room to me. "As much as you could be. You were hurting."

"And you were hurting as well." I replied. "I was just too much of a drunk self-absorbed ass to see it."

"I can't argue the drunk part." She smiled.

I smiled and sat down on the floor. She moved over and sat beside me.

"Still not sure if I've convinced myself you're real, you know, a ghost." I looked up at her. "Or if I'm just crazy?"

"I'm pretty sure both are actually true statements." She smiled as she inched closer to me.

"Thanks, I appreciate the vote of confidence." As I laughed, Brandon came down the stairs and sat beside me.

"Getting anything?" He looked curiously around the room.

"No." I replied as I quickly sat up straight. "It's been pretty quiet tonight."

"How about Theresa?" He smiled. "She have any insight on this case?"

I was stunned for a moment.

"Well?" Brandon insisted.

I finally looked up at him with frustration. "Christy has a big mouth."

"Christy only confirmed." He smiled. "I've been walking in on you talking to yourself for months now."

I shook my head.

"Not to mention watching you talk to yourself on camera these last few nights." He added. "Got to admit, I found that very entertaining."

"Asshole." I looked at Theresa. "He's an asshole."

She simply smiled watching our banter.

"She still here?" Brandon questioned.

"She's always here." I sighed. "And she talks more than ever now."

Brandon laughed while Theresa glared at me.

"Still haven't quite figured out if she's real, or if I've just finally lost my sanity." I looked up at Brandon. "Care to take any wagers?"

"Can't lose what you never had."

"Very true."

"Obviously I believe you." He sat next to me on the floor. "Or I wouldn't be in this line of work."

"Ha, this line of work." I laughed. "What do we do with our lives now?"

"How do you mean?"

"Well, we set out to prove the existence of spirits?" I said with an almost disappointed tone. "Been there, done that."

"Really?" Brandon looked around the room. "Where's your proof? I've seen nothing. We've still never gotten anything on film that proves it beyond a shadow of a doubt."

I turned to Theresa, shook my head and sighed.

"He's got a point." She explained. "Technically you don't really know if I'm here, or if you're just a nut job."

"Seriously?"

"She saying something?" Brandon was feeling a little left out of the conversation.

"Nothing helpful." I glared at her.

"Even if you now have proof." She continued. "Do you think you stop there? Did Sir Edmund Hillary stop after he conquered Everest?"

I stared at her oddly for a moment, then leaned over to Brandon.

"Who the hell is Edmund Hillary?" I whispered to him.

"Wasn't he…" Brandon paused for a moment and scratched his head. "Wasn't he the Unabomber?"

Theresa lowered her head and rested it on her knees.

"You know, I don't mean to get in the middle of whatever discussion you two are having." Brandon continued. "But we've all decided it's time to go."

"Thank god!"

"Christy showed me the file on Theodore." He shook his head. It's not worth it. All the deaths, even William's, coincide with the file. I've got the three of them packing up the equipment upstairs, and I'm going to help you pack up down here."

"Smartest thing anyone has said all week." I was relieved everyone was finally on the same page.

I sure as hell didn't need any more proof to convince myself, and if we are going to continue the program, I'd prefer locations that weren't trying to kill us. Brandon began rolling up the video cables while I collected the cameras and microphones.

"She still here?" Brandon asked as he gestured around the room.

"Yep." I responded.

"She capable of helping with any of this gear?"

"Not likely." I went into the wine cellar to retrieve the camera and the tripod. As I began to detach the video cable from the camera, I felt a cold rush of air. Without warning the large Greek pillar began to tip over. I dove to the side and managed to avoid being hit, but the wine bottles were not so lucky. As it came down next to the wine rack, it managed to sheer the ends off of the bottles. Leaving dozens of jagged wine bottles with wine dripping from the ends.

Brandon and Theresa both rushed into the room.

"What the hell happened?" Brandon shouted.

"I'm not sure." I looked at the pillar. "Maybe the cable got wrapped around the pillar and when I pulled..."

Brandon looked at the pillar. The pointed part of it had actually penetrated the concrete by about a half an inch. He picked it up and moved it over to the corner.

"I knew this thing was an accident waiting to happen." Brandon said as he leaned the pillar in the corner so it couldn't fall again.

"No harm no foul." I said while I picked myself up and brushed myself off.

"No harm no foul? You remember how Ted's last victim died?" Brandon asked as he ran his finger over the pointed end of the pillar. "Impaled?"

"You okay?" Theresa asked.

"Yeah, I'm fine." I assured her and smiled. "Cat-like reflexes."

"Cat-like is right." Brandon smiled while cupping his hand under one of the wine bottles to retrieve a little wine that was still dripping. "I've seen how fast you cat moves."

"What the hell are you doing?" I laughed as I turned to see him drinking the wine from his hand.

"What, you want it to go to waste?"

We made our way back into the main room. Brandon finished winding the video cable onto the roll and brought it upstairs. I began putting the cameras and tripods in their case.

"You know the cable wasn't wrapped around the pillar, right?" Theresa asked.

"Yeah, I know." I replied. "But the other explanation isn't something I care to think about at this moment."

How close I had come to becoming part of the urban legend that surrounds this place. Seeing how the point of that pillar had lodged itself in the concrete a good half inch, I have no doubt in my mind it would have made quick work of me. We had never left an investigation early. But I was relieved we were getting out of here.

"You almost finished?" Brandon said as he came back down the stairs.

"Almost." I replied while loading the case.

Brandon came over and tried to help me fit the pieces into the case. He obviously wanted out of here as bad as me.

"In a hurry?"

"Duh. You're not?"

"Given our surroundings, I think being extra careful to watch what we're doing is just as important."

"Fine, you take your time. I'll be waiting outside by the van." He said looking over my shoulder at the last empty slot in the case. "Where's the third camera?"

"Shit." I looked around me. "I think I dropped it when the pillar fell."

"What would you do without me?" Brandon headed back into the wine cellar to retrieve the camera.

"I'm guessing I would drink a lot less." I joked.

Brandon stopped just outside the wine cellar door and looked at me and grinned. "You may very well drink less. But you would have a lot less fun!"

As he turned to go into the wine cellar, I felt a cold rush of air come from the other side of the room. I looked at Theresa.

"It's not over." Her eyes opened wide.

I looked back to the wine cellar to see Brandon on one knee retrieving the video camera.

"Looks like you cracked a lens." He shouted.

As I watched, I saw the same dark figure from our first night pass across the room and into the wine cellar.

I froze for a moment. Then, almost as if in slow motion, I saw the wine rack itself begin to tip in Brandon's direction.

"Brandon!" I shouted as I sprinted across the room.

Brandon turned to see the wine rack filled with broken bottles falling towards him. I dove towards him and managed to push him out of the way, just before everything went black. When I came to, I could feel the weight of the rack on my chest. I could see Theresa and Brandon were trying to move the massive rack when I suddenly felt pain in my chest.

"Stop!" I shouted and tried looking between the slats in the wine rack. "Don't move it."

As I was slowly becoming more conscious, I could feel the pain of what I could only imagine was several of the broken wine bottles impaled in various parts of my body. Every time I tried to shift to get a better look, the pain intensified, and I had to lay still. Brandon knelt down on one side and shined his light between me and the rack.

"Oh shit!" He blurted out as he could now see the bottles sunk in my chest. "We shouldn't try and move this."

"You think?" I said sarcastically and cautiously turned my head to the side and tried to smile.

I turned my head to the other side to see Theresa with her hands to her mouth, trying to remain calm. I'm guessing in an attempt to keep me calm.

"Nice job on the whole 'guardian angel' thing." I tried to make her smile. As she let out a small laugh, tears began to stream down her cheeks. She knelt down beside me and took my hand in hers.

"I'm going to call for help." Brandon stood up quickly and stumbled his way to the door.

"Wait!" I gasped. "Come here."

"We need to get help!" As he pleaded, I motioned for him to come down to me.

"Please." I begged, and against his better instincts, he knelt down beside me and took my other hand. I smiled. "The bad guy's not supposed to make it out in the end."

"Goddam it!" He released my hand and stood up briefly to yell upstairs. "Christy! Call nine-one-one!"

He knelt back down next to me and once again took my hand. I tried to keep my eyes open, but it was becoming increasingly difficult. I tilted my head up just enough to see the rack on me and the bottles lodged in my chest. I had joked so many times about getting my alcohol intravenously through an IV, but this is not quite what I meant. Maybe this was Karma. Everyone always told me that alcohol would be the death of me. This surely seemed to be a little bit of a poetic ending.

In all actuality, it wasn't as bad as I would have imagined. There was relatively no pain as long as I didn't move around too much. Maybe I was in shock, or maybe all those half full bottles of wine running directly into my bloodstream had given me a nice little buzz. I at least hope this was the wine rack that held the good stuff. I would really hate to find out that this was the rack filled with the Boone's Farm three-dollar bottles of wine. I laughed a little, but quickly grimaced in pain. Note to self, don't laugh while impaled by a wine rack.

"They're on their way, what…" Christy shouted as she came down the stairs but stopped mid-sentence when she reached our room and realized the situation. She put a hand to her mouth. "Oh, god."

She stood in the doorway and watched. It wasn't long before Bobby made his way down the stairs as well, aided by Jerry. Both could only join Christy in the doorway and stare on horrified and speechless.

"You guys could at least try to fake a calm look and make me think everything was going to be okay." I tried to smile in their direction. They all smiled and entered the room a little further.

"I've had worse." Bobby smiled and motioned to his crutch. I laughed at first, but quickly stopped as the sharp movement caused me added pain.

"You know…." I looked at Theresa at Brandon, then up at the others. "I'm going to miss the shit out of all of you."

"Shhh." Theresa leaned into me. "Save your strength."

"Don't talk buddy." Brandon said. "Help is on the way."

Bobby, Jerry, and Christy moved over to us and knelt down as well. Jerry tried to take what he thought was my free hand, but quickly withdrew with a shiver and looked across at Brandon.

"I think Theresa's holding that one." He smiled at Jerry and the others, who's eyes widened as they looked around at each other.

"Theresa's hand is actually starting to feel warmer." I smiled as I announced to everyone. But I was the only one that took confidence in this revelation. Theresa tried to muster up a half-hearted attempt at a smile, while Brandon simply lowered his forehead onto mine and began sobbing.

"Whoa, easy." I tried to turn my forehead. "People will get the wrong idea about us."

Brandon lifted his head back up, smiled and wiped the tears from his eyes.

"You know what I want?" I tried to force words out, but speaking was becoming increasingly painful, as I could now taste blood as I spoke. "You know what I want more than anything?"

Brandon and the others shook their heads, awaiting my response. As I tried to force the answer out, my lips were refusing to cooperate. I kept trying to give my answer, but no words were escaping. This was exhausting. As the others began to break down and weep uncontrollably, I realized why the words were no longer coming out, and I finally stopped fighting the inevitable.

Well, shit.

That wasn't the way it was supposed to end. I was supposed to impart some great wisdom on them that would leave them speechless and motivate them for years to come. Maybe even the rest of their lives. Do you know what I want more than anything? I just created the worst cliffhanger in the history of bad story telling.

It's like when you watch a series, and at the end of each episode they left the hero in one dire situation after another, to make sure you tune in next week to see how they miraculously solve the dilemma.

But then they unexpectedly cancel the series, so there is no episode next week! And you are stuck for eternity wondering what would have happened. How would they have gotten themselves out of that situation?

Now I've left my friends wondering for eternity what I wanted more than anything. Brandon will assume tequila. Theresa will probably lean towards forgiveness. The others will probably imagine something along the lines of reconnecting with Theresa and Michelle. When all I really wanted them was how much I love them all, and that I hoped they knew that. They were all truly the best part of me.

CHAPTER 20

The minister finished up his last few remarks as he looked down on my casket. It was already at the bottom of a freshly dug grave. Not sure if was supposed to be at the bottom of the hole already? I watched the men setting it up this morning and originally they were setting it on some sort of stand that would eventually lower it down to the bottom after the guests had left. But they seemed to have some sort of malfunction, so they just stuck me down here from the start. Kind of fitting, actually. Just get me down here and throw a little dirt on me.

Actually, seeing my coffin in the grave seemed to now finally driving this into my head that I would not just be waking up tomorrow morning in a cold sweat. I truly had died. I continued to watch my funeral from a safe distance. Not sure why I thought I had to keep my distance, if I'm being honest. Just felt like I shouldn't venture too close. Guess maybe I've watched one too many time-travel movies, with the whole 'like matter shouldn't occupy the same space' thing.

"We can take solace knowing he is with God." The minister said, while I looked around and chuckled.

"Really?" I questioned as I looked towards the sky and chuckled. "You actually going to let him get away with that crap?."

"I'm afraid he has to say that." A voice came from behind me and startled me. I turned to see an old woman standing behind me. "Wouldn't go over too well if he said you were rotting in hell or wandering aimlessly around the cemetery watching your own funeral."

"It'd be pretty funny though." I extended my hand to her. "My name is Sebastian."

"Rose, nice to meet you." She looked around at my service and shook her head a bit dismissively. "Not a big turnout. Were you kind of a prick?"

We both chuckled as I shook my head. "Don't know if I'd go quite that far? Let's just say I was not much of a people person."

"Fair enough. So, you think you're going to go…" She hesitated and nodded towards the clouds. "You know, up there?"

"Not sure." I glanced briefly towards the sky. "never really thought much about it."

"Well, if the answer is 'not sure', that probably means no. You generally don't if you don't believe."

I started to mill around the grave, as she followed me.

"Are you Catholic?" She asked.

"No, never really picked a flavor." I shook my head. "Figured they were all kind of the same."

"Good luck with that." She smiled and started to walk away.

"Who really knows, anyway?" I defended my position, and she hesitated and turned back towards me.

"I guess you will, soon enough." Rose smiled.

"Think about it. All of these 'bibles' were written by men." I continued. "How many men have you met in your life that don't stretch the truth?"

"My husband did always used to convince me this was twelve inches." She held up her thumb and forefinger, while I laughed in a bit of an awkward manner..

"Feed thousands with a loaf of bread, turn water into wine? Part a sea?" I added. "Yeah, I'm sure it happened just like that."

"I don't think the sarcasm is going to help your chances."

"I'm just saying that ultimately, these books are written by men.

260

Who's to say how accurate they are." I glanced briefly back at the pastor handling my service. "What if all these religions are actually praying to the same guy?"

"You've lost me."

"Christians, they are all about family supposedly. So, from the perspective of the guy writing the bible, his heaven is a place where everyone will meet up again eventually." I explained. "Muslims? Maybe the guy writing the Quran hated his wife, so he put in the bit about getting seventy-two virgins instead of seeing his wife again?"

I could see I'd stunned Rose into silence with my compelling, yet not so fact-based, argument.

"Buddhist's? They love the thought of past lives and reincarnation." I continued. "Maybe the guy that had written it all down was just some poor schmuck who wasn't happy with his life and was desperately hoping for a do over someday?"

"I can see you've given this a lot of thought?"

"No, actually, it all just kind of popped into my head at this very moment while watching my service." I smiled. "But think about it. All these religions are probably based on the same 'God'. It's just people that have decided to perceive the message differently."

"That's amazing." She shook her head, then took my hand in hers and patted it. "You drank a lot didn't you?"

I pulled my hand away quickly. Wasn't sure I liked what she was implying.

"Well, at any rate, good luck on your journey." She smiled and began to walk away again. "I hope you find the answer you're looking for."

As she walked away, I turned my attention back to my service. Watching as people I barely knew took turns hugging my friends and family, then moved on to their vehicles. Soon this area of the cemetery was empty except for what was left of my dysfunctional little family.

Brandon stepped up to the grave.

"This isn't right." He sobbed. "It should have been me lying here."

I was glad the others stepped up and put their arms around him and tried to console him.

"Show boating son of a bitch." He added sharply. "Always had to make it about him, didn't he?"

The others smiled for the first time since I'd been here. Bobby stepped up to the freshly dug grave and sat down, letting his legs dangle in. The others followed suit, except Jerry.

"I'll be right back." Jerry said as he began to head to the parking lot. "Save me a spot."

"Save him a spot?" Bobby laughed. "Don't think we have an issue with running out of available seating."

Jerry soon came back carrying a backpack.

"This isn't going to be a slumber party." Bobby joked.

Jerry pulled a very expensive looking bottle of tequila out of the backpack along with six shot glasses.

"You are the man!" Brandon cheered.

Jerry began filling shot glasses and passing them around. Brandon and Jerry were sitting on one side of the grave. Christy and Bobby were sitting across from them on the other side. After they had each received their shot glass, Jerry filled the last two shot glasses. One filled to the top and one barely at all.

Jerry handed the completely full shot glass to Brandon who put it at the head of the grave.

"That ones for Sebastian." He explained.

"Obviously." Christy smiled. "We should be using a mason jar."

Jerry then put the near empty glass at the foot of the grave.

"For you, sweetie." He started to mist up. "Because I know you're not much of a drinker."

The others smiled and misted up as well. Hell, I almost started to mist up myself just watching this. Well, you all know by now I am certainly not one to pass on a drink, so I sat down at the gravesite and let my feet hang in as well.

Brandon grabbed his glass and raised it to toast. "To the two best friends any of us could have ever wished for."

They all grabbed their glasses and downed their shots. I tried to grab mine but all I managed to do was knock it over. That was depressing.

They all looked at the tipped over shot glass. After staring at the tipped shot glass for a moment, they all then looked around at each other.

"Nah..." Bobby said. "Jerry put it on a bump or something."

"I did no such thing!"

As I listened to them discuss, I looked across my grave to the other shot glass let out a little bit of a sigh. I hadn't seen Theresa since I passed. I guess I was hoping she'd show up one last time.

No such luck.

I guess maybe she was allowed to move on once I passed. I got the feeling she was stuck behind trying to take care of me and keep me from self-destructing. I think she succeeded. At least I didn't drink myself to death. I actually died in kind of a noble way, saving someone else.

"You better remember that." I looked up to the sky. "I don't expect to be spending eternity down south."

Bobby grabbed the bottle of tequila and took a swig straight from the bottle.

"You know what I'm going to miss most?" Bobby said as he stood up with the help of one of his crutches.

The others shook their heads.

"Even after they split up and she had moved out, they couldn't stay away from each other." He wiped a tear from his eye. "They had this connection."

They all nodded. I had to admit, that was pretty sweet coming from Bobby.

"At least they can all three be together now." Christy spoke while sighing. "And in a better place."

I once again looked around at my surroundings. Better place? Maybe Christy wasn't so smart after all.

"Theresa is definitely in a better place." Jerry smiled. "Sebastian? I think the jury may still be out on where his permanent residence will be."

The others all smiled as well, as Bobby handed the bottle to Christy. She passed it across to Brandon without taking a drink.

"I'm going to have to drive you lushes home." She added.

Brandon took a long sip from the bottle. Then I watched in horror as he poured some into the gravesite on top of my casket, and took another long drink.

"That is so wasteful." I agonized.

"One thing is for sure." He continued. "He wanted us to carry on the team and the show."

"How do you know?" Jerry asked while reaching for the bottle and taking a sip.

"After Theresa had passed, he had me sit down with him and his lawyer." Brandon grabbed the bottle back and took another sip. "He left the equipment and the vehicles to the whole team."

It seemed to be the least I could do. What would Louie have done with it?

"And he left me the house with the stipulation it also continued to serve as our home base." Brandon said.

They sat stunned.

"Wow." Bobby managed to squeeze out.

"Yeah." Brandon confirmed.

"What about his family?" Christy asked.

"They are pretty loaded." Brandon shook his head. "And I think he wanted to make sure we had the means to carry on the team."

"Even with no show?" Jerry frowned as he grabbed the bottle.

"Well, that's a funny story." Brandon explained. "With all the press from this last investigation, and the clips that have gotten out there, I've been getting calls from at least two networks a day trying to pick up the series. Our network has even called and asked we come back."

"All of us?" Jerry looked amazed.

"All of us." He smiled and pulled Jerry in close to him to give him a hug. "Not like we'd pick those assholes though."

As Jerry began to tear up, this was all getting a bit to sentimental for me. I had to get up and wander around a little bit. I began to walk around the cemetery and think about where I go from here. Wherever here is.

I had to admit Bonaventure cemetery was beautiful. Don't think I'd ever really noticed before. The Spanish moss hanging from the trees gave it a southern gothic feel. As I walked I began looking at some of the epitaphs on the headstones. I started thinking maybe mine was a bit on the drab side. At first this one stumped me:

Wendell Harrison is filling his last cavity.

Then I realized poor old Wendell must have been a dentist. There was one that simply read 'I told you I was sick!'. I laughed as I read it, but my favorite was:

Here lies an Atheist. All dressed up and nowhere to go!

I started to think my simple 'beloved husband and father' was a bit on the boring side. I continued to wander around the cemetery, pausing briefly to take in a few of the other ceremonies that happened to be occurring. Looking at a few of the widows, I decided I definitely had the hottest wife of the bunch. Maybe I was lucky she went first. She would have definitely upgraded in her next marriage if I had gone first. She certainly couldn't have done worse.

As I walked up to one of the ceremonies to catch the last few words of the pastor, I noticed an odd old fellow also watching the ceremony. He turned to me as I walked closer.

"You an old timer?" He asked.

"Me?" I responded, caught off guard that I could still be seen.

"Yes, you."

"I was just…"

"What do you think?" He motioned to the guests. "I had a pretty good turn-out didn't I?"

Then I realized, this was in fact his funeral he and I were watching.

"Yes, it's a great turn out!" I flattered. "Twice as many people as mine."

"I'm Sebastian." I extended my hand as I introduced myself.

"Patrick." He said as we shook. "Patrick Fitzgerald."

"You obviously had some Irish in you." I joked.

"A couple times when I was in prison for sure." He said dryly as I froze, not quite sure how to respond.

He laughed and broke the silence.

"I'm kidding. You need to lighten up." He chuckled as he put a hand on my shoulder. "So how did you, well, you know?"

I stared at him oddly, not quite sure of what he was asking.

"Die?" He clarified.

"Oh, yeah." I responded with a smile. "A pissed off ghost tipped a wine rack over on me. I got impaled with the broken bottles."

"Oh, that's horrible." He said as he shook his head.

"Yes, I thought so."

"I was referring to the damaged wine." He said, then thought for a moment. "But I feel for you as well."

"Thanks. I appreciate it." I hesitated. "How did you die?"

"Heart gave out. Was with a sweet little twenty-one-year-old Latino hooker, and the old ticker just gave out."

Once again silenced as I had no idea how to respond to that. I thought for a moment. "At least you went out doing something you love."

"You really need to lighten up." He shook his head. "I died during a kidney transplant."

"Sorry. This is all still pretty new to me. I keep feeling like I'm going to wake up and be back in my bed." I looked around the cemetery. "What are we supposed to do now?"

"Beats me." The old man shook his head. "Some have been moving on right after their funeral. Others seem to linger for a while."

Patrick pointed to a spot just past some bushes.

"This morning the ground opened up right over, and took a guy." He motioned dramatically with his hands flailing around. "You could see a few of the taller flames actually making it out of the ground."

I looked at the spot he was referring to and gasped. Then quickly looked at the ground beneath my feet, as I felt them start to get warm. Patrick noticed me staring at the ground.

"You're a little too gullible, son." He smiled and started to walk away, as I took a deep breath and began to relax a little. He waved an arm over his head as he continued to walk. "Nice meeting you."

"You too."

As I made my way back to my grave, I could see the others packing up and getting ready to leave. One by one they each said their goodbyes, gave each other reassuring hugs, and made their way to the car. By the time I got to the grave, Brandon was the only one left.

Once he had seen the others all file into Christy's car, he squatted down at the edge of the grave one last time.

"I let you down." He said as he took a sip from the bottle. "I knew you were in a bad place, and I did nothing."

"There was nothing you could have done differently." I reassured him even though I knew he couldn't hear me. "I was a train wreck waiting to happen."

I hated seeing him like this. I continued to watch as he filled my shot glass one more time and put it at the head of my grave.

"To my best friend! I love you." He took one last sip from the bottle, then raised it. "I miss you, you crotchety son of a bitch."

I once again tried to grab my glass again to toast, but all I could manage to accomplish was to tip it over for a second time. Brandon stared at the shot glass, then a smile gradually took over his face.

"Don't worry my friend." Brandon said confidently. "You'll get the hang of it in time."

He arose and began to walk to the car with the bottle in hand. I watched until he got into the car, and they drove off. I sat and the edge of the grave and let my feet hang in, almost as if I was expecting something to happen. I looked to the sky.

"Well, what now?"

CHAPTER 21

There you have it. My life summed up in a mere two hundred and eighty-six pages. Don't laugh. There was a time in my life I could have been summed up in a paragraph or two. Those that knew me would consider this a great step forward. The man who was once as shallow as a kiddy pool, has acquired a little more depth.

I know this isn't the ending all the hopeless romantics were wishing for. Maybe you thought I lied at the beginning and there would be a miraculous twist at the end, and I would be spared? Not so much, huh? The opposite is probably true as well. I'm sure many of you feel I got exactly what I deserved. I can't argue that. Everything that's gone wrong in my life I've pretty much brought on myself in one way or another. The only problem is I eventually dragged others down with me.

The only issue I see now is, I seem to have found my way back to my house. As I walk the halls I can't help but wonder why? My profession has taught me that spirits that don't move on to their final destination are usually here because they have unfinished business. But I can think of no unfinished business I have here. The dishes aren't done, and I do have a full hamper of dirty clothes. But I find it hard to believe many of us stay back to take care of chores. Strike that. I find it hard to believe I would stay behind for that.

I feel lost.

What is it they say, when words fail, tequila speaks?

Well, maybe that's not exactly how the saying goes. But I'm sure it's something like that. I looked across the room and see my trusty sidekick. I glide across the room knowing there are always ways to improve an unacceptable situation. I try to focus harder on the bottle this time, and reach for it.

What the...

I focus even harder and try to pick it up again, this time knocking the bottle over as I helplessly watch it shatter on the floor.

I slowly step back from the bar.

"What good is a room full of booze, if I can't drink any of it?" I finally spoke my first words aloud since being back, not caring that they were audible to no one else.

Well maybe not no one.

Louie entered the room and looked up at me. He tried to rub up against me.

Unsuccessfully.

His look of frustration was almost as bad as mine. He tried to rub up against me again, but was left discouraged. He walked over to the broken bottle of tequila on the floor and sniffed, then immediately backed away. I guess he was okay with beer but not the harder stuff. He came back over to me and tried to brush up against me once again, but to no avail. Giving up temporarily, he retreated back to the couch and stared at me from across the room.

I can't drink my booze, and I can't pet my cat. All that's missing are a few members of the Swedish Bikini Team that I can't touch and I'd have the trifecta. This is going to be a very, very long...

Shit!

"I'm in Hell!" I shouted aloud.

Louie looked at me with a puzzled expression. Not like it's the first time he's seen me talk to myself, and I'm guessing it certainly won't be the last. I started to think out loud as to how I could have possibly ended up here.

"How could this be? I wasn't that bad a person, was I?" I looked to Louie for confirmation. I took him licking himself to mean he agreed with me.

I mean I was no saint. But I also wasn't Hitler or Manson. I guess maybe my argument invalidates itself when I have to refer to Hitler and Manson to make myself look good. Point being, there are far worse people out there that should be punching a ticket to Hades long before me. I can't imagine they have an unlimited amount of space, so I would think they would think about this kind of thing.

So, this is how it ends? Trapped and alone.

"Oh shit." I muttered aloud.

I had forgotten a key element to what my seventh circle of Hell would be. I had left the house to Brandon and the crew. Not only will I be spending eternity unable to pet my cat or drink my tequila. I'll have to spend my eternity watching Brandon eat Cheetos and pleasure himself.

I shuddered uncontrollably.

Suddenly a pointy headed man with a pitchfork dangling me over a pit of flames wasn't looking all that unpleasant. I bet Brandon doesn't even wash his hands between his two favorite hobbies. His, well...you know what, probably looks like a strange swollen little Oompa Loompa. I was really starting to gross myself out.

"Could really use a drink right now, dammit."

I made my way over to the bar once again for another futile attempt, but jumped back as I heard a noise at the end of the hallway. Cautiously making my way to the edge of the living room, I peered around the corner. As I looked down the hallway, I panicked. I went back over to the bar and quickly looked for something I could use to defend myself if it was an intruder.

The ice pick!

I grabbed for it.

"Shit!" I groaned as I was unable to grab the icepick.

How quickly I had forgotten my predicament.

273

"You do realize you're a ghost, right?" Theresa laughed. "One of the few advantages to passing on is not having to be afraid of things that go bump in the night anymore."

I turned to see her standing in the doorway.

"You are the thing that goes bump in the night now." She smiled.

I was stunned for a moment and could only stare at her. If in fact it truly was her. Was this just a sick joke I was to be tormented with? Flashes of an illusion I've come to know as my wife. It was certainly understandable having these issues while I was still alive, but I would think after death I would be able to block them out. I moved cautiously across the room while she smiled and shook her head.

"Unbelievable." She laughed.

As I got within arm's reach, I slowly reached out to touch her.

"Boo!" She shouted while lunging forward.

I must have jumped a good five feet off the ground at which point she completely burst into laughter. I quickly moved back over to her and touched her.

"It's you?" I smiled. "The real you?"

"Yes, whatever that means." She smiled and moved closer to me.

She reached out, put her finger beneath my chin, and kissed me on the cheek. As I closed my eyes I was overwhelmed with emptions. None of the least was confusion.

"I'm sorry." She said as she released me. "This shouldn't have happened to you. I guess I did a pretty crappy job of looking out for you."

"Don't be sorry." I reassured her. "I'm the one that should be sorry. I'm where I belong."

I looked around not really knowing what this was, or where I

274

actually did belong.

"You're the one that shouldn't have been here." I continued. "You're here because of my selfishness."

As I lowered my head, she moved closer once again.

"Once again your inflated ego is giving yourself too much credit." She smiled. "The one thing I've learned here is we don't control when or how we go."

I raised my head and tried to wrap my thoughts around what she was trying to explain to me.

"We all have a predetermined amount of time." She continued. "And when it's up, it's up. If it hadn't been the car accident coming to get you in the bar that night, it would have been a car accident the next morning going to the grocery store, or a heart attack, or a stroke."

I nodded my head and tried to follow her train of thought, but this was a lot to process. We had all been programmed for so long with what to do, what not to do. What to eat what to drink. Don't smoke, don't do drugs, etcetera. To find out none of it really influences how long we live if difficult. And in retrospect quite frustrating when I think of all the things would have liked to try, but I thought them too dangerous.

"You realize what that means?" I smiled while she shook her head. "All those times you bitched about my drinking, telling me it would kill me?"

"Yes, I realize that." She nodded.

"So, what happens next? Why are we still here?" I looked around the room. "Shouldn't we move on to somewhere?"

"That I don't know. I've been in this state of limbo since, well you know."

I nodded.

"I was thinking this was some form of hell." I said. "But I guess if you're here, this can't be hell?"

"That's funny." She responded laughing. "When I saw you here, I thought for sure it was."

She always was a smart ass. I didn't really care what it was. This limbo as she called it was better than the nothingness I had always pictured death to be. Things could definitely be worse.

"What do you do to entertain yourself?"

"Well, until recently, I haunted you." She smiled and began walking down the hallway and opened the last door. Entering the room, she moved to the shelf in the closet and pulled down a photo album to the floor. "I guess I still have my other hobby."

"Which is?" I asked not sure if I really wanted to hear the answer.

"I like to hang out in the ladies' locker room at the gym." She began to say.

"Hey, there's a hobby we can enjoy together!" I interrupted her as she glared at me.

"I like to hang out in the ladies' locker room." She continued. "And push on the scale when the vapid girls try to weight themselves."

I have to admit; this amused me far more than it probably should have. "Nice!"

As she sat on the floor paging through the album, I sat down next to her. Looking through the photos started to bring back a lot of memories.

"We were really happy for a time weren't we?" I smiled as I looked at the album.

"Yeah, and then we met." She chuckled again.

"Wow!" I backed away from her a little. "This version of you is certainly more sarcastic."

"I'm just kidding. I've got to give you shit when I can."

As we paged through our past life, Louie entered the room, moved over in-between us, and lad down on the photo album. Theresa quickly slid him off to the side.

"How do you do that?" I asked with quite a bit of frustration in my voice.

"You'll get the hang of it." She smiled. "It takes a lot of patience and self-control."

She looked me up and down.

"Then again, you may struggle with it." She laughed.

We had been so wrapped up in looking at the photos, we had completely missed the sound of the front door opening. As we looked behind us, Brandon was staring at the photo album on the floor. Both of us froze. Even Louie stopped in mid step and stared at him.

"Oh, don't treat me like I'm stupid." He smiled. "Just make sure to pick up after yourselves when you are done. I'm not your damn maid!"

He smiled and left the room. At the hallway he poked his head in one last time.

"By the way, I've ordered a bed for this room. It should be here next week." He said. "Not sure if you even sleep or not, but if you freaks are going to stay here, you might as well be comfortable."

"Bed? Singular? He's taking a lot for granted." Theresa scoffed while I laughed for a moment then watched Brandon head back down the hallway.

"I'll be right back." I smiled and followed down the hallway after Brandon.

He made his way to the living room and stood behind the bar. With eyes that were still very red, even after the long drive home from the cemetery, he smiled and grabbed the tequila and a shot glass. I watched as he poured himself a shot and quickly drank it. Don't mind telling you, I felt a little insulted. It was after all my booze. He looked at the bottle, then grabbed a second shot glass and filled both.

That's more like it.

"Cheers!" He raised his glass and drank.

As I reached for mine, all I could manage was to knock it over. He smiled and shook his head.

"Maybe you should practice first with glasses of water?" He posed. "This stuff isn't cheap."

Yeah, no shit. I'm the one that bought it. But he did have a point. Theresa soon joined us at the bar.

"How's our boy doing?" She asked.

"Oh, he's fine." I snarled. "He's drinking all my booze."

"Stop pouting." Theresa tried to calm me down while Brandon poured himself another shot.

Before he could manage to drink it, Theresa grabbed the glass and drank it. When Brandon looked back down at the glass it was empty. He smiled.

"I really hope that's Theresa and not Michelle." Brandon laughed. "Although being Sebastian's offspring, it's entirely possible."

I was still too busy being stunned watching Theresa take a shot of tequila. She noticed me staring.

"What?" She shrugged. "It's not like I'm going to have to drive anywhere."

"That's got to be blowing Brandon's mind seeing stuff float in the air like that." I said.

"From what I can tell, it doesn't work like that." She explained. "I was watching some of the footage you guys recorded at Wakefield, and things I know I had moved, didn't move slowly. It was just one second they were there, then the next second they were in another spot. Not sure about the specifics, but while you saw me pick up the shot glass, drink it, then put it back down. All Brandon probably saw was the shot glass was full one moment, then empty the next."

"Damn, so we can't make things levitate across a room and scare people?" I smiled.

"Sure we can." She continued. "We just have to move slower than usual while doing it, to make sure it's visible to them."

"But when I was alive, I was seeing you at normal speed, right?" I asked. "How was that happening?"

"I don't know really. There's a lot that I'm still working out." She replied.

Brandon headed into the office for a moment and came back with two flashlights.

"We have the red infrared flashlight." He put it down on one side of Theresa's shot glass. Then put the other flashlight down on the other side of the shot glass. "And we have the purple full spectrum flashlight."

We waited patiently for an explanation.

"I know you both know how the flashlight test works." He said.

Of course we do. But only amateurs use the flashlight test. The theory behind it is, you take a flashlight, the kind that you have to twist to turn on. And you twist until it just turns on. Then back it off just a hair until it turns off. So in theory, all a ghost has to do is make that last little turn to make it light up. It's a sham though. There are too many other

279

variables that can cause that connection to be bridged. Excessive moisture in the air due to high humidity is enough to bridge that gap and make the connection.

"Moron didn't think about the fact these aren't twist on flashlights." I looked at Theresa.

Theresa shook her head and proceeded to turn both lights on.

"Now you're just showing off." I pouted.

After a few minutes, she turned them both off.

"Excellent!" Brandon refilled her shot glass. "We're going to say the purple light is yes, and the red light is no. Got it?"

Theresa turned the purple light on for a few minutes and then turned it off.

"Good!" He slid Theresa's shot glass across the bar.

"He's being bit condescending." She frowned. "Is the shot like my reward for putting the square peg in the square hole? He does realize I can take my own shot whenever I feel like it?"

"Hey, at least you get a shot." I stared longingly at the shot glass. Wondering how long it would take me to learn this new lifestyle. "You know how long it's been since I've been able to have a drink?"

"I know I'm going to regret doing this." She picked up the shot glass. "Don't get lazy! You still need to figure this stuff out for yourself."

She moved in closer.

"Tilt your head back." She ordered, and as I did as I was instructed, she poured the shot into my mouth.

Oh my God, at last! All those theories about taste and the other senses being gone after death. Wrong! That was maybe the best tasting shot of tequila I've ever had. Of course it could also be the fact that it was the first drink I'd had in almost a week. Which I believe was a record for me.

"Damn I needed that! How about another?" I smiled as Theresa simply shook her head and turned her attention back to Brandon.

"Okay, we need to have some ground rules." Brandon's voice brought me back quickly from my alcohol-induced mini vacation. "Number one, my bedroom is my safe zone. None of you enter. I want to know I can shower, bring a date home, or other stuff without you being creepy."

"Ewww, like I would." Theresa grimaced.

"You know by other stuff he meant..." I cupped my hand and motioned it back and forth.

"Yeah, I figured that out." She glared. "Thanks for making it grosser than it needed to be."

Theresa quickly turned the purple light on and off. Brandon waited for a response.

"Oh, for God's sake." Theresa quickly realized her error and turned the light back on, left it for several minutes, then turned it off.

"Thank you!" Brandon replied.

I was willing to give him his own room and his privacy. Not like I wanted to see him have sex. But he's going to have to learn to elaborate on his demands down the road. Because he said nothing about me leaving gay porn magazines and unwrapped condoms all over the rest of the house when he brings dates home.

He's going to be a fun roommate.

"Two, seeing as it appears you can drink." He looked at the shot glass. "I expect you two to pull your weight around here."

Theresa and I looked at each other. Two flaws with his plan.

One, I don't think either of us is going to have an easy time getting a job. And two, we don't actually weigh anything, so the weight to pull would be zero.

"Voodoo Blue has always had a decent following." He continued. "But we've never been able to compete with the other ghost shows until now."

"What's he talking about?" Theresa asked hesitantly.

"I think he is asking us to go on the investigations and make things happen on camera." I smiled and nodded my head as I had to admit, I had already been thinking the same thing.

"With you two as our secret weapons..." He continued. "We can make every episode great!"

"Absolutely not!" Theresa stood up and began pacing the room. "The one thing we said when we started this was, succeed or fail, we were not going to fake things!"

"You're kidding, right?" I asked her.

"No. I'm not going to be part of a scam." She defended her position passionately.

I moved across the room to her and grabbed her by the chin.

"Seriously?" I smiled.

"I'm not budging on this!" She fumed. "You and I are better than this!"

She thought for a moment.

"Well, I am anyway." She added.

I put my hands on her shoulders and tried to calm her down, but she was having none of it.

"It's wrong to fake evidence for the show!"

"I agree with you! But you realize, we are ghosts, right? What exactly would we be faking? I explained while she looked at me curiously. "Wouldn't anything we do be considered 'paranormal activity'?"

She thought for a moment, then smiled and nodded.

"I didn't think about it that way." She moved back over to the bar." It still feels a bit dishonest, though."

"But it's not." I assured her.

She slowly nodded and turned the purple light on for a couple of minutes, then turned it back off.

"Fabulous!" Brandon jumped up and down. "We are going to be number one in no time! Pennhurst Asylum, Eastern State Penitentiary, Moon River Brewery. The list is endless. We will own this business!"

He pulled another shot glass down and filled all three. Theresa and Brandon drank theirs quickly while I looked on sadly. Theresa must have felt some sympathy as she picked up my glass once again.

"Tilt your head back." She demanded and I eagerly did. "I feel like the shot girl at the Rainbow club."

As I finished my shot I tilted my head back to its forward position and smiled.

"If you were the shot girl at the Rainbow, I'd be getting this shot from in-between your cleavage." I grinned, then began to think a little more seriously about it. "You know…"

"Um, no." She cut me off quickly. "You'll be getting them form Brandon's cleavage before you'll be getting them from mine!"

Okay, so I still had some work to do on her. I don't blame her. But things definitely seem to be moving in a positive direction.

This certainly isn't Hell. It certainly isn't Heaven. Not sure what it is or why we are still here, but I am not complaining. I have the woman I love back, sort of. And oddly enough, I even have my career back in a way. I'm still surrounded by the people I love and doing what I love. How many living people can say that? Let alone dead people.

And that's how the second chapter of my life began. I'm sure many of you are still skeptical. I can't blame you. I was a skeptic myself and I was a paranormal investigator by trade. In the end, it took dying for me to open my eyes and my mind. I hope all of you don't wait as long as I did. Whether or not you believe in the paranormal, the afterlife, or any of this. One thing should be very clear to you by now. Do what you love, and be with who you love. If you don't go for it now, who knows if you'll ever get the chance.

If you still need more proof. Take a look at the author's name on the cover of this book. Coincidence? I think not. Did Brandon really write this book? Hell no. That walking hard on is even more shallow than I used to be. Just catch up to him at a book signing and talk to him for five minutes. You'll quickly realize he isn't capable of forming a complete sentence, let alone an entire novel.

You see I had always known I was meant to tell this story, to be the righteous voice of truth, to help other lost souls find what I had....

...Okay, again I'm bull shitting you. You guys should know me well enough by now, that you catch onto my crap before I do. The truth is I happened to be looking at Brandon's computer one night. Well, you know... because he always has good porn on it. And before I knew it, I found myself typing away. By morning, I had spilled my thoughts out in the form of this book you just finished. Is it Shakespeare? Of course not. But it's the best I can do to help you all realize you need to live life to the fullest. The end always comes sooner than we want it to.

Always.

As for me, I'm sure you'll be hearing from me again. If there's one thing you should have learned by now, even my good choices end up being complicated. Like agreeing to help Brandon boost the show by going to the locations and creating activity. As with most of my life, I never really thought it through. Sounded like a good idea didn't it? I never thought that the spirits that are already haunting those locations might have a serious problem with us coming into their home. Some might even want retribution.

But that's a story for another day.